UNSCRIPTED WITH *Mila*

NEW YORK TIMES AND USA TODAY BESTSELLING AUTHOR

MELANIE MORELAND

ABC CORP

BOOK 6

Dear Reader,

Thank you for selecting Unscripted With Mila. There are many choices available, and I am honored you choose mine to read today.

Unscripted with Mila, out of all the ABC books, was the most difficult to write. Whether the subject matter touched on a loss of a dear friend or the end of a series, I am uncertain. I know I owe a debt of gratitude to those who helped shape the story.

If you are interested in receiving up to date information on new releases, exclusive content and sales, please sign up for my newsletter here at https://bit.ly/MMorelandNewsletter.

Always fun book stuff - never spam!
xoxo,
Melanie

MORELAND
BOOKS INC.

Edited by Lisa Hollett of Silently Correcting Your Grammar
Proofreading by Sisters Get Lit.erary Author Services
Cover design by Karen Hulseman, Feed Your Dreams Designs
Cover Photography by Eric D Battershell
Cover Model Kevin Hessam

This book is a work of fiction.
The characters, events, and places portrayed in this book are products of the author's imagination and are either fictitious or are used fictitiously. Any similarity to real persons, living or dead, is purely coincidental and not intended by the author. Any trademarks, service marks, product names or named features are assumed to be the property of their respective owners, and are only used for reference. There is no implied endorsement if any of these terms are used. The author acknowledges the trademarked status and trademark owners of various products referenced in this work of fiction, which

FOREWORD

Nicholas' condition is based on my personal experience of a close friend, in consult with mental health professionals and that of a sensitivity reader with bipolar. This book is not meant to be read as a medical journal. As with all mental health conditions—the symptoms can cover a vast range of treatment modalities.

For more information, please contact NAMI.org

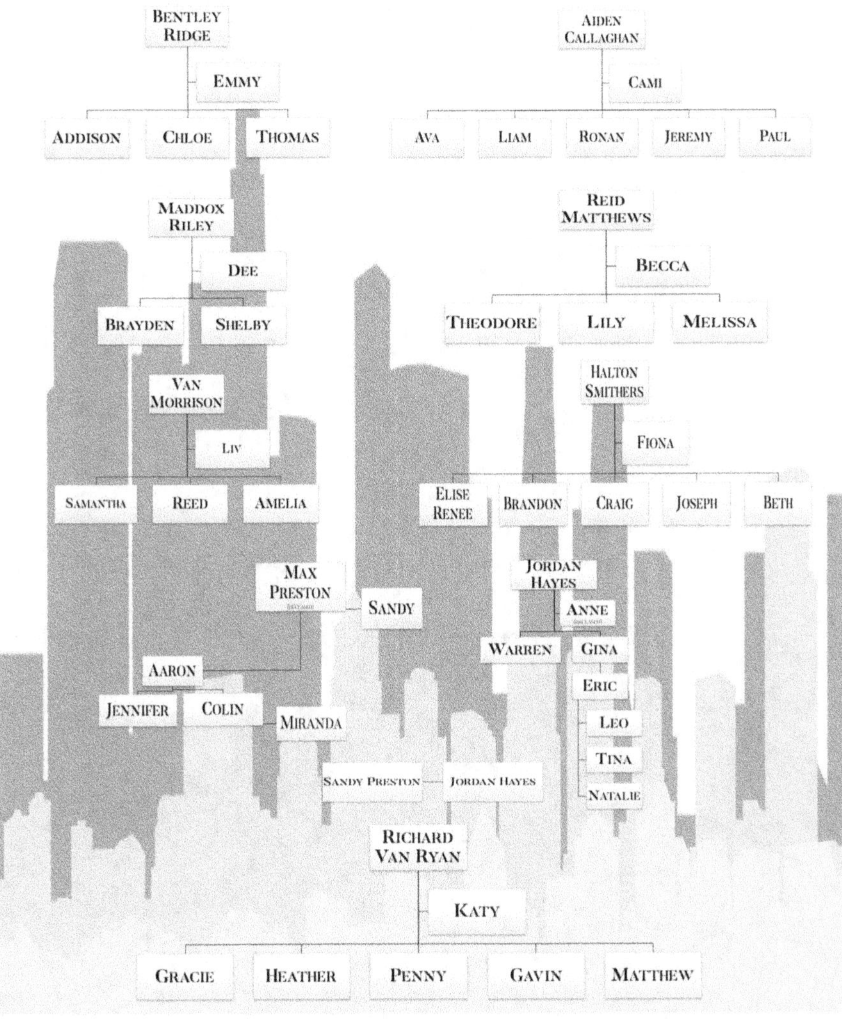

FAMILY TREE

The Contract VESTED INTEREST

NEW YORK TIMES AND USA TODAY BESTSELLING AUTHOR

MELANIE MORELAND

DEDICATION

*For Tracy who fought so hard and is missed so much.
Your smile will never fade from my heart.*

CHAPTER ONE

MILA

I huffed out a long breath and pushed my hair back off my face. I glanced around, moving things on my desk, finally spying a hair tie. I frowned at the computer screen, trying to come up with another word.

Apparently, snarl was a word I used too often in my books, and my editor, Lisa, made snarky comments about it in her notes. I had three other snarly bits, so I knew I had to start changing it up.

I pursed my lips and took a sip of coffee, then made a face. It was cold.

I had just made it, hadn't I?

A quick peek at my phone made me shake my head. I had brewed it two hours ago. Then I grinned. And written over two thousand words on the one sip I had taken.

Not bad.

"Ah." I grinned. "Growled. I like growly men." My grin stayed on my face as I finished the paragraph.

My mom often accused my dad of growling. He'd protest

and tell her she was wrong, but she wasn't. When he got annoyed when one of us wasn't listening, or some man stared at me, my sister, or God forbid, my mother, for too long, growls did escape his mouth.

My mom thought it was hot. Sammy and I always laughed. Sammy once said if a man couldn't withstand my dad's glare, he'd never survive this family.

She was right.

Of course, far more men looked at Sammy than me. She was gorgeous. Effervescent and funny. She looked like our mom, except her eyes were dark.

I looked like—well, I had no idea. I was adopted. Taken from a cold, scary apartment and a strung-out, drug-addicted mother who kept forgetting I existed. I had no recollection of what she looked like, except her hair was dark. Mine was honey-colored like my adoptive mom's, and oddly enough, my eyes were similar to hers as well—a golden brown with a dark circle around the iris. I was short and somewhat curvy, far more interested in writing and reading books than spending too much time on the treadmill. I did it every day, but I hated it. I knew if I didn't, my backside would be a balloon, never mind the fact that I would have to cut back on my snack of choice—cashews. I could eat them all day. I vaguely remembered my birth mother being taller and skinny. So I had no idea who I took after.

The day I met Liv and Van was my first, real, clear memory of my childhood that made me smile. Liv was so pretty and kind. She smelled good, her voice soft, and she let me sit on her lap and she held me. I hadn't been touched in so long except in anger that the feel of her loving embrace was addictive. I became attached immediately, and when they left, I recalled sobbing that the pretty lady was gone. But she returned again and again, and then she took me home with her.

Van was massive. He towered over me, his size frightening. But the pretty lady liked him and he gave me a cookie, so I decided he had to be okay. I had never known a man in my life. It had only been my mother in the apartment with me. The only time I heard a man's voice was when I was locked in the closet and someone else was there for a while.

I always hated it when she forgot to unlock the door.

But Van was gentle and kind. He had a wide smile and I wanted to get closer to him, but I was too afraid. When they took me home, I had an instant family. A brother named Reed and a sister named Samantha, but whom everyone called Sammy or Mouse. She shortened my name from Amelia to Mila. I loved her instantly. I liked Reed, even though he was loud at times. He turned into the best big brother a girl could ever ask for. Patient and sweet, protective and kind. He stood up for me everywhere, often getting into trouble for doing so. But he never backed down. I loved him fiercely, and we were very close now.

I adored Liv. I'd remained leery of Van, although he was nothing but kind and he called me "Pumpkin." It changed one day, though, when we were watching a movie as a family, and Van snuggled with Sammy. It fascinated me, seeing him cuddle her. She looked so happy with him. When she moved, I held out my arms, and Van took me onto his lap, wrapping me in a blanket the same way he did for Sammy. He held me tight, his broad chest the perfect spot to snuggle. I had never felt as safe as I did in that instant. All my fears faded away in his gentle embrace.

After that, he was my daddy. Liv became Mommy.

And my new life began.

I shook my head to clear my musings and saved my chapter. I headed to the kitchen, my footsteps echoing in the hall of the empty house. Sammy was off on one of her projects—helping a brother and sister save their ranch. I missed her terribly, although we had spoken a few times via FaceTime. She told me all about what she was doing. She liked the sister but insisted the brother was a pain in her ass. Except she said it with a smile on her face, and her eyes had a certain gleam I recognized.

I had certainly written about that gleam often enough. I had a feeling there was more to Sammy's annoyance with Luke Adler than she was willing to admit.

Time would tell if I was correct.

I popped a Keurig cup in the machine and waited as the coffee brewed, the scent filling the kitchen. I poked around in the fridge, happy to discover some leftovers from Mom that I slid in the microwave to heat up. I carried the hot casserole and the coffee to the table and sat down to eat.

My phone rang, and I answered my agent's call with a smile. "Hey, Andi."

"Kiddo—how goes it? Writing me lots of words?"

I propped the phone on the table, hitting speaker. "Yep."

"Excellent. When do I get it?"

I laughed. "Andi, you just got the last one. I'm only twenty K into this one."

"Just checking."

She rambled on a bit about numbers and some new foreign rights deals. I ate and sipped my coffee as she spoke.

"So, update on the movie."

"No casting changes?" I asked anxiously.

"No. You still have Nicholas Scott as the lead and Lacey Dunbar for Roxie. But production has been moved up. So far, the plans are, they're doing the scenes in LA in two weeks, then on to Vancouver for some of the outdoor filming. Then to Ontario, then whatever needs to be done for reshoots. They want you to fly down to LA for the shoot and be part of the read-throughs. Help the cast—give them insight."

"Wow, so soon?" I asked, anxiety curling around my chest.

"The studio is crazy for this book, kiddo. And you said you'd do it. You're not going back on that now, are you?" She paused. "I'll be right there with you, promise."

I drew in a long breath. "Yes, I'll do it."

"Awesome. We'll go to the studio, and you can meet Nicholas and Lacey, plus the supporting cast. Sit in on the read-throughs. I know both the leads want some direction. And I know you want Duncan and Roxie to be handled correctly."

"Yes, I do."

"And you can see where they're filming—see some of the sets and the exteriors. The actors prepping and all that. They still need a couple of locations for other exteriors, but I'm sure they'll find the right ones."

"So, when do we leave?"

"Two weeks Friday."

I bit my lip in worry. "What if I…" I let the sentence trail off.

Andi's voice dropped in sympathy. "Kiddo, I know you're shy. You can do this. And you haven't had an occurrence in a long time. If you do, I'm right there. And if it's too much, I'll take you home, okay?"

"Okay," I agreed.

"Good. Now go back to writing. I'll send you the details and see you at the airport in just over two weeks." She laughed. "And no doubt, I'll talk to you a dozen times between now and then. Ciao!"

I hung up with a sigh, the casserole no longer appealing. I pushed aside my plate and finished the coffee. I never said no to coffee.

Heavy footsteps on my porch made me smile, and I got up to get another mug to make a coffee for my visitor. There was a loud rap on the door, and my dad walked in. Still tall, still big, and still my favorite man on the planet.

He smiled, his eyes crinkling in the corners. He had aged well. His back was broad, his shoulders wide, and to this day, I was sure there was nothing he couldn't do. Certainly nothing he wouldn't do for one of us kids. Biologically, he might not be our father, but to us, he was the perfect dad.

"Hey, Pumpkin," he greeted me, pressing a kiss to my head. He slid a plate on the table. "Mom made pie."

"Oh no. What kind?"

He frowned. "Blueberry. Your favorite."

"Oh God, I have to go to LA in two weeks."

He rubbed his chin. "I think you can squeeze in eating a piece of pie."

"Then I have to really squeeze into my pants," I moaned.

Dad took the cup of coffee I handed him and laughed. "Mila, baby, you don't have to squeeze into anything. There is nothing wrong with you."

"My butt is big. And my hips—"

He interrupted me. "Your hips and butt are in perfect proportion to your waist, your height, and everything else." He met my eyes. "You know that. Why are you suddenly upset?"

"Los Angeles," I stressed the words. "Tinseltown, where everyone is glamorous and thin."

"And fake," he added, taking a sip. "You are beautiful,

natural, and you don't have to change a thing." He met my worried gaze. "Not a thing."

I smiled, letting my shoulders relax. My dad always told me how perfect I was. I loved him for that.

He leaned forward. "So, two weeks? That's faster than expected."

I nodded. "The studio moved it up. It's only for a short time then off to BC. I'll spend some time there, then head home."

"So you'll be gone how long?"

I furrowed my brow, tugging the foil-covered plate closer and lifting the lid. I could smell the blueberries and lemon. "I don't know. Three weeks, maybe? Four tops, I would think. Depends how long they want me around for."

I used my spoon from my coffee and cut off a bite of pie. The filling was thick and rich with blueberries. Sweet and tangy. The crust melted in my mouth. "Oh God, so good," I mumbled.

Dad leaned on his forearms. "Did you want Mom or me to come with you?"

"No," I scoffed. "I'm not a child."

"But the idea of going is making you nervous." He tapped my cheek. "You're pale."

"Yes," I admitted. "But I'll be fine. Andi will be there."

"I'll let Richard know you'll be close. He'll pop in and check on you." Dad grinned. "Probably sit down and tell them how to market the movie properly too."

"Dad, he's in Victoria. I'll be in Vancouver. It's a three-hour drive, at least. He can't just 'pop in.' Besides, we are only there a short time, then they're doing some filming in Toronto."

"He's partially retired. Katy will probably thank you for getting him out of the house."

I had to laugh. Richard VanRyan was a force unto himself. I could only imagine him on a movie set. He'd probably be discovered and have a second career as an actor. I said that to my dad, who threw back his head in amusement.

"You're probably right, Mila."

"I know I am."

"Seriously, if you need us, we're there."

I covered his hand. "I know."

"And if anything happens—"

I held up my hand. "It won't. It hasn't for a long time. Almost a year. I know how to control my breathing and stay focused." It didn't always work, but it helped.

"Your mom and I can be there in a few hours," he finished, ignoring my words.

"I know, Dad."

He nodded. "Now, you gonna share that pie?"

"You'll have to get your own spoon."

He grinned and snagged mine, slicing off a big hunk and chewing it. "I used to eat off your plate all the time. Nothing's changed." He grinned and cut off another piece, offering it to me. I let him feed me, smiling.

I had the best dad.

CHAPTER TWO

MILA

Sunday was our usual family brunch, and I walked toward the Hub, enjoying the nice day. The sun shone, and things were blooming, the houses all looking pretty with the bursts of color. Liam, Aiden's son, was an award-winning landscaper, and he always made sure the yards and common areas looked good. My uncles had bought this property, then added more and turned it into what they called the BAM compound. All the BAM men and their families lived there and many of us, the next generation, as well. But even those who didn't live here came and went all the time, and Sunday brunches were open to anyone who wanted to drop in. I never knew who I would see there.

Opening the door, I stepped inside, inhaling deeply. I could smell the coffee, the scent of bacon, the rich tang of cinnamon. Laughter and conversations were taking place. My brother Reed was talking with my parents, his wife Heather beside him, and I crossed the room, stopping for kisses and hugs with a few people. Reed stood, enfolding me in his embrace.

"Hey, Shortstack."

I hugged him back, grinning as he pressed a kiss to my head. "Stop it."

He laughed, shaking his head. "I swear you get shorter every time I see you."

I sniffed, sitting beside my dad. "I'm the same height I was last month, last year, in fact since I was fifteen and stopped growing. I highly doubt at thirty-two I have much chance of that changing. Besides—" I sniffed "—not my fault you're so full of manure you sprouted that high."

He chuckled. "Manure?"

I shrugged. "Manure, bullshit, all the same."

Everyone laughed, and Dad ruffled my hair affectionately. "You go, Pumpkin. Put him in his place."

Reed winked at me, and I smirked at him. I loved teasing him.

Aiden and his wife Cami came over, joining us. "Did I hear Mila say bullshit?" he asked, his eyes wide. "Can't be."

I shook my head in amusement. "I say a lot worse, Aiden. My readers would tell you that."

He shook his head. "Nope. Not going there. Not my little Mila. You used to ride on my shoulders and stick your lollipop in my hair to keep it safe and hold on to my ears. You were the cutest damn thing ever."

I gazed at him fondly. I remembered doing that. He, Maddox, even Uncle Bentley were all wonderful men to grow up around. My uncle Reid was the computer whiz who loved to show us all how to use technology. My brother Reed had worshiped him his entire life, and they remained close to this day. Halton was always around for guidance and wisdom. I had been very lucky to grow up in this family.

"You were always a good sport. Even when my lollys got stuck in your hair."

He grinned. "A quick soak in the pool got them out." Then he stood. "Food is ready. Thank God—I am famished."

Everyone chuckled. Aiden was always famished. So were his sons. It took a huge amount of food to fill them up, and it was always amusing to watch.

I filled a plate and got a cup of coffee, sitting beside Cami. She smiled at me as I sat down. My mom sat on my other side.

"Your dad tells us you're off to LA in a couple of weeks," Cami said.

"Yes."

"How exciting!" she exclaimed.

"It is." I chewed and swallowed. "A little nerve-racking too."

"I imagine so." Cami squeezed my hand. "You'll do fine. Just remember, they came to you. Your books are amazing, and once the movie comes out, you'll be even more famous!"

I rolled my eyes. "I don't really want that. I just want to write books."

"You will. You can do anything you want," she assured me.

We ate for a while, then I turned to Cami again. "I, ah, actually have a favor to ask you."

"Sure. What do you need?"

"Well, my usual wardrobe is leggings and loose shirts. Andi suggested that I try to bring some more, ah, professional clothing. And she says I need a couple nice dresses. I was wondering if you could help with that?" Cami had been a fashion designer before she retired. She still made articles of clothing for family, and I needed her advice.

Cami's eyes glowed, and she clasped her hands. "I would love to!" She sat back, eyeing me. "I have a couple of dresses that would suit you well. And we can go shopping for other pieces."

"I don't like restrictive things or anything too tight."

"No, we can do easy things. Pretty skirts, some nice pants, cool blouses. Mix and match. A couple knockout pieces for anything formal that comes up. LA will be hot, so we'll stick with all natural fabrics. Bold colors, simple cuts, easy to pack and take care of, but you'll look like a million bucks! Oh, this will be so fun. I know the perfect shops, and I will run up a couple things. Liv, you have to come with us."

"I wouldn't miss it for the world," Mom said.

"Um, I don't want to go overboard."

Cami laughed. "Don't worry, Mila. I got you covered."

After brunch, I wandered to the beach, sitting on the rocks and letting the sound of the lazy waves and the feel of the warm sun relax me. I loved my family and enjoyed the get-togethers, but I was always happy to be alone again. There was no doubt I was the introvert of the family. Bentley's son Thomas was quiet as well, and so was Maddox's daughter Shelby, but I was known as the loner. My words and books filled my life. I hated leaving the compound, although my mom and dad dragged me places, and Sammy and Reed made sure I left the house on occasion. When I was with them, I was okay, but on my own with strangers and in strange places, I became tongue-tied and awkward. I often wished I were more like Sammy—outgoing, adventuresome, and confident. But instead, I was quiet, shy, and preferred to observe rather than interact.

I doubted that would ever change.

My phone rang, and I slipped it from my pocket, smiling when I saw the caller was Sammy.

"Hey," I greeted her. "How's the ranch?"

"The ranch is spectacular. The owner is not," she replied. "What a grump."

"I assume we're discussing Luke, not Rachel."

She grunted, the sound furious. "Yes. He drives me crazy. He second-guesses everything, questions all my ideas, disagrees with them, then suddenly does something nice. I can't keep up."

I smiled widely, glad she couldn't see me. "I see. Sounds like someone has a crush and isn't sure what to do about it."

"I never said I had a crush. The man is a pain in my ass!"

"I never said you," I pointed out. "But we can talk about that as well."

There was silence on the line.

"You little witch," Sammy mumbled.

I laughed. "I have never heard you like this."

She sighed. "He is frustrating."

"But?"

"But so freaking hot, Mila. All growly and grumpy. His glowers and snark turn me on. It makes me want to press his buttons to see how far I can push him."

"And see what happens when he explodes?"

"Yes," she admitted.

"Are you ready for that? For what might occur between you if you set him off?"

"I know what I want to happen. And, at times, I think he wants it too."

"Sammy Morrison, are you planning on sleeping with him?"

She laughed. "Don't sound so shocked. We're consenting adults. A mutual itch-scratching session could be exactly what we need."

"Is that all it would be?"

"Yes. He's here and not leaving this place. I roam everywhere. Not a good match. But I certainly wouldn't mind riding that cowboy once. Or twice."

"Be careful."

"Don't worry. I always am."

"I meant with your heart, Sammy. Not protection."

She chuckled. "It's all fine, Mila. I'm not looking for anything permanent. Just a little stress-reliever."

Then she changed the subject, and I brought her up-to-date with my trip and all the shenanigans at brunch. "The boys got into a wrestling match over the last scones. By the time Liam was declared the winner, Bentley and Aiden had eaten them all. They dogpiled on Aiden. It was hilarious."

"And Bentley?"

I chuckled in remembrance. "He simply looked at the boys, almost daring them to tackle him. No one moved until he was walking past the pool."

"No," she breathed. "They didn't."

"Liam tackled him right into the water. Then Aiden jumped in, and suddenly, the pool was full of grown men acting like kids. Even Dad got in on it. It was so funny."

"I'm sorry I missed it."

"Mom videoed it. I am sure she will send it to you."

"Good. Okay, I hear Luke bellowing. I must have done something to displease him. Probably the suggestion I gave to Callie to add a taco bar to the menu. Clients would love it, and she was going to do a trial run on Tuesday. It will feature his damn beef, so it should make him happy, not all shouty. Gotta go!"

She hung up and I laughed. I heard the underlying excitement in her voice. She liked riling up Luke Adler. Making him all shouty. I had a feeling I was going to be hearing a lot about him in the coming days.

I stood and stretched.

Her words had inspired a scene for the romantic comedy I was currently writing. I hurried home to get the words out before I forgot them.

I stared at my reflection in the mirror, unsure at the image before me. The dress Cami had me try on wasn't like anything I normally wore.

Ever.

The rich red currant color looked odd against my pale skin. The dropped sleeves exposed my shoulders and neck, and the crisscrossed bodice emphasized my breasts. The full skirt swirled around my knees, the silky fabric cool against my skin.

"It's perfect," Cami murmured.

"Mila," Mom breathed out. "That looks gorgeous on you."

"It's not, ah, too much?" I asked, worried.

"No. It's just different. But if you have a formal event or dinner to go to, it will be perfect," Cami assured me.

I eyed the pile of clothes behind me. She had gone overboard, but I had to admit I had loved everything she had chosen. Simple pants and tunics. Cool, pretty skirts and tops. All in lovely colors and easy to care for. Low heels and nice sandals. I had tried on a couple of other, simple dresses, but this one was dressier. And definitely sexy.

"Good for an unplanned date as well," Cami murmured, tugging at the neckline. "I need to lift this a little. It sags, and I want it perfect." She began to pin it, muttering to herself. "An inch off the bottom as well. You have great legs. We need to show them off."

"I highly doubt I'll be going on any dates," I protested.

"You never know."

I didn't bother to remind her I hadn't been on a date in years. Nothing serious anyway. If I did get asked on one, I was always so quiet and awkward, I was never asked on a second one. I just wasn't girlfriend material.

I wasn't any kind of material.

I touched the fabric. "It's so soft."

"Silk," Cami said. "From a manufacturer I like. Breathes, doesn't wrinkle easily, and feels good against your skin. A lot of the skirts and blouses are made of it as well. But you have to dry-clean it."

"Okay."

"There."

I looked back at the mirror with a small sigh of relief. She had lifted the neckline and sleeves so it skimmed my shoulders and exposed my collarbone but not so much of my breasts. The dress was still sexy, but more understated. That, I could handle, although I wasn't sure I would ever have the occasion to wear the dress. But it was pretty.

"And I got you some nice jeans and a couple of poet blouses. White, crisp, classic. One has dark navy stripes to make you look taller. I added some jewelry pieces to wear with each outfit and put them together. You will look like a million bucks."

I flung my arms around Cami and hugged her. "Thank you. I only wanted a couple of things. Not an entire wardrobe."

She laughed. "It was fun. I've been dying to dress you for years. Leggings and tees are fine for the compound, but you need to dress for LA. It's part of the image. Part of the act. You feel more powerful if you look good." She tapped my chin. "Hold your head high, and keep your shoulders back. Show the world A.M. Archer. Leave Mila behind for a little while."

I nodded, knowing she was right. I had to be a different person, or pretend to be, while in LA. At least outwardly. And maybe she had a point. If I looked the part, people might not look so hard behind the mask and see the timid person holding it up.

I could do this.

"Okay."

CHAPTER THREE

MILA

My dad insisted on driving me to the airport, and I wasn't surprised to see Mom in the passenger seat when I opened the door to go out to the car. Dad lifted my cases into the trunk and pressed a kiss to my cheek. "She wanted to come see her baby off," he whispered.

"Her *baby* is in her thirties," I whispered back, but I couldn't help smiling. I loved that my parents still worried about me. And knowing Dad, he'd probably asked Mom to come along since he was the one who worried the most.

Dad opened the back door. "You'll always be our baby girl, Mila."

I winked at my mom, who was grinning. "Get in the car, Dad."

We chatted on the drive, which helped take my mind off my nervousness. Pearson Airport was busy as usual, and I texted Andi, who met us out front as Dad pulled out my luggage, setting it on the sidewalk. I hugged Mom and promised to let her know when I arrived and check in while I was gone. Dad talked to Andi, his head bent low. I approached them as Andi gazed seriously at him.

"I'll watch, Van. You know I'll look after her."

"She—"

Andi met my eyes with an understanding smile as she cut my dad off. "Will be fine, Van. I'll make sure of it."

I rubbed my hand on his arm. "I'm going to LA, Dad. Not some scary foreign land where I don't speak the language."

"Seems to me nothing is as foreign or as scary as Hollywood," he deadpanned.

I laughed because he was right. Andi scoffed and shook her head. "Say goodbye to Mila so we can go. I need coffee."

Dad hugged me, his large arms embracing me, holding me tight. He gave the best hugs. I could feel his love and strength. I leaned up on my toes and kissed his cheek. "Take Mom out for breakfast. Maybe some shopping. You'll both feel better."

I waved them off, smiling, hiding my anxiety. Andi took my arm. "Let's go, kiddo."

First-class check-in was fast, and soon we were in the lounge. Andi had two cups of coffee in front of her, her laptop open, phone beside her, and a plate overflowing with fruit, cheese, and croissants to the side. She frowned at my yogurt.

"That's it?"

"I might have more in a bit."

She patted my hand. "Everything is going to be fine, Mila. The hotel is booked, you have a car and driver at your disposal. No one is expecting you for a couple of days, so you can wander a bit and relax. We'll go to the set, and you can see how it all looks and get familiar with it. I know that helps you. And since no one has a clue what you look like, no one will bother you. I'll stick close."

"I know," I assured her. "I'm sorry—"

She cut me off. "Don't. I understand your anxiety. I'll help you as much as I can." She smiled at me reassuringly. "I know you prefer to be alone and you didn't want to do this. I appreciate the fact that you agreed. I think your insight on set will help. I know you want the movie to be done well."

"Yes, I do." That was why I'd agreed to this. I could have done a couple of Zoom meetings and stayed hidden, but Andi was right. My being there and talking as issues or questions came up made sense. This book was special to me, and I wanted it done right.

"It'll be fun. I am interested in how a movie is put together."

Andi grinned and picked up her second cup of coffee, the first one already gone. "That's the spirit." She sat back. "Now, go get some real food. I want to discuss this new manuscript you sent me. Girl, where on earth do you come up with these stories? I find it hard to believe you rarely leave the house, given the things you write." She fanned herself. "The alpha in this one? Wow."

I smiled and took her empty cup. I would fill it while I was up getting some fruit.

The flight was uneventful, and a car and driver were waiting for us. The hotel was luxurious, and my room was actually a small suite with a living area and a great workspace. My bedroom had a king-sized bed, and a deep, Jacuzzi-type tub was in the bathroom. Andi's room was down the hall. A large arrangement of flowers was waiting for me from the studio, as well as a big fruit basket, filled with all sorts of goodies.

I unpacked, hanging my new clothes neatly and putting my

far more familiar leggings and tees in one of the many drawers the walk-in closet held. I was glad I had listened to Cami. It was warm here, and if I had brought my hoodies, I'd probably melt. I had snuck one into the suitcase in case, but I was sure I wouldn't need it. The fuzzy socks were a must, though. My feet were always cold.

Andi knocked and came in, laughing at the fact that I already had my laptop open. "Got some words?"

"I just did a thousand. I had a scene in my mind. I wanted to sketch it out."

"How many did you do on the plane?"

"About five thousand."

"So prolific."

I grinned at her. "I gotta do something with all the voices in my head."

She smirked. "Those voices are fueling my retirement, kiddo. Let them talk."

She sat down, her ever-present tablet in hand. "Tonight, I'm having dinner and drinks with some colleagues. Over the next couple of days, we're meeting with some studio execs, dinner with the producer, breakfast with the director. We'll go visit the set, then some more meetings. Finally, we'll meet the crew and actors, and we'll start the process. I know John, the producer, says Nicholas and Lacey have lots of questions. So do the supporting cast."

I worried my lip, and she shook her head. "It'll be fine, Mila. They want to do the characters justice. The buzz is already happening." She frowned. "As long as everyone behaves."

"You mean Nicholas?"

She poured herself a glass of water, sipping it, tapping her long nails on the wooden tabletop. "I know you campaigned for him, but I am a little worried. He has quite a reputation. Ladies' man, difficult on set, far too fond of alcohol and illegal substances."

"His work is astounding," I argued. "He pours himself into his roles. And his costars dispute the rumors. They say he is unfailingly polite and wonderful to work with. He is going to be a brilliant Duncan. He has the right look, the perfect intensity. He was my muse when I wrote it."

He was more than my muse. At thirty-six, he was the perfect age for the role. Well-built, with broad shoulders and a slightly dangerous edge to his features, he even looked like the character I had written. He had dark curls that fell over his forehead in a sexy wave. His chocolate-colored eyes were expressive, smoldered on and off the screen, and his smile killer. But I wondered if anyone else ever noticed the difference when the camera caught him unexpectedly and he wasn't "on." I did.

She held up her hand. "I know. And I've never seen you so determined. I just don't want you to build him up in your mind. He's an actor. A chameleon. He can shed his persona as easily as you change a scene. Many of them play a part twenty-four seven. Don't confuse the tortured, intense, deep, soulful character you created with the alcoholic playboy he is in real life. He'll show you what he wants you to see."

I felt an odd sense of anger toward Andi. Toward everyone. I saw something in his eyes that it appeared no one else could see. A hidden, lingering sadness. Fear. Anxiety. Maybe only I could see it because I could relate. Sympathize. My early childhood had left a mark on me that no amount of time or love would ever erase. I'd moved past it and built a life, but the stain lingered.

"I don't expect anything of him, except to play the part

with the intensity and layers I wrote it," I assured her, keeping my anger in check. "I highly doubt we'll have much interaction other than the meetings about the characters. But I stand firm in my gut instinct that he'll own this part."

She chuckled. "Okay, Miss Tiger. I hear you. Now, do you want to come with me for dinner, or are you going to stay here and relax? The pool is wonderful, and room service is top-notch."

I loved to swim. My dad had taught me when I was little, saying I was a natural. His little fish, he would call me. I spent as much time in the water as I could when I was younger. Even now, I swam every day. Uncle Aiden had installed a resistance spa pool in the Hub, and I was in it daily. Uncle Bentley and I were the ones who used it the most, often crossing paths early in the morning as we entered the Hub to swim. If he was done first, he usually made a pot of coffee, and we would sit and talk once I was finished. He was the most serious of my uncles, his reputation as a stern, cold businessman well deserved.

Unless you knew him.

Then, he was Uncle Bent. Warm, funny, and caring. He loved hearing me talk about my books and had often helped me work through a scene I couldn't plan out. He was adamant, though, about not being involved in any of the "spicier" parts of the books. I adored him. I adored all my uncles and cousins our blended family contained. I was a lucky woman to have grown up with the BAM men and the family we shared.

Andi cleared her throat, and I realized I had been lost to my thoughts—a regular occurrence for me. She smiled at me, and I returned her grin with one of my own, my earlier ire forgotten. She was looking out for me, the way she always did, and I appreciated it.

"I'll stay in."

"What a shocker," she teased. "Please don't write all night, forget to eat, and not leave the room, okay?"

"I won't. I'll write a bit, maybe walk around the grounds, have dinner and a swim, and an early night."

She stood, leaning over to kiss my cheek. "Right. You'll write for hours, grab a snack and a swim, then write again until dawn."

"That's what I said."

She was laughing as she left the room.

A knock at the door of the suite startled me, and I looked up with a grimace. A glance at my phone told me I had been lost for over four hours. My word count had grown significantly.

I went to the door, not surprised to see a room service trolley.

"Hello." I smiled in greeting.

The young man on the other side of the door grinned. "Compliments of Andi Reacher. She left instructions if we hadn't heard from you by nine to send this up."

I had to laugh. Andi knew me well. I waved my hand, and he rolled in the cart, setting the tray on the empty dining table.

Luckily, I had some money in my pocket, and I tipped him, lifting the lid after he departed. The plate contained various cheeses and crackers, some fruit and nuts, and there was a sandwich on a separate plate, beautifully arranged. The filling made me laugh.

Peanut butter and jam.

I picked up a triangle and nibbled at it, glancing toward my laptop, the pull strong. I lifted the tray and headed back to the desk and sat down. I wanted to finish this scene, then I would be done for the night.

Time passed quickly, and when I saved my work, I was almost eight thousand words further ahead than I had planned to be. This boded well for the trip. I had eaten the sandwich, nibbled some fruit and cheese, but most of the larger plate was still full. I put the lid back on it and slid it into the fridge the suite came with. I wandered out to the balcony, inhaling the warm night air. It was so different from home. The sounds were foreign to my ears. The steady hum of traffic in the distance, the scents around me unusual. I wondered what my parents were doing. I had let them know that I arrived and all was good, and Dad had mentioned they might have plans that night but hadn't decided. I could picture them on their deck, looking at the water, or sitting with their group at the Hub, sharing Chinese food or a barbecue. I felt a little pang of homesickness, then I shook my head. This was an adventure, and I needed to enjoy it.

I rolled my neck and shoulders, feeling the stiffness from sitting so long and typing. Below me, the pool was still, and I knew it closed at nine. But Andi had told me there was a second, adults-only pool farther back on the grounds, and it was open until midnight. I had my passkey, and the thought of swimming and getting the kinks out was tempting. I could see only a few people walking around, and they all looked as if they were headed to their rooms, not the pool.

Inside, I checked the map, changed into my suit, and put a long cover-up over it. Passkey in hand, I headed in the direction of the pool, stopping the same room-service guy, who pointed me in the right direction. "You'll see the gate," he instructed. "You'll probably be the only one there. The hotel is booked for a movie crew, and most of them haven't arrived. They rarely use the pool anyway. Far too busy."

"Oh, how interesting," I muttered and headed in the right direction. I found the pool, hidden away, the path lit by solar lights, the trees overhanging the way stirring only slightly in the light breeze. I opened the gate, pleased to see he had been right and I was the only one there. The pool was long, perfect for laps. The one side was canopied in low-hanging trees, casting shadows in the corners, the faint lights flickering on the water's reflections.

I pulled off my cover-up, secured my hair clip, and got in, sighing at the feel of the water. Cool enough to be invigorating, but warm enough not to jolt me as I slipped under the surface. I began to swim, all other thoughts escaping my head as I did lap after lap. Finally, I stopped, heading toward the darkened corner. There were steps there, and I sat down, enjoying the silence, the feel of the water, and the breeze on my shoulders.

Then I felt it. I wasn't as alone as I thought. I could sense someone else was nearby. Watching in silence. A nervous tremor passed through me, and I looked around, my gaze finding the form of a person sitting across the pool from me, submerged in the water, the glow of a cigar hanging from his fingers a bright spot in the dimness.

He lifted a hand in greeting. "Hello."

I recognized his voice immediately.

Nicholas Scott was sitting across from me.

"Didn't mean to startle you. I came in while you were swimming," he said. "You must do that a lot."

"Do that?" I repeated, my voice almost husky.

"Swim. You're like a little fish."

"Oh. Yes. My dad says that all the time." Then I grimaced. *My dad.* I sounded about thirteen.

I felt about thirteen. Tongue-tied and standing in front of a boy at school I had a crush on—unable to talk. If Sammy were here, she'd glide through the water, introduce herself, and carry on a proper conversation. Charm him.

But I knew that wasn't going to happen.

He moved, sliding off the step and wading toward me. I swallowed, pushing myself back into the shadows.

What was he doing?

He stopped a few feet away, as if he sensed my unease. "So, you like to swim."

"Yes."

He nodded. "I like to come out here and relax."

I cleared my throat. "You-you don't swim?"

"For fun. I'm not regimented like you."

"I'm not regimented," I replied. "I just like to swim. It relaxes me."

He tilted his head, taking a draw on his cigar. The aroma hit me, reminding me of my uncles and Dad. They liked the occasional cigar, and as much as I disliked smoking, I had to admit, I liked the scent of a good cigar. He studied me, a frown on his face. "Why would a pretty girl like you need to use so much energy in order to relax?"

Pretty? Nicholas Scott thought I was pretty?

"Do you need glasses?" I asked without thinking.

He looked startled, then he began to laugh. The sound was low, rumbly, and sexy as hell. He reached up and ran a hand through his hair that, even damp, fell in curls over his forehead. He peered at me, one eye open and focused through the puff of smoke around his head. "No."

"You shouldn't smoke. It's not good for your voice. Or your health."

He blinked. "I do a lot of worse things for both," he drawled and stepped closer. "Does it offend you?"

"No, but this is a non-smoking area," I pointed out, my voice almost squeaking.

He nodded, then extinguished the cigar on the cement beside him. "I'll dispose of it," he assured me. "But you won't tell on me, will you?" he teased.

"Um, no."

I pushed up to the next step, moving away from him. He noticed my actions and held up his hand. "I won't hurt you." Then he extended his arm, his hand hanging between us. "I'm Nick, by the way."

I hesitated, then let him take my hand. His large palm and long fingers closed around mine, encasing it in warmth. I felt a slow shock run up my arm as our skin connected. "Mila," I murmured.

"Mila," he repeated with a smile. "What a joy to meet you."

What a joy? No one had ever said that to me before. It sounded so personal. Intimate.

My heart raced, and my breathing picked up. Our hands remained locked together, his warmth sinking into my skin. The corner we were in was cast in darkness, the branches of the tree filtering out the moon and overhead lights. His face was angles and shadows, his silhouette a dark form in front of me. I felt my nipples tighten at the closeness of him, the shiver that raced through me having nothing to do with the breeze and all to do with his close proximity. He was taller than I expected, his shoulders wide and his muscles defined, even in the low light. He frowned as he looked down at our hands, then allowed our fingers to slowly separate. He stepped back, shaking his head as if to clear it.

"You're a guest here?"

"Yes."

"For how long?" he asked.

"I-I don't know."

"Are you here with someone?"

"Yes."

He frowned, the action making him look angry in the dull light.

"Boyfriend? Husband?"

"No. A-a business associate."

"*Are* you married?" he demanded, his voice low.

"No."

Our gazes locked. Even in the semi-darkness, I could see the intensity of his gaze. His presence was overwhelming. I swallowed, my throat dry. I should tell him who I was. Explain we would be working together.

Yet, I couldn't get words to form on my tongue. My shyness had kicked in, locking me into silence.

I took in a deep breath, startled as he moved closer. He was too close, yet I wanted him closer. I shook my head. He was too much. It was all too much.

And yet somehow, it wasn't enough.

The intensity hit me, and I knew I had to get out of there.

I pushed myself up and out of the water. "I have to go," I burst out, racing around the pool and grabbing my cover-up.

I headed for the gate, ignoring his plea of, "*Wait!*"

I rushed away, not relaxing until I got to my room, satisfied he wasn't behind me. I dropped my head into my hands, shaking my head.

"What a moron," I whispered.

I was certain he must think me mad. I groaned as I realized we would see each other on set, but I comforted myself with the fact that we'd been in the shadows and he would have had a hard time seeing my face. Besides, I was wet, and he probably wouldn't recognize me. I pushed my hair away from my face, frowning as I realized my hair clip had come out at some point during my race back to my room. Dammit, I liked that one.

I sat down, shocked to see I was trembling and breathless. I felt a longing in my chest I couldn't explain. It had to be the surprise encounter. I had never told anyone about my secret obsession with Nicholas Scott. The first time I had seen a picture of him, something in my chest had fused together. I followed his career closely, celebrating his victories, cheering for him from afar. I cried during his bad times, the sensation of there being more to his story than people knew strong and unshakable. Somewhere deep inside myself, I thought if I could meet him, I could help him. But I hadn't been prepared to see him so soon after I got here. It startled me.

My reaction had to be hero worship.

That was all.

Right?

CHAPTER FOUR

NICHOLAS

I picked up my coffee mug, draining the last of the liquid from it and setting it back down on the table. I glanced at the hotel grounds from my vantage point on my balcony, not surprised to see how quiet it was. I knew the studio had a bunch of rooms rented out for the cast and crew. I was grateful to have a room here. I would be driven to and from the set, and it would help me avoid the paps and reporters that always seemed to flock around me while I was filming. It seemed odd to some people that I preferred life on a set, but I was protected—insulated, even—from a lot of things. Security watched out for me. Meals were prepared. There was always a gofer to run an errand and to pick up something I required. Another one to get me coffee or a cold drink. And often, other cast or crew members to shoot the shit with to help pass the time. And if not, I had my sketchbook. I could draw for hours.

I tapped my pencil as I studied the drawing I had picked up half a dozen times today. It was a study of shadows, the focus of a face I had barely been able to make out last night, and yet the memory lingered.

She had hidden in the corner like a frightened rabbit. Her very posture warned me not to move too quickly. She was ready to run at the drop of a hat. When I'd arrived at the pool, at first I had been disappointed to find someone else there. The last two nights, I'd had it all to myself, and I liked sitting in the water, gazing up at the sky, sneaking a cigar MJ would have no idea about, and enjoying the quiet. I had sat down in the water, watching the small figure glide back and forth—up and down the pool in steady, strong pulls. I lost count of the number of lengths she swam. When she stopped and climbed up the steps across from me, I had a glimpse of her profile and figure. She was short. Curvy. Her hair was dark, pulled back into a knot on her head. She wasn't breathing fast, so swimming was obviously something she was used to doing.

I had no idea why I approached her. I was surprised at her reaction, the fear evident on her face as I went closer. I held out my hand, expecting some sort of recognition. Instead, her eyes had remained apprehensive, her posture tense. Until we touched. Something hit me, something unexpected. Something intense and warm. It felt as if I had touched home. And from the flare in her eyes, I guessed she felt it as well.

It was the oddest sensation.

But before I could press her, before I could find out her full name and room number, she was gone. Rushing in her panic to get away, almost tripping over herself to put some distance between us. She hadn't even noticed that her hair clip fell out, rattling on the cement surrounding the pool. I climbed out and picked it up, intent on handing it into the front desk.

Except I never did.

I inquired if there was a guest with the name Mila but was

informed no. For some reason, I slipped the hair clip back into my pocket and thanked the girl behind the counter, who was watching me with an eager expression, hoping I would stick around and talk more.

Instead, I left before she could find a reason for me to stay.

Now, the hair clip sat beside my sketchbook, the only vivid detail in the sketch aside from the wide eyes I drew from memory. I guessed they were dark—everything about her had been dark in the dim light. The glimpses I'd had of her face had been too cloaked in shadow to recreate. I picked up the hair clip, studying it. It was pretty. Pink with white and gold swirled into the base. Heavy and thick, leading me to think her hair must be long. Her voice had been soft, lilting.

Shy.

I wasn't used to that in this business. Most of the women I dealt with could hold their own. Break my balls without much effort. You had to be strong in this industry.

Something, I was reminded of almost daily, I was not.

I blinked, bringing myself back to the present and the mystery girl. I wondered if she would be at the pool again tonight.

I certainly planned to find out.

There was a firm knock at my door, and I shut my sketchbook and slid it and the hair clip into a drawer before opening the door and greeting my agent as she breezed in.

I followed her to the balcony, watching with amusement as she poured herself a cup of coffee and took a long sip.

"Bad morning?" I asked.

She sighed, overdramatic and loud.

"I had a meeting with the studio and the author's agent. I got read the riot act again about you, Nicky boy." She wagged her finger. "A lot is riding on this movie."

I hated it when she called me that. No matter how often I told her to stop, she still did it. I knew she loved the fact that it made me upset. I refused to let her see that reaction anymore.

"I'm aware."

"None of your bullshit this time."

I tamped down my ire. I had no idea how to explain my *"bullshit"* to her so she understood. How to make them all understand.

I hated all the lies and deception. I got tired of saying it. Living it. Sometimes I was so tired, I wanted to give it all up. That was when the darkness hit the hardest.

"I'll do my best."

"Really, Nicky. Someone pushed hard for you for this role. Keep your nose clean, your pants on, and concentrate. Knock it out of the park. I know you can do it. Stay focused. This will lead to something else great. I know it."

I blinked at her words. *My nose clean and my pants on?*

"Do you believe your own PR, MJ?" I asked her. "The lies the studio leaks out, the ones you support?"

She stood, a frown pulling at her face. I was worried her skin might tear away from her bones if she frowned any harder. Botox didn't like to move.

"I know who you are and what you're capable of if you don't self-sabotage," she hissed at me. "I don't want any of your attitude or meltdowns this time around. I barely contained the damage last time. I have no idea how you got this chance, but you aren't going to fuck it up for me, you understand?"

"I would hate to fuck up your plans," I assured her, the sarcasm in my voice evident.

She glared at me, then dropped her head. "I only want

what's best for you, Nicky boy. This role is a chance to redeem yourself."

"The truth would redeem me."

"The truth would kill your career faster than you could blink. Hollywood lies when it says it loves tortured souls, my friend. They want actors, not patients."

I snorted. "They cater to drunks and drug abusers every day. Hell, they create most of the issues. But they can't deal with me?"

She shook her head. "No, they can't. And they always win, Nick. Remember that. You love acting. Don't mess this up."

Then she switched subjects, not wanting to discuss the one thing I needed to talk about.

"We'll go on set in the morning. The author arrives day after, and you'll meet them." She pulled a folder from her bag. "Speaking of which, you have to sign this."

I scanned it fast. "Really? An NDA? I can't reveal the gender or true identity of the author?"

"Nope. That was the only way they agreed to come here and meet with you and Lacey. Privacy is their number one priority." She leaned close. "I heard one of the studio heads slip up and say *him*. I think it's some big-time businessman who doesn't want the world to know he dabbles in mommy porn." She pretended to shudder. "How embarrassing."

I frowned. "Did you even read this book? It's not mommy porn. It's deep and emotional. Gripping."

"And some intense sex scenes."

"Those are secondary to the writing. I read a few other of his or her books. The writing is incredible."

She waved her hand. "Whatever, Nick. It's a role and a chance to redeem yourself."

I signed the document and handed it back to her. I really

had no choice in the matter, and I was too tired to argue with her.

The file went into her crowded briefcase. "Good, we're all set. I have to go."

She headed to the door, pausing before she left. "Just don't fuck it up."

MILA

I gazed around the movie set in wonder, trying to take it all in. The lights, the cameras, all the various equipment. The cavernous building echoed with the sounds of people talking, yelling, bellowing out directions. And there was only a skeleton crew. I could only imagine how the building would hum once they started filming and the entire crew plus the cast was here. Andi was busy talking to someone, and I wandered, peering at the main set of the film. It was as if the garage had come alive from the descriptions in my book. Even the sign was correct. I felt a flutter of excitement as I investigated, trying to stay out of the way. I pushed my hands into the pockets of the cotton hoodie I had bought at the hotel. It was light but offered me the comfort I needed today. Since my encounter with Nicholas, I had been on edge. I had avoided the adult pool last night, instead swimming before dinner in the other pool. I stuck to one side and did my laps while Andi was on the phone, sipping a drink at a table beside the pool.

When she asked if I wanted to come with her this morning, I said yes, but I planned to stay away from everyone. I had a pass around my neck, so no one questioned my being there, but they had no idea who I was and I wanted to keep it that way.

Someone yelled out something, startling me, and I backed into the shadows of one corner that seemed emptier. I bumped into something, and I turned, seeing a couple of empty director's chairs. I scrambled into one, sitting safely out of the way and watching the bustling going on around me. I pulled my legs up to my chest, resting my chin on my knees. It was all fascinating. I had studied the terms and hierarchy of a movie set, and it blew my mind how many people it took to create a movie. The vast number of departments with the various positions that fell within the scope of each area never seemed to end. Some of the terms I found amusing. The grip, key grip, dolly grip, best boy grip, best boy electric, set decorator, the shopper, the prop master, PAs. The list went on and on. Everyone had their own role to play aside from the actors.

"Hey." A rough voice startled me.

I looked up, my breath catching as I realized, once again, I had run into Nicholas Scott in the shadows. Today, he looked angry, an annoyed frown crossing his face. His eyes were cold, with purple thumbprints under them.

"If you're going to take a break, make sure you look to see whose chair you're sitting in," he snapped.

I jumped out of the chair, my heart racing. He reached over, spinning the chair, and I saw his name printed out on the back.

"Gofers have their own places to rest. This is mine." He sat down, crossing his legs and opening the script he carried. I couldn't help but look at it—notice all the notes jotted in the columns of the pages. The sticky notes attached to the edges. The question marks I could spy. I longed to take it from his hand and look it over, and if I were anyone else, I probably would. Laugh and introduce myself. But instead, I managed to mumble an apology and begin to back away.

"Wait," he said. "Do I know you?"

"No," I pushed out between tight lips.

He scratched his chin, the gesture making me stare at his long fingers as he ran them over the scruff that highlighted his angular jaw. "Maybe we've been on the same set."

Before I could answer, he flicked his hand. "Get me a cup of coffee. Enough cream it looks like caramel. Light caramel. And the tiniest pinch of sugar. Minute."

I blinked.

He glanced up. "That's your job, little gofer. Even if we're not filming yet. I want a coffee." He shook his head, dismissing me. "Now."

I knew where craft services was located. Andi had made a beeline for it as soon as we arrived, needing her caffeine hit. But it wasn't my job to get him coffee. It wasn't my job to get him anything. But I turned and hurried away, my cheeks burning. He hadn't recognized me from the pool. No doubt, he'd forgotten all about me the moment I left.

I saw none of the charming, charismatic man from that night today. He was dismissive and cold.

And he thought I was a gofer.

I should just let him stew and get his own damn coffee, but I poured a cup, adding cream until it looked like light caramel, along with a little bit of sugar, and carried it back, handing it to him. I had to clear my throat to get his attention, then he took the cup from my hand. I made sure our fingers didn't brush, but I still felt the warmth of his skin close to mine. He took the cup, peered at the contents, and took a sip. Then to my shock, a smile tugged on his lips.

"Ah, perfect." He took another sip. "Usually, it's shit." He closed one eye, studying me. "What's your name, little gofer?"

"W-what?"

"Your name. I want you to get my coffee while we're filming. You got the cream just right. That never happens."

I shifted, tugging the hoodie over my head a bit more. "They call me Shortstack," I said for some reason.

He grinned, the gesture changing his face entirely. He barked an amused laugh. "I see why." He frowned as he stared at me. "Are you sure we haven't worked together?"

"I gotta go." I spun on my heel and hurried away.

His laughter floated behind me. "See you later, Shortcake."

Twice, I heard him asking for me while I was on set. Once, I actually went and got him another coffee when I heard him complain about a cup someone else had brought him.

He smiled widely when I handed it to him. I tried not to react to the warmth and sexiness of it. Or the fact that I felt that sensation when our fingers brushed together briefly.

"You always hide under a hoodie, Shortcake?" he asked.

"Stack," I replied. "It's Shortstack."

He shook his head. "I'm not big on pancakes. But I love cake. I think I prefer my name."

I tamped down the thrill his words caused. Nicholas Scott had his own nickname for me.

I only shrugged and hurried away.

When we left the set, I sighed in relief. Andi looked at me quizzically.

"What's wrong, kiddo? Too much?"

"No, it was great. I can only imagine how crazy it will be when there are more people there."

"The actors arrive tomorrow. I heard Nicholas was around at some point. He likes to scope out the set early, I was told."

I hummed, not speaking.

"He was in a bad mood, from what I understand. Kept shouting for some poor assistant. Shirley, I think I heard."

"Huh," I muttered.

"Tomorrow, we'll meet with the director for breakfast. Then you'll meet the cast the day after."

"Okay."

She glanced at me. "You okay, Mila? You're pale."

I sighed. "I'm fine."

She frowned but didn't say anything. She tapped out some messages on her phone then looked at me, her voice cautious. "I know today and tomorrow you want to be comfortable, but…"

I laughed as she trailed off. "I will wear one of the outfits Cami put together for dinner tonight and our meetings, Andi. I won't go in looking like a bum."

She joined in my amusement. "You don't look like a bum, Mila. You look cute, actually. But about seventeen in your hoodie and leggings. I want the cast to meet the author. Not my shy Mila. Can you do that?" she asked gently.

"You want me to play a part as well," I replied.

"No." She shook her head. "I want you to believe you belong here. That you deserve what is happening. I want you to embrace and enjoy it."

Her words hit me, and I wasn't sure how to respond.

She leaned over and grabbed my hand. "You are so talented, Mila. So deserving of this. I believe in you. Your family does. Your legions of fans do. You have to believe it too."

Tears filled my eyes.

She was right—no matter what my family said, or the fact that this deal had happened—I always felt as if I wasn't quite good enough. That someone was going to stand up and point their finger and call me out for being a terrible writer.

"Thank you."

She squeezed my hands. "Remember that. Every time you doubt yourself, remember that. I believe in you." Then to lighten the moment, she scoffed. "And I'm the most jaded bitch out there. If I believe in you, that's saying something."

We both laughed, and I wiped at my eyes and looked out the window.

I sighed in relief as I walked into my room later that night. I had been a nervous wreck about having dinner with the producer and his wife, but it turned out to be a nice evening. He was charming and gregarious, and he loved to talk. I didn't have to say much. He was enthusiastic about the movie, the crew, the cast. He had worked with the director, Amber Grey, before. I was thrilled it was a woman, and I knew her work. She was a sharp, intuitive director, and I looked forward to meeting her and hearing more of her vision for the movie. She was also no-nonsense and ran a tight set.

I stripped off the clothes I had worn, letting down my hair and rubbing my aching scalp. I looked at my reflection in the mirror, unused to seeing myself with makeup on. I had to admit, I looked more grown-up and sophisticated. The outfit Cami had put together helped. The pants and poet shirt with the chunky jewelry had given me an air of smartness while still letting me be comfortable. The silk was soft against my skin, and I'd followed her advice to wear my hair up. Andi had approved, especially when I'd draped a shawl over one shoulder, the pop of color making the outfit perfect.

I kicked off the heels, groaning in relief. Even though they were low, I still found them difficult to walk in, and my legs and feet were hurting. How Andi marched around all day in stilettos was a mystery to me.

I rolled my shoulders, threw on the robe the hotel provided, and walked out onto the balcony. Below me, the lights reflected off the still water of the pool, the area empty. I couldn't help but look over to the corner where the other pool was hidden. I could see the low lights but heard nothing carrying over the air. No sounds of splashing, nothing. I bit my lip in hesitation. The day had left me keyed up yet not wanting to write, my mind too tired. I had done so much sitting and being Amelia. I wanted to swim and tire my body out.

I made a decision and changed into my suit, pulling the robe back on over it. I headed to the other pool, going out the back door and taking the shorter route now that I knew it. I stopped at the gate, peering in, but the area was deserted, the surface of the water undisturbed. I swiped my passkey and went inside, closing the gate behind me. Dropping my robe on a lounger, I dove into the deeper end and began to swim, losing myself to the soothing rhythm of the strokes. I lost count of my laps, finally stopping when my arms grew tired and my body was relaxed. I treaded water for a moment, then swam toward the corner, sitting on the steps and letting the night air kiss my shoulders and arms. I dropped my head back, realizing I had forgotten to put my hair up. I had inquired at the front desk, but my clip hadn't been turned in. I had others, but it was my favorite—especially for swimming as it held my hair in place firmly.

I would have to find another.

It was quiet and peaceful in the dim light of the corner. Tranquil.

Until the surface of the water rippled, and a voice interrupted my moment.

"Hiding in the shadows again, Mila?"

CHAPTER FIVE

NICHOLAS

The night after I'd met Mila, I'd slept badly and was in a foul mood when I woke up. I decided to head to the set and study the script. I always did better surrounded by the sights and sounds of the production. It helped to center me. Ground me to the character. Some actors spent as little time on set as possible, but I tended to remain as much as I could. Study the dailies. Commit the next day's filming schedule to memory. Ignore the emptiness of my real life and immerse myself in the life of the character I was portraying. It was far more acceptable, no matter the role.

The highlight of the day was meeting the PA who had the nerve to be sitting in my chair when I got to set. Obviously new to the business, she had no clue, and she didn't correct me when I called her "little gofer." The name suited her—she seemed too young to be a professional PA, so I stuck to the nickname. There was something familiar about her, but I couldn't put my finger on it. She was short and curvy. Her eyes were an unusual shade of golden brown—almost caramel, much the way I told her I liked my coffee. I had no idea the color of her hair since she wore a hoodie that covered her head, as if she were hiding. Every time I saw her, part of her was cast in shadow, so I couldn't get a good look at her and figure out how or where I recognized her from. No one seemed to know her when I shouted for her, but she appeared a few times with a coffee for me, somehow getting the taste perfect each time. Something intrigued me about her, and I was sure we'd met. But she danced away every time I pressed her and, at some point, disappeared for good. Tony, another PA, got me another coffee, and I threw it away, the cream wrong, and the flavor off. I came back to the hotel and napped for a bit, had a solitary dinner, then went back to the script. I had hundreds of notes, questions to ask the writer. I looked forward to meeting him or her and getting a chance to pick their brain. The intensity of this role spoke to me; in fact, at times, it felt as if it had been written for me, the pain and conflict in his head so similar to what I felt so much of the time.

Eventually, I got restless, and I abandoned the script, sitting on my balcony, edgy and waiting. I knew what I was waiting for, even if I couldn't admit it to myself. Another strange woman who intrigued me.

Mila.

She hadn't shown up at the pool the night before, and I wondered if she had checked out. But in case she simply didn't swim last night, I stayed on my balcony, sipping a bottle of water, and waited. Watching. I was about to give up when my patience was rewarded, and I saw movement below, a small figure scurrying down the path toward the adults-only pool area. I knew it was her. She looked like a child running down the path, but I knew she was anything but.

I followed her, closing the gate quietly, and observed her slice through the water, lap after lap, until I assumed she was exhausted. She sat in the corner again, lifting her head, her long, dark hair fanning out in the water behind her. She was unassuming and nonchalant in her sexiness. I had the feeling she had no idea how incredibly appealing she was—at least to me.

I scrutinized her for a moment, feeling like a stalker, yet also incredibly protective of the minute woman. The hotel and grounds were safe and well patrolled, yet I felt an odd pang of anger that she was out here alone. I could be anyone watching her. Alone with her in the shadows. I discarded my shirt and stepped into the water across from her, disturbing the smooth expanse of liquid.

"Hiding in the shadows again, Mila?"

She startled, a small gasp escaping her mouth. Sitting up straight, she put her hand to her throat in shock. I waded toward her, as if pulled by an unseen thread. I needed to be closer to her.

"Are you done exhausting yourself?"

She lowered her hand, our eyes meeting in the dull light. "I like to swim."

"Obviously. You are aware you shouldn't be out here alone, right?"

"I'm not alone. You're here," she replied, an edge of snarkiness to her tone.

It made me grin. "I could be the big, bad wolf."

She relaxed back against the stairs. "Try, then. Do your worst. I grew up with a father and an uncle who taught me how to defend myself, and lots of cousins willing to help me practice." She cast her gaze over me slowly, perusing me with her eyes. "And all of them have forty pounds of muscle on you, and I can take them." There was a definite challenge in her tone and her expression. "I can take you too."

I felt the heat of her gaze on me as if she was physically touching me. I had been ogled by women most of my adult life. Objectified on a daily basis since becoming an actor. Yet, no glance had ever affected me the same way. My body tightened of its own accord, and the flames of desire licked at my skin. I was grateful for the cool water surrounding me, stopping me from showing exactly how her contemplation was affecting me.

It was extraordinary.

I held up my hands in supplication, even though I was sure she was joking. "No need to take me down. Simply pointing out you're alone out here. I could be anyone."

"And who are you, exactly?"

Her innocent question caught me off guard. It was one I asked myself every day. Wondered if I would ever have the answer.

I shrugged, forcing a smile. "Just a guy who likes late-night swims."

"Yet I haven't seen you do a lap."

I dipped under the water, the temperature refreshing. "Didn't want to interrupt the marathon."

"I'm done."

I turned and dove under the water, doing a few laps in a lazy front crawl. I really had no interest, but I refused to back down from her silent challenge.

At the end of the pool, I glanced back, making sure she

was still in the corner. She hadn't moved, her silhouette outlined in the shadows. Taking a deep breath, I plunged underwater, kicking off the side, and swam in her direction. I emerged from the water at her feet, pushing my hair back and grinning. "There. Laps done."

She snorted, an indelicate sound coming from her mouth as she scoffed. "I wouldn't call those laps. More of a dog paddle."

I laughed at her words. She was amusing. "You want a race?"

"A race?"

"Sure. You and me. A race."

"Why?"

"Call it incentive. Four laps. Winner gets crowing rights."

She pursed her lips, and I held out my hand in challenge. "Unless you know I'll beat you. Given the fact that I'm taller, stronger, and—" a grin pulled at my lips, already knowing how she would react "—a man."

As expected, her eyes flared, and I swore I caught a glint of gold in them catch the light. She tossed her hair like a bull getting ready to gore the matador bothering it, and she let me pull her from the step. The difference in our heights became apparent—she was well over a foot shorter than I was. The same intense sensation of intimate warmth flowed under my skin when our hands made contact, and I felt the longing to feel more of her pressed against me.

But she swept past me, and I followed her to the edge of the pool. "I'll give you a head start," I offered, tongue in cheek. "For the, ah, height challenge."

"Don't bother," she almost snarled, making me grin again. "On three."

She counted, and we were off. Slicing through the water, both of us doing the breaststroke. I liked to swim and was decent, but the small woman beside me was part fish. She belonged in the water and churned through the laps as if they were nothing. In fact, she was leaning against the side of the pool, waiting with a smirk when I touched the edge at the end.

"I won." She playfully splashed me.

"Hey," I protested. "Bad sportsmanship." I splashed back.

The next thing I knew, we were having a water fight. Two adults acting like children, splashing, laughing, ducking, weaving. I felt free and light. Caught up in the moment. I dove under the water, grabbing her by the waist and pulling her close to me as I broke the surface. I held her arms to her sides, rendering her incapable of splashing me. "Gotcha."

Our eyes met and locked. The air around us changed, going from playful to intense in the blink of an eye. My throat felt thick, and I had to swallow. It seemed as if my air intake was being cut off, and I had to force my lungs to work. Mila's breathing picked up, her eyes like saucers in her face. Who moved first, I didn't know, but suddenly, my mouth was on hers, her full lips opening under the pressure of mine, and I was kissing her.

I hauled her as tight to me as I could, the feel of her in my arms perfection. The taste of her was unique. Minty, sweet, life-affirming. My tongue slid along hers, and she whimpered, touching her tongue to mine in a hesitant yet sexy way. I groaned as I explored her, wanting more. Wanting my tongue as deep inside her mouth as possible. Needing her body pressed against mine as tightly as I could. I wanted to embed her into my skin. Devour her until I forgot about anything else. Until I could taste her from memory.

Except, she suddenly broke away, pushing from me. Her breathing was deep, matching my harsh gasps of air.

I reached for her, but she escaped my hands and headed for the edge of the pool. Once again, she grabbed her robe and rushed away, leaving me behind. There was something oddly familiar about her retreating figure. Something I couldn't quite put my finger on. But I was certain I had seen it before. More than once.

Perplexed, I let her go, somehow knowing I had to. Hating every second, but certain we would meet again.

It felt like destiny.

I tried not to laugh at the word.

Destiny was what happened to other people.

Right?

MILA

I stared at my reflection in the mirror, touching my lips with a trembling hand.

He kissed me.

Nicholas Scott.

He kissed me and held me tight in the pool, his passion and desire evident.

And I kissed him back.

Me. Mila Morrison. I kissed the object of every fantasy I'd ever had, and he had no idea who I was.

I was the girl in the pool.

Not the writer of the character he would play in the film.

Not the little gofer he ordered around earlier.

I was just the girl in the pool who teased him.

I wondered how he would react when he realized they were all the same person.

A knock at my door brought me out of my musings, and I answered it, smiling at Andi.

"Hi. Almost ready."

"You look tired."

I shrugged, brushing off her words. "Up early. I didn't sleep much either. Huge scene playing in my head."

She frowned. "You need to stay rested."

I shut my eyes at the worry in her voice. "I'm fine."

I reached for the hoodie, then paused. "It's just a casual breakfast, right?"

"Yes. We're having breakfast with Amber at the studio, then we'll drop by the set for a bit, and tomorrow you get introduced." She grinned. "You can wear your hoodie today and be incognito, but tomorrow, you are A.M. Archer."

I was wearing a pretty T-shirt and capris, but I felt better with my hoodie over top. I knew tomorrow would be different and part of me was dreading it, but it was the reason I'd come, so it had to happen.

I pulled on the soft cotton but left it open. I pulled my hair into a ponytail and sighed. "Okay. Ready."

We were quiet on the drive to the studio. We met with the director, Amber, and I liked her right away.

"Mila or Amelia?" she asked. "Which do you prefer?"

"Mila," I responded. "My family only says Amelia if I'm in trouble."

She chuckled. "Gotcha."

Amber had breakfast catered in her office, and we discussed various aspects of the film, the locations, and her vision.

"We're still scouting the small town," she admitted,

draining her third cup of coffee. "Nothing's felt right yet." She smiled ruefully. "I'm afraid finding a town as quaint as what you described with the family complex by the water doesn't really exist."

I had to laugh. "But it does. That's where I grew up. Port Albany."

"Really?"

I opened my phone and showed her some pictures. She got excited as she looked them over. "Would your family allow some filming to happen on the property?"

I paused, considering it. Did I want a film crew in my town? On our property?

"It would be done with the least amount of invasion into their lives," Amber assured me. "I would be very respectful that it is your home."

"I could ask Uncle Bentley," I offered.

"Just exterior shots. And some around the town. We'd pay, of course."

I texted my dad, Uncle Bent, as well as Aiden and Maddox. BAM owned the land, so they had the majority shares and the first right of refusal. It was midday there, and I knew someone would get back to me. If they said no, it was fine. If they were interested, I was sure Amber could be trusted to stick to her word.

Before I could put my phone back in my pocket, it buzzed, and I had to laugh as I read the reply.

I glanced up, meeting Amber's gaze. "My uncle Aiden wants to know if he can be one of the extras."

Amber was busy looking at pictures of Port Albany on her computer. "Get me in there, and your uncle can have a walk-on part."

He would love that. Uncle Bent replied as well, his wording more cautious.

"They have questions."

She peered at me over her glasses. "I have all the right answers. Give me their contact information, and I will call them today."

"Okay."

CHAPTER SIX

MILA

On set, Andi and Amber walked over to the set decorator, and I mumbled something about a coffee. I tugged up my hood, headed to the craft table, and poured a cup, adding the cream. I had already seen that Nicholas was in his chair in the corner, and I headed that way, pausing before I spoke. He was studying the script again, a pen held in one hand as he read the pages, his mouth moving silently. He looked tired today. Even more tired than the day before. I edged closer, wanting to offer him comfort but knowing I could only do so in the form of a cup of coffee.

As if sensing me, he glanced up. Unable to stop myself, I smiled. "Hiding in the shadows again, Nicholas?"

I wondered if my words struck a memory for him. "So you know who I am."

I had to snort. "Since you made sure I read the back of your chair yesterday, that pretty much guaranteed it." I held out the coffee. "I got this for you."

He snatched it from my hand, almost groaning as he took a sip. "Finally, the good shit."

"Seriously," I muttered. He reminded me of Halton, the coffee snob of the family. He would shudder over the quality of coffee served here and insist on making it himself. I could only imagine him and Nicholas together.

"If the coffee is so terrible if someone else makes it, get it yourself."

He shook his head. "Nope. It's a perk. Someone else gets it for me. And I've decided you're getting me coffee for the rest of the shoot. Make sure you stick close."

I snorted. "I have other priorities bigger than you."

His eyebrows rose slowly, expressing his disbelief. "Bigger than the star? Pretty sure I can call bullshit on that one." He narrowed his eyes, silent for a moment. "And where have you been? You keep appearing out of nowhere. I looked for you— no one seems to know who you are."

"Maybe because you call me by the wrong name." I deflected.

He glanced at my pass, frowning. "Why does that say visitor?"

"Lost my other one."

He drained his cup, tossing it in the bin beside him. "I need another one of those, Shortcake."

"Too much caffeine isn't good for you. Maybe a juice? A water?"

He frowned. "Coffee, little gofer. Now."

I rolled my eyes and, because I was an idiot, got him another one. He watched me walk toward him, his head tilted as if studying me. I handed him the cup, feeling nervous. Was something familiar about my walk? Did he recognize me?

"Stay close," he demanded. "I'm going to need lots of these today."

"The other ones can't be that bad. Just tell them how you want it." I cleared my throat. "Politely."

"Are you suggesting I'm rude?"

"Snippy is a good word. Demanding. Impatient. They all work."

"If you like your job, I suggest you shut up," he said, trying to look angry, but failing. His lips were quirking in amusement. "Or try being a writer. I hear that pays well."

A small laugh escaped me, and he sat up straighter. "Come closer," he demanded.

"I have to go. I have things to do."

He frowned, beginning to rise from the chair. "I said, come here."

I turned and ran. Dodging through equipment, people, and moving fast. I heard his bellowed, "Shortcake!" but I ignored it.

He recognized my laugh. He wasn't sure from where, but he knew it. And it was only a matter of time before he knew for certain I was the same woman he had kissed in the pool last night.

And I wasn't sure what he would do when he figured it out.

Luckily, Andi was waiting for me, and we left the set. I spent the afternoon wandering some stores while Andi was busy. I bought gifts for my mom and Cami, as well as my other aunts. My driver waited outside each store, taking my few bags and stowing them in the trunk. It was warm, the sun bright, and on impulse, I bought a pretty, floppy hat—the brim wide enough to shade my face and shoulders. I paused outside a store, staring at a dress that caught my eye. It was incredible. The softest shade of yellow, it flowed and swirled in the gentle breeze of the fan that blew on the mannequin. The bodice was a halter, with beading that caught the light and glittered. The skirt was full and jagged, layers of material ranging from the pale, creamy yellow to a brilliant orange at the very last layer, with some sort of glittering fabric hidden within the tiers. It reminded me of a beautiful sunrise.

I was tempted. I peeked in the store, looking around nervously. I pushed open the door and stepped inside, the cool air welcome. An older, skillfully made-up woman approached me.

"The dress in the window?" She smiled. "I saw you admiring it."

"It's beautiful."

"Would you like to try it on?" She studied me for a moment. "The color would look striking on you."

I took in a deep breath. "Please."

The next morning, Andi came into my room, coffee in hand, talking on her phone. I had spent the night writing, hiding in my room, refusing to look at the pool. Not giving in to the temptation of going to see if he was there. It was a dangerous game I was playing. I had barely slept, and I felt tired and emotional.

Andi hung up and frowned at me. "Kiddo, what's wrong?"

"Nothing."

"You are as white as a sheet. Have you slept at all? You pulled another all-nighter?"

"I'm fine. I was writing, and time got away from me." I shrugged, brushing off her concern. "I'll sleep later. Give me five minutes. I need to finish getting dressed."

She muttered something about my dad, and I shook my head. "He is used to seeing me sleep-deprived, Andi. It wouldn't worry him—well…it wouldn't surprise him. He knows what happens when I get on a roll."

I headed to my room and got dressed. I chose a simple skirt and lacy blouse, needing to feel feminine and in control. I left my hair down, brushing it until it shone a burnished gold. The soft rust color of the blouse suited me, and the kick pleat on the taupe skirt made it different. I slipped on low heels and even added a swipe of gloss and mascara. I looked polished and professional.

Andi agreed, nodding her approval. "Cami needs to dress you all the time."

I laughed. "This would not be comfortable writing attire."

"But perfect for meeting the cast." She looked past me. "What's in the garment bag?"

"Oh." I grinned with a sheepish shrug. "An impulse buy. I'll never wear it, but I had to have it."

"May I?" She indicated the bag.

"Of course."

She pulled down the zipper and lifted out the soft yellow dress. In the sunlight, the hidden glitter sparkled, the layers of colors on the skirt breathtaking. "Kiddo, this is spectacular."

"I couldn't resist it. I was only going to try it on, but it fit as if it was made for me. I loved it and decided to splurge. Maybe I'll wear it to Sammy's wedding."

"*Sammy's* getting married?" she asked, surprised. "When did this happen?"

"No. Well, she says no. But I have a feeling this Luke is

going to give her a run for her money. He sounds like exactly what she needs."

"Wherever you wear this, you'll be the star. It's beautiful. Maybe even while you're here."

"I doubt that. I have no plans for a big night out. But one day." I zipped the dress back into the bag. "It was indulgent, but I couldn't resist."

"You deserve to indulge." She patted my arm. "You ready to go in and meet everyone officially?"

I sucked in a deep breath. "Yes."

"Then let's go."

It was warm and bright, and I wore my sunglasses and floppy hat. Andi teased me about looking like a movie star, and I ignored her, knowing she was trying to make me smile. I found the sun here hot, and I was feeling a little out of sorts today, not that I would admit that to Andi. I had waited too long to buy the hat, and the sun always had an effect on me—as if it drained me, leaving me light-headed and tired. I'd made sure to eat this morning, and I drank a lot of water last night and today. I was certain by this afternoon I would feel better. Once this meeting was over and I could get down to the reason I came here—talking to the cast about their roles and answering any questions. If I was honest with myself, coming face-to-face with Nicholas was what was making me the most nervous. Would he recognize me as either the gofer he liked to order around or the woman he kissed in the pool? Every encounter, we'd been in the shadows. I introduced myself as Mila in the pool, but no last name. I used Reed's nickname for me as the gofer. It seemed harmless, but now I wondered. Unless luck was on my side and he never gave either woman another thought or connected us as the same person.

We went to the studio and were escorted to a large room. The table was equipped with papers, pens, pencils, sticky notes. On the sideboard were coffee, water, juice, sodas, and an array of breakfast foods. I wasn't hungry, but I took a cup of coffee and some water.

Amber breezed in, looking effortlessly beautiful. Her long blonde hair was in a ponytail. She wore leggings and a tunic, the sleeves rolled up. A baseball hat was backward on her head, glasses on top of it, and her feet were encased in steel-toed boots. She looked casual, stylish, and ready for work. She was smiling and friendly, kissing me on the cheek and helping herself to pastries and coffee, chatting the whole time.

"So excited to get this going," she enthused. "I have some ideas to bounce off you, Mila. I spoke with your uncle. Three of them, in fact. So charming. You Canadians and your accent. I love it."

I shook my head. "We don't have accents."

She sat down, talking around a mouthful of pastry. "You do! The way you say your r's and *about*. Never mind the *eh* bit. I love it. Anyway, Aiden and I spoke at length, along with a Halton?"

I nodded. "He's a lawyer."

"Yes. They agreed to let us do some filming. Aiden walked me around the town via Zoom. It is perfect and will cut down on the filming needed elsewhere. I'm sending a crew to meet with the town officials and get the permits. Aiden and Bentley are going to help." She grinned. "I am assuming they carry a lot of weight there."

"They do," I agreed, sipping my coffee. "Our family owns

a lot of the businesses and housing in the area. They turned it into a project to make the town prosper."

"And your complex! My God, what was it like to grow up there?"

"We lived in Toronto while I grew up. We moved in my teens. I love it there. I do much better in small towns than big cities." I dropped my voice. "Or new places and crowds."

She patted my hand. "You're among friends here. Lacey and Nicholas are eager to meet you. I know they have questions. As do some of the secondary cast. And the pictures of the town have inspired me for some scenes."

"I'm glad. It's a magical place."

The door opened, and Lacey Dunbar walked in. Petite, pretty, with blonde hair that was cut to her chin, she had a smile that lit up the camera. She was effervescent, her dark-brown eyes lit with humor. She was the perfect foil against the dark intensity of Nicholas's character.

She dropped her script on the table, hugged Amber, shook Andi's hand, then flung her arms around me. "Oh my God. I am so happy to meet you. Your book—all your books. I love them, and I am thrilled to be doing this movie." She stepped back, meeting my eyes. "I have so many questions."

"I hope I can answer them."

"I'm sure you can." Then she grinned. "And I won the pool."

"The pool?"

"I bet A.M. Archer would be a woman in the prime of her life, simply wanting her privacy. I also said you'd be as cute as your characters." She winked drolly. "Nick won't be as happy."

"What was his guess?"

"An older woman living vicariously through her characters.

Maybe writing from memory. He said the author was too sensitive to be a male."

"Well, I hope he isn't disappointed."

"I'm shocked he isn't here yet. I heard him earlier, bellowing on set. Looking for someone named Shortcake or something." She rolled her eyes. "He bellows a lot, but it's all show. He's a great guy."

"That's right. You've worked with him before."

She nodded. "Brilliant actor." A dark look crossed her face. "Misunderstood by a lot of people, and sometimes…" She trailed off.

"Sometimes?" I prompted.

She shook her head. "Nothing. My own musings. I need coffee then we can get this started!"

She moved away, and I tamped down my frustration. I had a feeling she was about to divulge something about Nicholas. Something important. I would have to try to find a way to wheedle it out of her later.

I went to the sideboard, pouring myself another cup of coffee. The actor playing against Nicholas as his best friend came in and introduced himself, shaking my hand with a wide smile. With his shock of red hair and dimpled chin, he was the ideal sidekick for the main character.

"Bradley Holmes. Good to meet you. You are quite the mystery, Ms. Archer. Or do you prefer Mrs.? Miss? A.M.?" he asked in a teasing tone.

I smiled at his query, waving my hand. "Mila is fine," I assured him.

Behind me, the door opened, and without looking, I knew it was him. The hairs on the back of my neck stood up. My entire body began to hum with him being in the same room. I swore I felt his intensity. Sensed his penetrating stare on the back of my head. For a moment, I was frozen, then I blinked to clear my head and took a sip of my coffee, striving for calm. With a fast breath for courage, I turned around and met his eyes.

Nicholas stared back, and I had no doubt how he felt about finding me here. His dark eyes were filled with ice, and they spoke volumes.

Anger didn't cut it.

Fury barely touched it.

Wrath came close.

CHAPTER SEVEN

NICHOLAS

I grunted as I stirred my coffee, having given up asking any of the runners for one. They never got it right. There was either too much cream or not enough. Often no sugar. Or some of them totally fucked it up and brought me a cup with enough sugar added to send me into shock. The only one who got it right so far was Shortcake, and she was nowhere to be found this morning. Again.

She was a mystery, it appeared, and not only to me. No one else seemed to have heard of her. It was as if I was the only one to have had any interaction with her, yet I swore I saw her talking to an agent I had seen on set and a few other people.

She was familiar to me somehow, reminding me of someone. I still hadn't figured it out, but I would. Some of her gestures were unique, yet I felt I already knew them. She stuck to the shadows, seemed shy, her voice quiet, but at times, I saw the flash of a feistier personality. But when I pressed her, she ran away.

Much like Mila had done the two times I'd seen her in the pool. It was strange how similar the two women seemed when they raced away from me.

I took a sip of coffee, casting my gaze around the set. The author was arriving today, and I knew Lacey was anxious to meet with her. Or him. There was a lot of interest and even a pool on the identity of the writer. I'd gotten in on it, certain it was a woman, but older. The sensitivity in the writing suggested someone with experience and wisdom. But regardless, man or woman, I had a lot of questions to ask as to my character, then I doubted we would see the author again. Or if we did, it would be in passing. They often came in, did their duty, and left. A few hung around for some filming, but they ultimately found it boring and departed back to their keyboards.

I scanned the vast room again, but there was no sign of the little gofer. It was a shame since I enjoyed sparring with her. Plus, the coffee thing. Even I didn't mix it as well as she did.

My thoughts drifted back to Mila. The sparring I had done with her. Namely with her tongue in my mouth.

That was another mystery. I had never met a woman like her. Another one who liked the shadows. She said little yet intrigued me more than any person I could recall meeting. She drew me to her like a moth to a flame. And I wanted to get burned by her. I felt emotions I had never experienced with her. The strange feeling of needing to watch over her. The sense I had met her before, somehow already knew her. It wasn't possible, yet that was how it felt. And the few moments of pure, unadulterated joy I felt with her. A simple water fight in a pool. I hadn't enjoyed myself that way for years. The women I knew were too invested in how they looked and acted to be so spontaneous. To get their hair wet and giggle like a schoolgirl. To let themselves be real with me.

And although I had kissed her, held her in my arms, Mila was a complete enigma to me. I wasn't sure I would recognize her in daylight, aside from the fact that she was small and had dark hair. At least, I thought she did. It had been wet the two times I'd seen it. For all I knew, it was red or light brown. Even her eyes had been obscured by the shadows of the trees and dim lights. They, too, were dark, I thought. Yet the sense I knew her went deeper than her physical attributes. It was as if something inside me recognized her.

I shook my head at my thoughts. I sounded deranged.

I was feeling a bit deranged. Even obsessed.

I couldn't stop thinking about Mila. How she felt in my embrace. How she tasted. I wanted to know more about her. I wanted to sit with her and talk. Get to know her. I had tried to find her in the hotel, attempting to charm the front desk clerk, but she insisted there was no one registered with the first name Mila, and I could only assume she was staying under a different name.

I also wanted to know why when I thought of Mila, the little gofer invaded my thoughts as well.

It had to be because both of them were mysteries, and each ran from me.

I saw Lacey head toward the conference room, and I drained my coffee, tossing the empty cup in the bin.

I needed to stop thinking about anything but this role. It was time to go meet the author and get some questions answered.

At least I would solve one mystery and finally know the answer as to the author's real identity.

I picked up my well-read script, covered in notes, and

headed toward the other side of the studio, stopping to grab another coffee. I had a feeling I would need it.

I saw the infamous A.M. Archer from behind as I walked into the conference room. I was right and it was a woman, but unless her face showed me something different, far younger than I expected.

Her back was to me, the curve of her shapely butt somehow familiar. Her skirt hugged the swells of her ass like a lover. She was tiny, barely reaching Bradley's shoulder, and he was a good six inches shorter than I was. She wouldn't break my chest. Her hair was spectacular, falling over her shoulders and halfway down her back. The colors were indescribable. Caramel, gold, blonde, soft browns all woven together. It was one hell of a dye job. She had shapely legs and wore low heels.

What I didn't expect was the sound of her voice or her words.

"*Mila is fine,*" she said to Bradley.

Mila?

As in the pool nymph Mila?

I highly doubted I would meet two Milas so close together. Which meant the woman I had kissed in the pool had to be the author. It also meant she knew exactly who I was. Why I was there.

And she'd decided to play me. Have a little fun with the lead actor.

Anger, cold and insistent, dripped into my chest. It canceled the disappointment that hit me first. And the surprise that the seemingly shy woman I had kissed had written the steamy script in my hand.

She was a pretty damn fine actress herself.

She turned slowly, and our eyes locked. Another shock hit me as I took in her wide eyes and saw her face fully.

Mila was not only the author and the pool nymph; she was also Shortcake. There was no denying those full cheeks and big eyes. The color of which I now saw clearly. Golden in their tone with a dark rim around the outside, they were as unique as the face of the woman they were set in. She was a fairy brought to life with her lovely hair, pretty eyes, and full mouth.

For a moment, nothing changed. Our eyes stayed focused on each other. No one else in the room moved. It was as if they felt the raging emotions between us.

My confusion. My anger.

Her…*fear?*

I blinked at the maelstrom of emotions in her gaze. It was like looking in a mirror some days. I felt her anxiety as if it were my own.

Then it happened. Her face went white, her left eyebrow quirked, her eyes rolled back in her head, and she pitched forward.

There was no thought, nothing but instinct. The anger I was feeling vanished. The script in my hand went one way, the coffee I was holding another. I was on my knees in front of her, catching her falling form before she hit the floor. I felt the heat of her coffee splash my chest and my arms. I ignored the burning sensation as the hot liquid hit one cheek. I encased her protectively as my joints took the brunt of the impact.

Then I held her close, refusing to let go until she woke up.

I needed to be the one to lay her fears to rest when she opened those incredible eyes.

Somehow, I knew it as strongly as I needed my next breath.

Chaos broke out around me. Amber ordered everyone out of the conference room. "Keep this to yourselves," she ordered. "I'll let you know what is happening."

A woman dropped to her knees beside me. She was the one I had seen on set a couple of times. She pushed at my arms. "Let her go."

"No," I snapped. "Get a doctor."

"She doesn't need a doctor. She'll come round in a minute."

"How the hell can you be so sure?"

She met my gaze, hers upset but calm. "Because I know her. I'm Andi—her agent and friend. I know what she needs."

Mila's eyes fluttered open, and she jerked at finding herself in my arms. Her gaze flew to the woman beside me. "Andi?"

"It's okay, kiddo. You're okay."

"Oh God, no. It happened," Mila whimpered.

"It's okay," Andi soothed her. "Everything is going to be fine."

Mila's eyes met mine. She pushed at me. "Let me go, please."

"Are you sure you're okay?" I asked, not wanting to release her.

"Yes. This, ah, happens."

"What is *this* exactly?" I demanded.

"None of your business," Andi replied, tugging on my arm to let Mila go.

Before I could retort, Amber leaned over me. "You should have your arm and face looked at, Nicholas. That coffee was hot."

Mila gasped, going white again. "Oh, I am so sorry!"

Terrified she was about to faint again, I shook my head, reassuring her. "It's nothing," I grunted as Andi stood, helping Mila up. I rose to my feet, my hands outstretched, worried Mila would fall again. But Andi wrapped an arm around her, leading her to the end of the large table and away from me.

"Nicholas," Amber said, her voice and stance every inch the director in control. "Go to medical. I can't have your face marred for filming."

"But—"

She cut me off. "Her agent has her. She probably forgot to eat or was overly nervous. I'm sure she's fine. I'll come get you when she is ready to talk to everyone."

I had no choice but to leave, but everything in me hated it.

I headed to medical to get some salve, then to my trailer, where I pulled on a fresh shirt. I wasn't surprised when I hurried back to find the room empty. I sought out Amber, who told me that Mila's agent had taken her back to the hotel. "She'll be back tomorrow. We're doing some read-throughs today." She handed me my coffee-covered script and a clean one. "You might need this one."

I followed her to the table to start work, but my mind wasn't on it.

All I could think of was how pale Mila had looked in my arms. The fear that had been in her eyes before she passed out.

I couldn't explain why, but I needed to find her.

This time, I wasn't giving up.

We received word that the meeting was rescheduled for the next day. The cast sat together, talking, discussing various aspects of some of the scenes, ideas we had. Lacey was calm, Bradley unconcerned, but I couldn't stop thinking about Mila. All the facts I had discovered.

She was not only the author, but the woman from the pool, as well as the little gofer. Three very different personalities, yet the same. The author had a strong voice and was determined. The woman in the pool was soft and sexy. The gofer shy and eager to please. But through all the voices, there was a sweetness. A timidness I suspected was the real Mila. But why would she hide who she was?

The fear I had seen in her eyes before she passed out haunted me. The way it affected me was unsettling. I swore I felt her anxiety.

"…you coming?"

I blinked at the sound of Bradley's voice addressing me.

"Sorry?" I asked.

"We're going for a drink. You coming with?"

"I'll pass, thanks. I, ah, have plans."

He clapped me on the shoulder. "Have fun. It was an interesting day. We'll see if the lady has a case of the vapors again tomorrow."

I felt a flash of anger at his words. "Hey, have some respect. She could be ill."

He held up his hands. "Just a comment. It was an unusual way to meet someone."

"Since we don't know what happened, maybe you should keep your mouth shut."

He frowned. "Wow, I had no idea you were so touchy on the subject."

"She deserves more than to be joked about."

He paused, then picked up his script. "Didn't mean to offend."

He walked away, and I glared at his retreating figure. I headed to my trailer, glancing in the mirror. There was a red splotch on the side of one cheek, but it would fade. My shirt had protected my chest, and my arm was fine. Still a little warm to the touch, but fine.

I couldn't explain my anger. Why the thought of Mila being teased over what happened upset me. I also didn't understand my worry. I didn't know the woman. Not really.

Why her health was so troubling to me was unclear, yet my concern was real.

I paced my room, unable to settle that evening. I walked the grounds, hoping for a glimpse of Mila or Andi. I tried the front desk again, but not even the name Archer got me anywhere. I sat in the lobby, watching the various people around, recognizing some of them from the set. My patience was rewarded when Andi stepped from the elevator. I followed her to the front desk, getting as close as possible to overhear her conversation.

"Can you make sure the dinner for 1401 is delivered by eight? And put a DND on her line, please. No visitors either."

"Of course. Anything else?"

"No."

I slipped around the corner as Andi turned and headed toward the front door. I waited until I saw her climb into a waiting car, then I headed upstairs, dropping by my room for a minute before heading to the fourteenth floor. I was certain I knew who was getting dinner at eight.

It was the same person I had been looking for and who was currently alone in her room.

At least, for now.

I knocked on the door, waiting anxiously until I heard her soft footfalls approaching. The door opened, Mila already shaking her head in vexation. "I told you I'm fine, Andi. Why…" She trailed off in shock at seeing me standing there.

"Not Andi, I'm afraid," I replied, studying her. She was still pale but looked okay, although the word weary came to my mind.

She gripped the edge of the door. "Nicholas. What are you doing here?"

"I came to check on you." I indicated the room. "Are you going to invite me in?"

She leaned her cheek on the hand resting on the door, the worry in her expression doing something to me. The urge to cup her face was strong. So strong, I had to physically stop myself from reaching out to her. The sensation made me tense, and my voice was sharp when I spoke again.

"I really don't want to have this conversation in the hallway. But we're having one, regardless. Where it takes place is up to you."

She nodded. "Come in."

CHAPTER EIGHT

MILA

To say I was shocked to see Nicholas at my door was an understatement. I could feel his emotions, tightly contained, as he strode past me. It was in the set of his shoulders, the way his hands were fisted at his sides. He was still furious.

I shut the door, taking in a deep breath. I followed him, sitting on the sofa as he looked around. "Nice place," he muttered.

I nodded, unsure what to say.

"I just have a regular room. But then again, I'm not the real star here, am I, Mila? Or do you prefer Ms. Archer? Or Shortcake?"

I sighed, accepting his anger.

"Mila is fine. That is my name. Shortstack is what my brother calls me. You changed it to Shortcake, Nicholas."

"And the Archer?"

"For my privacy. For my family's privacy."

He narrowed his eyes. "Are you married?"

"No!" I frowned. "I let you kiss me the other night. Do you think I'd do that if I were married? Or even involved with someone?"

"I have no idea," he replied coolly.

"Well, I wouldn't."

"Why the subterfuge?"

I rubbed a hand over my eyes. "Can you at least sit down? I'm getting a crick in my neck looking up at you."

He sat across from me, still glowering.

"You're the one who mistook me for a gofer."

"You could have corrected my mistake."

"I know. But you were funny with the whole coffee thing. I should have said something. I'm sorry."

"And the pool?"

I had to look away from his gaze. "You were larger-than-life. The last person I expected to see. The man I had fought to have cast as Duncan. Right there." I looked at my feet. "I'm a little shy. I didn't know how to tell you who I was, and I thought I wouldn't see you again outside the studio, and you wouldn't recognize me when we met."

I was startled to feel his fingers under my chin, lifting my head and making me meet his eyes. "You were the one who wanted me for the role?"

"Yes."

"Why?"

I felt the rush of blood flood my cheeks. "You were my muse while I wrote the book."

He looked shocked. "Me?"

I decided to be honest. "I've followed your career. I've always been a fan. You have the right intensity to play Duncan." I shifted, warming to my words. "You're not Nicholas on the screen. You're the character. You melt into the role. I'm sure it's not, but it seems effortless. I wanted that for this film. I wanted you. I pushed very hard for it."

For a moment, there was nothing but the heat of his stare. "Even with my reputation?" he asked quietly.

"I don't listen to gossip. I make up my own mind."

Something passed over his face. An expression I couldn't identify. But I could see pain and worry behind it. Anxiety. "I hope I don't disappoint."

I shook my head. "You won't."

He dropped his hand, and I instantly missed his touch. He didn't say anything for a moment.

He pulled something from his back pocket, holding it out.

"My hair clip!"

"You dropped it. I was hoping I'd see you again to give it back. I didn't have it on me earlier," he added with a slight edge to his voice.

"I'm sorry," I whispered. "I just didn't know how to tell you."

"What happened today? Can you explain it to me?" he asked.

She sighed and nodded. "I have a condition."

"What kind of condition?"

"It's called vasovagal syncope. It causes a sudden drop in blood pressure, and I faint."

He leaned forward, gripping my knees. "Is it serious?"

"It can be, but mine is not. I've had it most of my life. When I get overly stressed or something else triggers it, I drop." I shrugged, feeling self-conscious. "It hasn't happened in a long time."

"What triggers it?"

"Various things. Usually for me, it's when I'm anxious or emotional. I have also found when I'm tired or get too much

sun, that seems to make me more vulnerable to it happening."
I paused. "Today was a culmination of all of the factors."

He stroked my knees, his touch searing me through the fabric of my leggings. "And you were worried about meeting the cast today?" he asked softly.

"Yes."

"Meeting me? Officially?"

"Yes."

"I set you off?" he asked, sounding upset.

"You were so angry."

"I thought you'd played me. Had a laugh at my expense. I hate being lied to. Despise it."

"I didn't mean to—"

He cut me off, squeezing my legs. "I know, Shortcake."

I felt my lips quirk. "I'm not getting you coffee."

"Oh yes, you will. But not right now." He paused. "What can I do?" he asked. "To help you?"

"What?" I asked, confused. "Help me?"

Suddenly, he was on his knees in front of me, between my legs. He looked up at me, concern etched on his face. "Seeing you fall scared me. I couldn't get to you fast enough. All that anger was gone, and the only thing I felt was terror. Fear you'd hit the floor before I could get there. Worry that something was dreadfully wrong. Nothing else mattered in that split second but you. I want to know how to prevent this from happening again."

Unable to stop myself, I traced the slightly reddened skin on his cheek. "I'm sorry I burned you."

He cupped my hand, pressing the palm into his skin. "It's fine. I'm fine."

"So am I. Today was one of many incidents. When I was younger and scared of my own shadow, I passed out almost daily. I had therapy to help me deal with stress, learned tricks to stay calm, and the episodes slowed down. Today was—" I huffed out a long breath "—today was an anomaly. I hope," I added ruefully.

"You scared me."

His quiet confession moved me.

"I'm sorry."

"Are there signs I can watch out for?"

"I don't understand."

"I don't know. Like when your eyebrow quirked. Was that a tell?"

"My eyebrow quirked?"

"Yes."

"I have no idea, no one's ever mentioned that. The doctors never said anything about tells. Usually, I don't even know it's going to happen. I just go."

"But you're not ill?" He swallowed heavily. "This isn't fatal?"

"No. As I said, I have had it most of my life. It started in my early teens. I see a neurologist regularly."

"My mother had cancer and didn't tell me. She didn't want to 'trouble' me while I was making a movie. That role led to another one, and she kept it from me. It was aggressive, and she was dead in six months. I found out too late and barely got to say goodbye." He met my eyes. "I hate being lied to. I don't need protecting."

"Nor do I. I'm not lying. My family is well aware of my condition. So is Andi."

"That's why she didn't panic."

"Yes."

"Is that why you want to stay out of the limelight?"

"That, and because I hate it. I'm shy. I don't do well with crowds or people. Coming here was a huge step for me."

"The woman who writes those books isn't shy."

"It's my persona. Like your roles, I can adapt."

"The one I met in the pool was intriguing."

"It was dark. I felt…safe with you somehow. More comfortable than I expected. You were funny. Sweet. I liked how you made me feel."

"I thought you were incredibly sexy. Alluring. A mystery I wanted to solve."

"I suppose you've solved it now. I'm just me. Nothing very special."

He stroked up on my arm, his fingers light. He cupped my cheek, gazing at me. "I like the woman I see right now. I think she is pretty special."

I felt the warmth of his caress. His fingertips were callused, yet his touch was gentle. He had an expression in his eyes, a heat to his gaze that matched the warmth building in my chest. It flickered and coursed through my body, lighting it up the same way it had in the pool when I was alone with him.

His grip tightened, his other hand settling on my waist. The air around us turned warm, bubbling with our attraction. His head inched closer, and I gripped his arm, already anticipating his lips on mine. I trembled in desire, feeling it unfurl in my stomach, casting its grip throughout my body.

Then a loud knock sounded on the door. "Room service."

We broke apart. His mouth had been so close, I could feel his breath on my skin. Almost taste him. A part of me I didn't recognize wanted to say screw it, forget about the door, pull him back, and feel his mouth on mine. Lose myself in his kiss.

But he stood. "Your dinner. You need to eat."

He went to the door and returned with a tray. He slid it onto the table, waving me over.

I sat down, and he lifted the lid. He chuckled. "Breakfast?"

"I love breakfast for dinner."

"Well, enjoy."

I stopped him from leaving, not wanting him to go yet. "Stay."

He hesitated.

"Andi always orders me too much. Eat with me. Look," I said, lifting lids. "I have pancakes and eggs, bacon and hash browns. Toast. She even added sausage. I'll never eat all this. Please."

He sat down, eyeing up the feast. "Only one fork."

I picked up a piece of bacon, biting down on the salty, delicious morsel. "We can improvise."

He picked up a sausage, rolling it in a pancake and dipping it in the syrup. "Okay, Shortcake, you win."

I poured a cup of coffee, automatically adding the cream, a touch of sugar, and pushing it his way. "There you go, Mr. Hotshot Movie Star."

He sipped it and grinned. "Told you you'd be getting me coffee again."

I laughed. "I guess you did."

***

As we ate, he asked questions. "You mentioned siblings."

"A brother and sister."

"Are you the baby?"

"Yes."

"Do they have the same disorder?"

"No. We're not blood siblings." At his curious expression, I explained.

"My mom already had my sister when she met my dad. He adopted Sammy after they got married. Then they adopted Reed. Then me."

"Wow."

I nodded around a mouthful of toast. "Reed was older than Sammy, so she is really the middle child. We tease her about that all the time. She went from number one to the invisible one. And if you met her, you'd know she is anything but invisible."

Nicholas chuckled.

"Do you have siblings?"

He shook his head. "Nope. Just me. I think my agent is the closest thing to family I have. She is also my business manager."

"Have you known her a long time?"

"I can't recall not knowing her. She is like a sister to me. Or at least…" He trailed off with a shrug. "She was."

"Ah."

He chewed and swallowed, then frowned. "We certainly argue like siblings. She watches out for me, though." He paused. "I think."

"You think?"

"MJ is always on the lookout for number one. I'm well aware that isn't me anymore. But she does a good job, so I guess I can't complain. I haven't always been the easiest client for her."

"Certainly one of her most famous."

He shrugged. "Famous or infamous? Sometimes I wonder."

Before I could question him more, he changed the subject back to me.

"Were you close growing up? With your siblings?"

I huffed out a long breath. "Once I settled into the family, yes. We grew close. My brother was my protector. So was Sammy. They watched over me. Given my history and the issues I had, they were cautious."

"Issues?" He pushed away the plates between us, regarding me with his serious expression. "What kinds of issues?"

"It's not really pleasant conversation," I replied. "I don't want to bore you with it."

"I'd like to know. I guarantee you, Mila. Nothing about you is boring."

I blinked at his words.

"Maybe we can move to the sofa at least and get comfortable."

He stood, offering me his hand. "Okay."

Nicholas

Mila looked nervous as she curled into the corner of the sofa. Her color had returned to her face, and I had made sure she ate well, secretly thrilled at the fact that she loved breakfast for dinner. I did as well. It was something I could cook for myself and was fast and easy. We had that in common. I had a feeling we had more in common than she realized.

"So, you were adopted?"

"Yes."

"How old were you?"

"Three."

"Did your parents die?"

She huffed out a sigh. "My father walked away from us. My mother never wanted me. She was a drug addict and died not long after Van and Liv took me in. She couldn't be bothered with me, really. I don't recall a lot except being cold, hungry, and scared all the time."

I frowned, reaching for her hand. "I'm sorry."

She shrugged. "I was pretty young, so my memories aren't very clear."

"Was she—" I had to swallow before asking "—abusive?"

"Not physically. She yelled a lot—I remember that. Ignored me. Refused to touch me unless she had to. She was far too busy trying to figure out how to score her next hit than worry about things like feeding me or keeping me clean. I recall being locked in a closet a lot. She used to forget to unlock the door at times." Mila fidgeted a little.

I had to physically hold myself back. I could picture a baby Mila. Sweet, scared, locked in the dark. Lonely and afraid. Often the way I felt as an adult.

The list of things we had in common grew.

"I remember how it felt the first time Liv, my mom, gave me a bath. She sang to me, washed my hair. Dressed me in warm pj's and tucked me in. Left a light on so I felt safe. I hated the dark back then. It felt so strange to feel clean. To be touched. I craved it." She smiled sadly, looking at our hands. "I still do."

I moved closer so our legs touched. I felt the warmth of her skin on mine, even with the material that separated us.

"So Liv and Van adopted you, and your life changed."

"Yes. You never really outgrow the abuse. You put it behind you, you move on, but it lingers. I was always the smallest, the shyest at school. I never made friends easily. Even once I grew up and entered high school, I was still awkward."

"I bet you were adorable. Sweet and shy, so pretty. What color was your hair?"

She frowned and flipped her hair over her shoulder. "This color."

"That's natural?"

"Yes."

"It's spectacular. I was sure you had it professionally done when I saw you earlier."

"No. It's just mousy brownish blonde. It never makes up its mind what color to be."

I gaped at her. "It is anything but mousy. It's like a sunrise. Golds, blondes, reds. All woven together. Beautiful."

She looked truly startled. "Oh," was all she said.

"You must know that."

She shrugged. "My family says nice things. I guess I don't see them."

"I see them."

She fiddled with the hem of her shirt. "Thank you."

"So, back to school."

"I hated school. I loved learning, but the rest of it..." She shook her head. "The kids, the bullies. Gym class was awful. I was picked on all the time. Called names. My episodes had started, so my activity was restricted. I wasn't allowed to climb ropes or do some of the intense activities since we never knew when I'd go down. I spent a lot of time on the bench or helping out. Kids don't like it when you're different. And they pick on what they don't know."

"You were bullied."

"I was ostracized. Bullied from afar. My brother and sister defended me when they could. I think if Reed could have stayed and gone to classes with me, he would have. It was easier when they were around." She smiled. "Reed and

Sammy were often dragged into the principal's office for defending me. I think they had my parents on speed dial. But eventually, the bullies got tired of me and ignored me. I was fine with that. I didn't care about their parties or social cliques. Who was dating whom. I put my head down and worked. Got good grades. Made it through those awkward years." She looked sad for a minute. "Luckily, I had a couple of good friends, and we looked out for one another. When we moved to Port Albany full time, it was easier. I had some cousins at school with me, and they watched out for me too."

"Cousins?"

She explained her family dynamics to me, and I shook my head. "I can't even imagine. All those people? All those families coming together as one? Living in the same place?"

"It happened slowly. More of us live there now. Most of the parents have retired to Port Albany. Lots of us live in the complex. Some come and go. Others are married with families of their own and come visit often. There is always someone around."

"Wow."

I couldn't imagine having people around to talk to all the time. Share. A place to call my own where I was accepted.

"When did you decide to become a writer?"

"It sort of happened by accident. I think I lived in my head so much, I invented stories to entertain myself. I loved to write, and I kept notebooks of little stories. I entered a contest one day in the local paper for a short story, using a fake name, and I won. I let my mom read it, and she loved it. I started writing more. Once I graduated and started working, I hated it. I hated the nine-to-five thing. The office. The monotony. Most people would be thrilled. A family business. A secure job. But I hated it. I didn't want to go to university. I didn't know what I wanted to do, but when I wrote, I lost myself in the worlds I created. I loved it, and my parents encouraged me to follow my dream. I submitted a manuscript and got rejected. Over and over. But one day, Andi read my book and contacted me. She helped get me in the door, and well, the rest is history."

"So here you are," I murmured.

"Here I am."

I realized I was still holding her hand. That at some point while she was talking, we had turned to each other, hands clasped, bodies close. Her head lay on the sofa cushion. Mine leaned on my arm I had draped over the top. Our hands rested on our knees that were pressed together. It had gotten dark outside, and the room was dim, the only light coming from the lamp in the corner.

"Does the dark bother you now?' I asked. "Do you want me to turn on another light?"

"No, I love the dark now. As long as I know I'm safe, I'm okay."

"You had a rough start," I observed.

"But a good finish."

I smiled. "Is this the finish or another beginning?"

"You mean the movie?" she whispered.

"Or something else," I admitted. "I'm drawn to you, Mila."

"Which Mila?"

"All of them. The sweet, shy woman. The playful girl. The clever writer. The siren in the pool."

"I didn't know I was all those."

"And more, I think." I let my fingers drift over her cheek. She smiled and leaned into my caress. I recalled what she said about needing to be touched. I lifted our entwined fingers and kissed her knuckles. "I'd like to find out."

"How?"

"By getting to know you. Letting you get to know me. I know you feel this draw too."

"I do, but…" She trailed off.

"But?" I prompted.

"I'm only here for a while."

"Then we get to know each other for a while."

She searched my eyes. "I don't know if I can do that. I tend to get attached."

I laughed, the sound slightly bitter. "You'll get tired of me, Mila. Everyone does."

She frowned. "That isn't true."

"It is. I'm a lot to take on."

She was quiet, and a thought struck me. "I know you're not married, but maybe you have a boyfriend back home? I've overstepped?"

She shook her head. "My last boyfriend was almost six years ago, and he thought I was far more trouble than I was worth, if I recall his words right. Before that… Well, there isn't much to report before that."

"First off, he was obviously an idiot."

She smiled, although it didn't reach her eyes. "Obviously."

"And second, I find that hard to believe. A beautiful woman like you. Clever, smart, successful."

She shrugged. "As you know, with fame, comes many people more interested in the by-product of success than the person behind it."

I nodded thoughtfully. I had experienced that many times. Women were interested in being seen with me for publicity. For access to the right parties, the right people. Some were open about it. Others played a good game. I couldn't recall ever sitting and having an honest conversation with any of them.

Or enjoying their company the way I did Mila's. It was an odd sensation.

"He used you."

"He worked at one of the building supply businesses in town, and he knew my family. He knew what I did. Who I was. I didn't think it mattered to him, but it was what he was really interested in. The money. The life he thought I would give him so he didn't have to work. But he didn't get very far. I have safeguards in place for my money. My family didn't like him, so that was a warning sign. I fainted once, and he was embarrassed by my 'weakness,' as he called it. And when I refused…" She trailed off and cleared her throat. "Let's just say, he wasn't the person he led me to believe he was."

"Refused?" I asked, curious. "To give him money?"

"To sleep with him."

"You have every right to say no."

"He didn't think so. He thought he should be the one to relieve me of my so-called burden."

"Sorry, I'm not following."

Her cheeks colored, but she met my curious gaze. "My virginity."

I was struck dumb. Mila was a virgin?

I blinked. "But you write—" I indicated the manuscript on the table. "Vividly."

"I have a good imagination. I talk to my sister. My aunts and friends. I read."

"Ah." I took a sip of water.

She paused. "And I use porn sites a lot."

I almost fell off the sofa, choking on my water. The image of Mila watching porn lodged itself in my mind. I shook my head to clear it.

She had to be pulling my leg.

"So you've never—" I twirled my finger "—ah, done *that?*"

"No."

I swallowed, my throat suddenly thick. My pants felt constricted as well, and I shifted a little to hide that fact from Mila.

"But you've kissed before. I mean, you were great at it."

She laughed at my obvious discomfort. "Yes. I've done other things, but I have never had actual sex. It has always felt very intimate to me. Precious, even—as corny as that sounds. I haven't met the right person."

I could only nod. I wanted to ask her more, discover more about her, maybe steer the conversation back to this topic, but she yawned. Wide and hard, her eyes almost watering. Internally, I shook my head. She'd had a long, difficult day. Had an episode. Been upset. She was exhausted, and here I was, wondering how to get her to talk to me more about the whole imagination and porn site thing and her virginity. Somehow, I thought it fascinating. And frankly, a total turn-on.

"I should go," I said instead, forcing my thoughts down. "You need to rest."

"Thank you for checking on me. You were so angry, I wasn't sure you'd speak to me again."

Her words stopped me. I cupped her face again. "I was worried, Mila. I couldn't stay away."

She covered my hand with hers, the palm warm and soft against my skin. Our eyes locked, and the tension between us mounted again.

"I want to kiss you."

"Is something stopping you?" she murmured.

I closed the distance between us, covering her mouth with mine. I slid my tongue between her open lips and groaned at the taste of her. I cupped the back of her head, weaving my fingers into her rich mass of hair, the silkiness of it heavy in my hand. I tilted her head back, diving deeper into her sweet mouth, exploring it. I hooked an arm around her waist, pulling her onto my lap. She draped her arms around my shoulders, kissing me back with the same intensity I was showing her. She tugged at my hair, played with the strands at the back and slid her fingers along my neck, making me shudder. I delved my hands under her shirt, ghosting up her back, feeling the delicate structure of her spine under my fingers. The heat of her skin, the velvetiness of it. I wanted to feel her completely bare and pressed against me toe to chest. I was lost in a vortex of sensation. Her on my lap, my cock pressed between us. Her breasts rubbing against my chest. The heat of her soaking into my skin. The scent of her swirling around me. The sweetness of her mouth and the sensual drag of her tongue on mine.

I wanted her. More than I could ever remember wanting another woman.

Then her phone rang, the ringtone blaring out in the room, startling us. We separated, our breathing heavy, our eyes wild.

"That's Andi," she said. "If I don't answer—"

"Get it."

She crawled off my lap, answering brightly. "Hi."

She listened for a moment, tugging a hand through her heavy hair. "No, I'm good. Just getting ready for bed."

I stood, walking away from her. I walked onto her balcony, overlooking the pool. The area was mostly deserted, the night air cool on my skin. I sucked in some much-needed oxygen, allowing my body to calm. Mila joined me, standing to one side.

"On her way back?"

"Soon."

"I should go."

She hesitated. "Yes, I suppose so."

Her hand was resting on the balcony railing. I covered it with mine, squeezing it. "You need to rest."

She nodded, and with a groan, I turned and pulled her into my arms. I held her tightly, loving the way she burrowed into me as if she belonged there. "I'll see you tomorrow, Shortcake. And we'll figure out where we go from here."

"Are we going anywhere?"

"If you want. You can decide."

She tilted back her head. "What do you want?"

I was honest. "You. Any way I can get you. As a friend. A mentor. A strictly professional level." I paused. "A wholly unprofessional level. Your lover. Whatever you want."

She blinked, not speaking. I pressed a kiss to her temple. "I'll see you tomorrow," I repeated. "Sleep well."

Walking away from her was the hardest thing I had done in a very long time. I stopped at the door and looked over my shoulder. She had followed me inside and was by the balcony door, the lights behind her, casting her in a burnished glow. I was certain I had never seen anything as beautiful as she was right at that moment. Her hair was a mess from my hands, her lips swollen and her cheeks pink. Unable to help myself, I lifted my phone and took a photo.

Then I winked and left.

I had a feeling sleep wasn't going to be what was happening when I returned to my room.

Not for a long time.

CHAPTER NINE

MILA

I watched the sun come up, the light hitting the water in the pool. The sunrises here were different from back home, the colors more yellow and orange than in Port Albany. I missed the pinks and purples that were so prevalent there. I rested my arms on the balcony railing, feeling nostalgic. I missed home.

I hadn't slept well again. Andi had made me relax all day once we'd gotten back from the studio after the incident, so I wasn't tired. I had done some writing, but my mind wasn't on the story. It was somewhere else in this hotel—on Nicholas.

Some of the words he'd said stuck with me. Echoed in my head.

"You'll get tired of me, Mila. Everyone does."

On occasion, I caught true sadness in his eyes. Heard it in his voice. I wanted to ask him, but I wasn't sure I should. If he would tell me.

But I knew there was more to Nicholas Scott than he let

people see. There was something deep and profound in his expression. His voice. Something he kept hidden.

I wondered if he had anyone to talk to about it.

I ran a hand through my hair. I had no idea how he would act around me today. How I would react to seeing him. What last night meant—if anything.

My phone rang, and I saw my dad's number. I answered, forcing my voice to sound light.

"Hey, Dad."

"Pumpkin. How are you?"

I rolled my eyes. "Let me guess. Andi called you."

"She said you passed out."

"I was nervous. I didn't eat, and I'd had too much sun the day before. I'm fine. Feeling perfectly normal today," I lied.

"Are you sure?"

"Dad," I murmured. "I'm fine. Honest. Andi shouldn't have called you."

"I made her promise me she would if anything happened."

"Well, you can stop worrying. It was the first incident in a long time, and I'm sure it will be the last. I got lazy," I said, trying to brush it off.

"Was it meeting the cast? Andi said you and the lead seemed to strike sparks."

"I was a bit overwrought," I admitted. "But they were all so nice." I ignored the remark about Nicholas, but Dad didn't let it rest.

"And the lead?"

"I was shy," I said. "I pushed for him so hard, and it was a big moment." I laughed lightly. "I tossed my coffee at him by accident, so no doubt that made a big impression."

"Are you sure? Mom and I can come down. Richard could be there this afternoon."

"Dad, no. I am fine. I promise. Really, I wish you wouldn't worry."

"We'll never stop worrying, Mila. You're our baby girl."

His words took away the annoyance I was feeling. I knew they worried. They did about all of us, but especially me.

"I know, and I love you for it, but really, I'm fine. I slept like a baby, and I already had a big breakfast. I plan on staying upright for the whole day."

He paused, and I held my breath, hoping he bought it. I had slept like crap and hadn't eaten anything so far.

"If you need us, we'll come."

"I know."

I heard a knock, and I headed for the door. "Andi's here. I have to go."

"I'll call tonight."

"Okay."

I opened the door, and Andi came in, studying me. "You're still pale."

"I'm fine." I put my hand on my hip. "Do not call my dad again. Now he's worried."

"He made me promise."

"I'm giving you a direct order. As your client."

Her eyebrows shot up. "Well, well."

"I mean it. Unless I pass out and end up in the hospital, no calling my parents. I'm an adult."

"Okay, kiddo. I hear you." She smiled. "They love you. You're very lucky to have them."

"I know. But I am going to have this the rest of my life. I hate them fussing."

There was another knock, and I opened the door, frowning at the room service waiter. I was about to tell him he had the wrong room, when he handed me a note. It was short and sweet.

> Shortcake,
> Eat. Wear a hat. I'll have long sleeves on today.
> I look forward to seeing you later.
> Nick

I managed to hold in my grin, and I dug in my pocket and tipped the waiter. Andi watched as I lifted the lid, smiling at the toast and bacon. I had told Nicholas how much I loved both bacon and toast last night. He obviously remembered. I piled the bacon onto the hot bread and covered it with another slice and took a bite.

"I'm glad to see you eating."

"You want some?" I indicated the plate that still held a small pile of bacon and the extra toast.

"Were you starving when you ordered this?" she asked, picking up a piece of bacon and chewing it as she poured a coffee. "And what was the note?"

"Oh, ah, just a recommendation I asked the kitchen about."

She sipped her coffee, staying silent as I ate my bacon sandwich and drank a cup of coffee. "Okay, we have a meeting with the cast at ten. You're okay with that?"

I felt the flutters in my stomach at the thought of seeing Nicholas again. I tamped them down and nodded. "Yes."

"Both leads and Bradley will be there. You're prepared?"

"Yes. Really, I'm fine."

She studied me. "Are you sure you're okay? You look…different."

"Different?"

She nodded. "I can't put my finger on it. But something is different."

"You're seeing things." I stood. "Let me brush my teeth, and we can go."

"I like the outfit again."

Today, I wore a skirt and a loose blouse. It was feminine and lacy, and I loved the creamy color with the bright material of the skirt. Andi's gaze focused on my neck, and she frowned. "Did you scratch yourself? The side of your neck looks red."

My hand flew to my neck. Nicholas's scruff had left some marks. I thought I'd covered them up and even wore my hair down to hide them. "Blow-dryer got too close," I mumbled. "Not used to using one."

She laughed. "The things we go through for beauty. Okay, you get ready. I'll make sure the car is coming."

I escaped to the bathroom and added more concealer to the offending pink patch. I tugged on the neckline, doing up another button on the shirt. Andi was right. I did look different. Brighter. My lips were still a bit red, maybe even a little swollen from Nicholas's mouth.

I giggled softly to myself. I felt like a teenager, sneaking around with her boyfriend so her parents didn't catch them.

I had never experienced that growing up.

What was Nicholas Scott doing to me?

At the studio, I sat in the conference room, trying to be calm. But every time the door opened, the butterflies in my stomach erupted, only to settle down when it wasn't Nicholas who came into the room. Aside from asking if I was feeling okay, no one mentioned yesterday. Amber sat with us, and I spoke with Bradley and Lacey, listening to their thoughts and giving mine on their characters. Andi sat at the end of the table, constantly busy on her phone. I was grateful to have her there, knowing if I needed her, she would be close.

Lacey looked puzzled, glancing at her phone more than once. "I wonder where Nick is. He was the one with the most questions," she mused. "I thought he'd be here."

Bradley smirked. "He had plans last night. Maybe those *plans* kept him up late." He waggled his eyebrows, trying to look funny.

Lacey rolled her eyes, and I frowned. He'd had plans for after he saw me? Or had I been his plans?

Before I could say anything, Nicholas hurried in, carrying his script under his arm. He looked upset, tired, and anxious.

"Sorry," he said. "Got stuck in another meeting. I hope I didn't hold things up."

"I'm kinda done," Bradley announced, standing. "I didn't have a lot of questions. At least not yet. I'm going to head to my trailer. Thanks, Mila."

"Sure."

Nicholas cleared his throat, and our eyes met, his intense gaze locking on mine. "I apologize."

"Not a problem," I replied, hoping I didn't sound as breathless as I thought I did. "I was just going to get another coffee."

Lacey stood. "I'm going to get a smoothie from craft services. Anyone else want one?"

I shook my head. "No, the coffee here is good for me, thanks."

Amber jumped from her chair. "Great idea. We'll take a fast break and get back at it."

They left, and Andi walked to the window, talking on her phone. I headed to the sideboard, pouring coffee for myself. Nicholas sidled up next to me.

"You got one of those for me, Shortcake?"

I laughed quietly, already pouring a second cup. He watched me as I stirred in the cream and sugar, and I slid it his way, making my own. We stood next to each other, sipping our hot beverages.

I felt the flutter of his fingers brush along mine.

"Hi," he whispered.

"Hi," I whispered back. "Thanks for breakfast."

He squeezed my pinkie. "Just returning the favor."

I glanced at him. "You okay?"

"I am now."

Then he stepped back and headed for the table. I followed him, sitting down, trying not to laugh as he hooked his foot around the leg of my chair and slid it closer to him while not even looking. He was busy opening up his script and pulling a pen from behind his ear.

Lacey and Amber returned, and Andi sat back at the end of the table, not seeming to notice how close Nicholas sat to me. No one did.

Nicholas turned to me. "I have a lot of questions, Mila."

I drew in a deep breath. "I hope I have the answers."

He cocked his head, studying me, a grin pulling on his lips. "If anyone does, it'll be you."

NICHOLAS

I grilled Mila for two hours. Lacey got bored and left. Amber came and went, and Mila's agent, Andi, spent the time on the phone or her laptop, often disappearing and getting straight back to work once she seemed sure Mila was okay.

I had been late, cursing and upset that I was delayed.

MJ had shown up unexpectedly, a pile of scripts clutched in her hands. "I need you to go through these. I think the top one is a winner."

I frowned. "I told you I wanted a break when this was done."

She shook her head. "If this goes well, you need another one right away. I want you to keep working. Smooth out your reputation."

I had shut my eyes, gathering my patience. "My reputation is fine."

"If this movie does well, we need to cash in on the good PR." She held up a script. "This one is angsty and gritty." She frowned. "It's a pretty long shoot. You'll have to do some training and lose some weight for the second part of the movie, but it's doable."

I shook my head. "No. I don't want a grueling schedule."

She became irate. "Too bad, Nicholas. You need to listen to me——"

I interrupted her. "No, you need to listen to me, MJ. If I don't think I can do it, I'm not going to."

"Then you can kiss your career goodbye."

"Stop being so overdramatic," I insisted. "That's my job." I tried to tease her into a better mood.

She glared at me. "Then do your job. Stop wasting my time."

She stormed out, and it took me a while to relax. I glanced through the script, rolling my eyes. Doable? I would have to train intensively, and the weight loss would be significant. As I'd learned the last time, I didn't handle those extremes well.

Had she forgotten, or did she simply no longer care?

It hit me that perhaps she never really had—at least not for a long time.

That led to more thoughts, and I forgot the time, making me late.

Mila pursed her lips, shaking her head, bringing me out of my woolgathering.

"I never thought about it that way," she mused. "I saw him as deeper than that. Complex and trying to handle everything on his own." She huffed out a long breath. "Not because he wanted to, or even made the conscious decision to, but because he didn't know how to do it any differently. How to ask for help," she explained. "Does that make any sense?"

"Yeah," I replied. "I get that."

"Do you?" she asked. "Know how to ask for help, I mean?"

I sat back, surprised by her question. Amber was out of the room, and Andi was on the phone again at the other end of the conference room.

"I don't know," I replied honestly. "I'm not given the choice most of the time."

She nodded, looking thoughtful.

"Do you?" I queried. "Have someone you can turn to?"

"Yes," she stated firmly. "My family. They would help me, no matter what."

"You're very lucky."

"I know."

Our gazes held, and I slid my hand onto her leg, entwining our fingers briefly. I had found it torture being this close and not able to touch her. Walking in here, I wasn't sure how she would react to me this morning after last night. She had been on my mind all night. The last thought in my head when I finally fell asleep, the first one when I woke up. It was her name I groaned low in my throat as I stroked myself in the shower.

I had heard the slight hitch in her voice when she greeted

me. Saw the soft color on her cheeks, the welcome in her shy, sweet gaze. The urge to cup her face between my hands and kiss her full mouth was strong, but I'd managed to resist. I wanted to know if her blush warmed her skin. To trace the heat with my lips and discover how far down her neck the pink went. I settled for sitting close and inhaling her floral perfume, listening to her voice, losing myself in her world. She was magical as she talked about the characters and her vision. The shy woman melted away, and she became animated, her voice taking on a different tone. She used her hands to emphasize her points, was adamant in her beliefs, not offering an apology for her thoughts. I loved seeing this side of her. It was so different from the more timid version she usually showed.

"You can ask me," she whispered, squeezing my hand and bringing me to the present again.

I smiled, glancing over to make sure Andi was still busy on the phone. I liked her. She seemed to be a straight shooter, and I had half listened to her when she was talking to someone. Always polite, but firm. She represented her artists well. MJ was abrupt, bordering on rude at times. She insisted she had to have balls to "play with the big boys," but it seemed to me that Andi did the same thing without the attitude.

It gave me pause, wondering if perhaps it was time to look for new representation. I had always been loyal to MJ. She was there when no one else would look at me. We'd fought together. She'd stuck with me through some rough times. Celebrated my achievements.

Or at least, she used to.

I tried to recall when that changed. When our relationship changed. When we went from fighting together to fighting each other.

I shook my head. I was maudlin this morning.

Satisfied that Andi was still busy and not remotely concerned about Mila and me, I leaned a little nearer. No one had objected when I sat next to her this morning. It gave me the chance to touch her occasionally. I liked having her close.

"Have dinner with me."

"What?" Mila responded.

"Dinner. Tonight."

She glanced at Andi. "Where?"

"I don't care."

"I'm not sure it would be a good idea…" She trailed off.

"There are lots of places we can go and not be discovered," I urged her. I knew her need for privacy was for her own anonymity, not because she didn't want to be seen with me.

Her lovely eyes lit with mischief. "Oh, a clandestine dinner. Will there be passwords and secret handshakes?"

I chuckled. "A good meal, some conversation, and if I have my way, my mouth on yours as often as I can get it," I said honestly.

She blinked. "Oh."

"Is that a yes?" I asked, hearing Andi say goodbye to whoever she was on the phone with.

"Yes."

Andi sat down. "You two behaving yourselves?"

I smiled at her. "Mila's insight is helping me see my character better. I still have tons of questions, though." I glanced at my phone then at Mila. "You should eat, though, right? I don't want you to faint again. I can get you something from crafty."

She shook her head, and I glanced at Andi, who looked surprised at my words. I cleared my throat, covering my slipup.

"I assumed yesterday happened because of no food and the heat hitting you."

"Oh, um, yeah," Mila mumbled.

Andi stood. "You should take a break, kiddo, and walk around. We can sit down again after lunch if you still have questions, Nicholas?"

"Yeah, I do. Plus, I was hoping Mila was going to be around during some of the filming so I could pick her brain on occasion." I glanced at Mila. "Yes?"

"We haven't determined how long," Andi said smoothly. "But some time is planned."

"Good." I winked subtly at Mila, reaching under the table to squeeze her fingers again. "That is good."

I managed some more time with Mila in the afternoon. Andi was busy talking with Amber, so I got Mila's number and arranged to meet up with her at six.

"What will you tell Andi?" I asked, curious.

She laughed. "That I'm writing. She never disturbs unless it's an emergency. And if she did and I wasn't there, I would tell her I was swimming." She looked concerned. "You sure no one will see us?"

"Nope," I assured her. "I have a plan."

"Okay."

"Meet me by the side door at six."

"How should I dress?" she asked.

"Super comfortable."

"Okay."

At ten past six, I was waiting, smiling when she appeared, rushing my way. She was in leggings and a long top, her hair piled up on her head, looking somewhat messy. Not a bit of makeup on. Sneakers. Natural. Perfect.

I did what I had been dying to do all day and cupped her cheek, kissing her sweet mouth. I dragged my lips across her cheeks, finally knowing that her blush did make her skin warm. I nuzzled the soft spot behind her ear, grinning when I felt the heat intensify.

"Hi, pretty lady."

"I was writing," she murmured. "I got caught up in a scene. I'm sorry I made you wait."

I chuckled, kissing her again. "Ten minutes is nothing. I'm used to being kept waiting far longer."

"I hate being late, but I usually am if the words are flowing."

"We can go back upstairs, and you can write."

She frowned. "And what would you do?"

I shrugged. "Watch you. Study the script. Make sure you ate."

She shook her head. "Wow. Not what I expected, but no. I want to go out. I don't want to ruin your plans."

I bent and kissed her again, wondering how I had gotten addicted to her mouth so fast. "As long as you're there, my plans are complete."

She blinked. "Oh."

"But I would like you to take a break. We don't have to be gone long."

"I want to go with you."

I held out my hand. "Then let's go."

Mila peered around my SUV, then at me.

"What?" I asked.

"I would have thought you'd drive a convertible or some expensive, sporty car," she admitted.

I chuckled. "I'm sure you've seen photo shoots of me beside cars like that. I had one a few years ago, but it attracted attention. I like this one. It's comfortable, blends in, and I feel safe when I'm driving it."

"Road safe or protected from the world safe?" she asked, indicating the tinted windows.

"Both."

"Do you like being an actor?" she queried.

"I love acting. I hate the world around it," I admitted.

We drove in silence. I liked the fact that she was quiet. She didn't fill the air with idle chatter. She didn't even ask where we were going, instead trusting me to take her wherever.

She looked curious as I pulled off the road, guiding the SUV down a dirt path.

"Are you a serial killer? Planning on dumping my body?"

I chuckled. "Yep. And you fell for it."

"Damn. I really wanted to finish that chapter."

Then she gasped as the road opened up and the view appeared. The cliffs overlooking the ocean were one of my favorite places to escape to. She leaned closer to the window, gripping the dashboard and staring at the vista. I parked the vehicle.

"I brought a picnic. No one will see us, and we can be together."

"It's so beautiful."

"I wanted to share it with you." I paused. "I have never brought another person here."

She turned and pressed her mouth to mine. "Thank you."

I smiled against her lips. "You're welcome."

We climbed out of the SUV, and I grabbed the picnic basket and blanket from the back. I spread out the blanket on a flat piece of ground as Mila wandered to the edge, looking out over the ocean. I joined her, wrapping my arms around her and pulling her back to my chest. "Not too close," I murmured.

"Where I live is surrounded by water but not like this. It's so wild. Open," she breathed out. "Breathtaking. Inspiring."

I was pleased. "Yeah?"

"Yes."

"Good. We can explore a bit after. Come eat."

She let me lead her to the blanket, and we sat down. Her eyes widened. "This looks amazing!"

I grinned. "I had a place I know make it."

They had outdone themselves. We had small croissants stuffed with tempting fillings, chicken and avocado roll-ups, a mini charcuterie board, a pretty tomato salad, chocolate-covered strawberries, tiny cream puffs. A bottle of my favorite white wine, chilled. Napkins, utensils, everything we needed to enjoy the small feast. They'd even provided real glasses for the wine, and I smiled as I handed her the red rose I'd asked them to include.

Her blush was soft as she took it from my fingers. She lifted it to her nose and inhaled the fragrance. She met my gaze. "Thank you for tonight," she said simply. "I had a wonderful time."

"It's just started."

"It's already the best night I've had in a long time."

I handed her a plate. "Me too, Shortcake. Me too."

We ate and chatted. About nothing. The view. The small town she lived in and the family she grew up with. Our favorite colors. Ice cream. Her small feet. My larger ones. We laughed as we stretched out our legs, comparing them.

"Your toes are very long," she observed.

"Yours are little stubs. Pretty color, though."

She wiggled her toes, leaning back on her hands. "I like to paint my toenails often. Today felt like a burnt-orange day."

I slid my hand over hers that rested between us. "Like the sunset." It was already getting dark, but I had thought ahead and brought a couple of battery-powered lanterns with us. They added a cozy glow to the air.

"It was spectacular here."

"I know."

We strolled along the cliffs but far away from the edge. I wrapped my arm around her waist, tucking her close to my side, and carried a lantern in the other. It was different. I couldn't recall the last time I wanted to be this close to a woman. Needed to touch her constantly. All during dinner, we had touched. Fed each other bits off our plates. Shared small kisses. Held hands. She touched me often while talking. My arm, shoulder, or the top of my leg. I kissed her knuckles, tucked stray strands of hair behind her ear, stroked her cheek. Pulled her earlobe while teasing her.

"No episodes today?" I asked. "I was watching. Your eyebrow never twitched."

"No, I was fine. I wasn't nervous today after you arrived."

I stopped walking, turning to face her and gazing down. "You were before I got there?"

"I wasn't sure how to act. After the pool. Last night."

"How did you expect me to act?"

She shrugged, looking self-conscious. "I don't have a lot of experience, Nick. It could have been a momentary lapse of judgment. A moment. I wasn't sure if…" She trailed off.

"If?" I prompted gently.

"If you felt something too, or if it was just me."

I slid my fingers under her chin, lifting her head. "I felt it too," I assured her. "I know there is a lot of press out there about me, Mila, but it's just that. PR. MJ is of the mindset no press is bad press. She encourages the rumors and stories to keep my name in the media. Most of it is just BS. I'm not a playboy."

I bent and brushed her lips with mine. "I don't know what is happening right now, and I'm not questioning it. I'm just trying to live in the moment and enjoy it." I kissed her again. "I don't do that very often."

"You don't?" she whispered, rolling up on her toes and kissing me back.

"No. My life is scripted, Mila. I do what I'm told. Go where I'm told. Play the parts I'm told to play. I lose myself in the characters so I can forget what a miserable life I have outside the set."

"You hide yourself?"

"I have to."

She played with the hair at the back of my neck, making me shiver. We both were keeping our voices low, sharing secrets, the rest of the world disappearing for now. Allowing the other person to see our vulnerabilities.

"The only place I feel like Nicholas is with you. And you come totally unscripted." I smiled, tracing a finger down her cheek. "Unscripted with Mila."

She returned my smile with one of her own. It was wistful and shy. "Sounds like a book."

"A best seller if you ask me."

Our eyes locked, silent words in our gazes. Trust, tentative and warm, flowed between us. Other emotions swam in the depths of her incredible gaze. I wondered if she saw my internal struggle. I had so much to tell her. So many things she needed to know about me. As if she felt the tug-of-war in my head, she cupped my cheek, tracing along my jawline.

"We'll figure it out," she whispered. "It's okay, Nicky baby. It's okay."

"What did you call me?" I asked.

"Um, baby?"

"Nicky. You called me Nicky." No one had called me that since my mother died, unless it was MJ during one of her rants. Then, it was used in a derogatory manner. Nothing like the sweet way it fell from Mila's lips.

"I won't if you——"

I cut her off. "I want. And no one has ever called me baby like that before."

"No one has ever called me Shortcake."

I couldn't resist her anymore. I yanked her close and kissed her hard, sliding my tongue into her mouth and tasting her sweetness. She whimpered and clutched at my shoulders as I tightened my grip on her. I slid my fingers into her hair, tugging on the messy strands, liking the fact that I broke the elastic keeping them bound and feeling them fall over my skin like a wave of silk. I dove deeper into her mouth, into her, feeling complete and whole. Not denying the desire I felt for her, exulting in the knowledge she felt it back for me.

We kissed until we were breathless. Until we had to stop before I carried her to the blanket and made love to her until she cried out my name. I pressed my forehead to hers, our ragged breathing mingling.

I took her hand, and we sat down, the darkness closing in.

I felt her yawn, and I chuckled, pulling her tight to my chest. "Boring you already?"

"I didn't sleep much last night," she confessed.

"Too busy thinking of me?" I teased.

"Yes."

My breath caught in my throat, and I held her tighter. "I kept thinking of you too," I confessed.

"What were you thinking about?"

I nudged her head to the side with my chin and placed my lips to her ear. "You want to know how I couldn't stop thinking about how you felt against me, Mila? How you tasted? The incredible way you smelled? How you dropped your little porn-watching information like you were telling me it was going to rain in the morning? Do you want to know how I wrapped my hand around my cock and stroked myself, remembering all that? Wishing you were there with me? Thinking about how much I want to watch you watch porn and pleasure yourself?"

She moaned softly, pressing back into me. My cock was hard, trapped between us. I dropped a hand to her thigh, stroking the warm flesh I could feel under her thin leggings.

"I thought about it all night. Imagining it. Wanting it. Wanting you."

"I don't touch myself," she whispered.

"Oh God." I shut my eyes, my hand drifting closer to her center. "You use a vibrator?"

"No. I-I don't have to do anything. I get so turned on, I orgasm."

My hand stilled. The air in my chest constricted. My cock hardened to the point of being painful.

"What?" I asked.

"Watching it, porn, sometimes makes me orgasm."

I buried my face in her neck. *"Jesus."*

My next statement made her laugh. "I want to see."

"Um…"

I pressed my lips to her neck, nipping at the juncture and licking away the sting. "All of it, Mila. I want to feel you come on my cock. Watch you as you fall apart. See what you look like as you climax. Hear my name as you scream. And I want to watch you as you come from watching someone else orgasm. Promise me, one day I'll get all that." I pulled on her earlobe, tugging it with my teeth. "Tell me you want that too."

She gasped as I boldly cupped her, groaning at the heat under my hand.

"Yes," she whispered.

I ran my finger along her seam with a groan. I moved my hand to her waistband. "Tell me to stop," I demanded. "Tell me to move my hand away."

She wrapped her arm around my neck, pulling my head down to hers and kissing me. I hooked my feet around her, pulling her legs open and delving my hand inside the material, finding her wet and bare.

"Oh God. You're so turned on right now, you're wet for me, baby." I stroked her, all pretense of trying to be a gentleman falling away. I was so excited, my entire body felt as if it was a live wire. "Sweet little Mila, shy and soft. Who knew fire like this burned inside you?"

I kissed her again, deep and desperate. She whimpered as I circled her clit, the hard nub almost vibrating under my touch.

"Has anyone else done this for you, baby? Stroked your clit? Made you tremble?"

"No." She arched against my hand. "Please don't stop."

"I'm not stopping until you come on my hand. Cry out my

name." I slid a finger inside her, cursing at how tight she was. "Jesus, I want to feel you wrapped around my cock."

She whimpered again, and I banded my arm around her waist as she began to undulate her hips. The friction against my cock was incredible. The heat and wetness of her an aphrodisiac. I pressed my thumb to her clit and kept sliding my finger inside her. When she whispered "More," I carefully added a second finger, stretching her. Her reaction was to press back into me harder and move her hips restlessly.

"Is that what you need, baby? My fingers inside you? Your clit to be played with? You're going to come for me soon, I can tell. Your sweet little clit is so hard. So needy. Next time, I'll suck it. I can't wait to taste you." I groaned as she moved faster. "Do you feel my cock on your back? I'm going to come too, Mila, my dirty girl. All over myself."

I kept kissing and licking at her neck. Her mouth. She grasped my thighs, moaning and gasping, her fingernails digging in through the cotton. Then she stiffened, crying out, arching her back and sobbing my name. My orgasm hit me, and I came, hot and thick, trapped between her back and my shirt, not caring in the least about the mess we were making. I grunted and cursed, holding her tight as she jerked and spasmed against my hand.

And then we were still. Breathing hard. Overcome. Neither of us spoke until I felt her shiver. I slowly withdrew my hand and wrapped my arms around her.

"First off, tell me you don't regret that."

"No."

"Second off, promise me we'll do that again. Maybe in a more private place where we can take longer and I can make you come harder."

"Harder?" she squeaked.

"So hard you'll see stars."

She patted my hand. "Already did."

"Then fucking Jupiter."

She laughed softly. "Okay, then."

"And third, tell me how brilliant I am that I keep a spare set of gym clothes in the trunk and just this morning picked up my dry cleaning. I have towels and a clean shirt for you." I leaned down and kissed her neck, liking how she shivered. "Not that the idea of you walking across the lobby wearing some of me doesn't turn me on yet again."

"A clean shirt would be appreciated," she said in her prim tone that always made me laugh. "I'm a little damp."

"Okay, my dirty little girl. One cleanup, fresh clothes, and maybe a cup of coffee somewhere before I take you back to the hotel."

"Or we could just stay here," she said, snuggling into me.

Her words made me smile. I wrapped her in my arms, kissing her temple. "For a while, Shortcake."

"Okay."

I kissed her again. "Okay."

CHAPTER TEN

MILA

Nicholas held my hand all the way back to the hotel. We didn't talk much, and I felt his sidelong glances my way on occasion.

I wasn't sure what to say to him. I had never done anything quite like that before. I had barely dated, never mind such an intimate, highly erotic encounter.

The thought of it made me shiver. I ached a little from his endeavors, but I liked it. His dirty talk and the way he touched me had been incredible. How I responded had shocked me, yet with Nick, it felt so right.

We felt so right.

"Damn," he suddenly said and sped up, going past the hotel.

"What's wrong?" I asked.

He pulled over a few blocks up and parked. "Photographers," he hissed. "Fucking paps in front of the gate of the hotel." He slammed his hand on the steering wheel. "How the fuck did they find out I was here?"

"Is there a chance it's not for you?" I asked, trying to keep the mood light. "Perhaps another celebrity is staying at the hotel that they're after."

He ran a hand through his hair. "No, I recognized one group. They're after me constantly. In my face. Screaming things, taunting me. Trying to get me angry so I'll say or do something stupid and they can catch it on film."

"Has that happened?"

He sighed, leaning his head back on the leather. "Yes. A couple of times."

He looked over at me. "My windows are tinted, but they'll be able to look through the front and see you there. I know you don't want that, and I certainly don't want them splashing your picture around and making remarks."

"Then I'll get out and walk. They don't know me, so I'll go right past them and into the entrance. I have my guest pass. You wait and drive in a few moments later."

"I don't want you walking."

I laughed. "Nick, I walk a lot. I've been for walks here. It's perfectly safe."

"I'm back to Nick?" he asked, lifting one eyebrow.

"I think the other is for, ah, special occasions."

He grinned. "I like special occasions with you." Then he became serious again.

"I should be escorting you back to the hotel."

"You can watch. Make sure I get in the gate. Give it ten minutes and drive through. If they take a picture of you, you'll be alone." I glanced over my shoulder. "Or I can crawl in the back seat and cover myself with the blanket."

"Not fucking likely."

"Walking, it is."

I put my hand on the door, and he leaned over, stopping me.

"Mila…"

"What?"

His eyes were filled with turbulence. His eye color was listed as brown, but his irises were anything but plain. Up close, they were almost cognac in color, with a dark-brown rim. Gold and green flecks made them even more unusual. They held so much pain at the moment it made me ache.

"What is it, Nicky?"

"I don't want you to go. I want to talk to you more."

"I'll meet you at the pool."

A relieved smile crossed his face. "Yes. Perfect." He glanced at the people milling on the sidewalk a few blocks down with a frown. "With them around, this is going to be even harder than before."

"We'll figure it out."

He kissed me swiftly, then drove past the hotel again, parking so I couldn't be seen getting out of the car.

"An hour?"

"Yes."

"Okay."

I scrambled out, shutting the door, then headed toward the hotel. I saw Nick turn the car around so he was facing the gates, and I knew he was watching me. Making sure I got in safe. I slid my hand into my pocket, finding the pass, and strolled past the photographers. As I suspected, they didn't give me another glance. I was invisible. A nobody.

The guard on the gate recognized me and opened it before I showed him my pass. He nodded and I stopped. "What is all this?" I asked innocently.

"Someone leaked the name of one of the guests staying

here. It happens. Be careful and don't interact with them, miss."

I nodded and wished him a good night. I walked into the lobby and spied Andi on the phone, pacing. She saw me and headed in my direction with a frown on her face. I walked toward her, the back of my neck prickling.

"Kiddo. Where have you been?"

"Out for a walk."

"I checked on you hours ago. You weren't in your room. You aren't answering your phone. I was getting worried."

I patted my pockets. "I must have left my phone in my room. Sorry. I was stuck and needed a change of pace. I went for a walk and had something to eat."

"Where is your purse?"

"Oh, I must have left that too. Luckily, I had some cash in my pocket."

"You got in okay?"

"Yes. What's with all the photographers?"

"Someone leaked that Nicholas was staying here. Apparently, they're lying in wait."

"Oh, how awful."

"Well, he gives them enough fodder. They keep coming back."

"Maybe they provoke him," I replied, needing to defend him.

She either ignored my tone or didn't hear my anger. "Let's grab a drink."

She pulled me to the bar and ordered us each a dirty martini. I sipped the salty drink in appreciation, and she eyed me in speculation.

"I don't recognize that shirt."

I looked down. It was Nicholas's shirt. It was pale blue, and

I had rolled up the sleeves and tied it at my waist, leaving the tails out.

"One of my dad's. I forgot to change when I left the hotel."

"No phone, no purse…" She shook her head. "You need to be careful. After yesterday…" She trailed off.

"I'm fine."

There was a small commotion outside, and I startled as I saw Nick's SUV pull up out front through the large windows of the lobby. He climbed out and hurried inside.

"Oh boy," Andi breathed out. "He looks pissed."

He stormed in, his mouth pulled down in a frown. He was heading to the elevator when he spotted me and made an abrupt turn in my direction.

He faltered when he saw Andi behind me, but it was too late to change course. He stopped in front of us. "Ladies, good evening."

"Having some trouble, Nicholas?" Andi asked.

"You could say that."

A phone rang, the ringtone familiar. It was my dad's ringtone. He had put it on my phone years ago, and I left it because it made me smile. It was a funny hip-hop song that repeated "my dad is da best" over and over. It was unique.

Unique enough Andi recognized it. And we both knew the sound was coming from Nick's pocket.

She looked at me, then at Nick. "Why do you have her phone?" She turned her head. "You said you left it in the room."

"I was, ah, sure I did." The prickling in my neck became stronger.

I blinked, and the room went black.

NICHOLAS

Mila's eyebrow twitched slightly. Without a thought, I was beside her, grabbing her before she passed out and fell out of the chair. I propped her up so her head was on my shoulder. I made sure no one saw anything.

Andi was off her stool instantly, standing beside me. She picked up her drink, acting like everything was normal. I kept my arm around Mila, doing the same thing.

"She'll come out of it in a minute."

"I know."

"Why do you have her phone?"

"She left it in the conference room. I was bringing it to her."

"Nicholas?"

"Uh-huh?"

"As hard as Mila pushed for you, I need to tell you that you aren't that good of an actor."

"Huh. That's a shame."

"Were the two of you out?"

"I wanted to talk to her more about the role. I saw the epic fuck show happening at the gate and dropped her down the block so she wouldn't get associated with me."

She took another sip of her martini. "Is she?"

"Is she what?"

"Associated with you?"

I drew in a deep breath. "You'll have to ask her."

Mila roused, looking around, startled. I turned my head, ghosting my lips over her temple.

"It's okay, Shortcake. Everything is fine."

Andi smiled at her. "No one noticed. Finish your drink, and we'll go upstairs. Everything is fine."

"I don't want it."

I reached for it and downed it in one gulp, shuddering at the taste, but I needed it. Seeing Mila unconscious did something to me. I hated the feeling of helplessness. I didn't care what she said; it was scary.

She slid from her seat, plucking the olives from the glass. "I'll eat these."

"Good. That was nasty."

"Not an olive fan?" Andi smirked.

I shook my head. "Nope."

She directed her attention to Mila. "You okay to walk?"

"Yes. I'm okay."

I handed Mila her phone. "I'll say good night."

Andi snorted. "I don't think so. You're coming with us. We all need to talk."

I had no choice in the matter. I followed them closely, my hand ready to catch Mila if she went over again. In the elevator, she leaned against the wall with a sigh. "Sorry," she mumbled.

I slipped my arm around her and kissed her temple. Andi already knew, so there was no point in pretending. "It's fine. Everything is fine."

Andi looked over her shoulder at us as she walked out of the elevator.

"I'll be the judge of that."

"Fuck," I muttered. But I followed.

Tonight was full of revelations.

What was one more?

In Mila's room, I sat beside her on the sofa, holding her hand, stroking the skin gently. She was still pale, which bothered me. Andi was busy again on her phone, pacing outside on the balcony.

"Busted," I mumbled. "That didn't take long."

Mila sighed, rubbing her head. "Did they see you? The paps, I mean?"

"Yeah. Called out some slurs and tried to get me to interact, but I didn't. Luckily, the guard at the gate recognized me, so he got me in fast. They didn't get a lot of pictures."

"How did they find you?"

"MJ," I confirmed. I had called her from the car, and she had been unapologetic about her tip-off. I had cursed and raged. She had laughed and told me to grow up.

"No press at all is the only kind of bad press, Nicky boy," she had sneered. "We need you out there."

Then she had hung up, not caring she'd thrown me to the wolves or that I was upset.

"What a bitch," Mila murmured.

I didn't reply. She was right. MJ was a bitch, and although that had worked many times in my favor for negotiations, lately, it had become personal. I felt like a piece of meat, my only value the money I brought to her. She used to care about my well-being, but now I wasn't so sure.

I lifted Mila's hand and kissed it, just as Andi came in and sat across from us.

"Obviously, you two were out."

Mila lifted her chin. "Yes."

"Not running lines either."

Crossing them was more like it, but I kept that information to myself. "I asked Mila to have dinner with me. She agreed. We went somewhere private." I flipped my fingers toward the front of the hotel. "I didn't expect the shitshow out there. I did my best to protect her from it."

"Who is protecting you?" Andi asked, shocking me with her question.

I blinked at her words, unsure what to say.

"His agent tipped them off," Mila said, leaning forward. "For publicity."

Andi frowned. "Sounds like you need a new agent. But that's beside the point. When did this happen?"

Mila sat back, tilting her head. "Nick was concerned yesterday. He came to check on me, and we talked. Shared dinner."

"You lied to me, kiddo."

"You never asked directly."

Andi waved her hand. "Semantics. We have always been truthful with each other."

Mila frowned, her voice low. "I didn't really know what to say. It felt too private to share."

"No more lies. Tell me what I need to know to protect you."

Mila reached out and clasped Andi's hand. "I will. I'm sorry."

Andi patted her knuckles. "Okay, then."

I watched in fascination. By now, MJ would have been screaming or telling me off. Making threats. I wondered what it would be like to have an agent you were actual friends with. Someone who cared. It had been too long since I'd had that connection.

Andi sat back, crossing her legs, looking between us. "You two are cute, but I suggest caution." She pursed her lips. "Should I remind you we're only here a short while?"

"Should I remind you I'm a grown woman and can make my own choices?" Mila retorted.

Andi's grin surprised me. "Well, well, there she is. Okay, kiddo, message received." She stood, brushing off her pants, looking directly at me. "Mila wants to remain invisible for her family's privacy and her own peace of mind. You want the attention? You do it on your own."

"I don't. I never do."

"Then tell your agent to back off."

I wished it were that easy.

"In the meantime, I spoke with the hotel. There is a staff entrance at the back that is well protected. You can come and go from there. They might catch on, but it will cool their heels for a few days." She leaned down and kissed Mila on the cheek. "We'll talk in the morning."

Andi fixed me with a look. "You hurt her, you'll answer to me."

"I have no intentions of hurting her. We didn't plan this, Andi. It's really fresh for both of us."

"Your reputation—" she began.

I cut her off. "You, of all people, know how a rep can be blown out of proportion. Manipulated. How everything can be orchestrated to look like something it's not. There are times when nothing is what it seems."

She studied me. "Maybe we need to have a conversation. It sounds as if you need some advice."

"Maybe we could do that."

She nodded and picked up her purse. "If this is going forward, we need to talk. My number one goal is protecting Mila. Ensuring her safety and well-being."

"Andi," Mila interjected. "I'm fine."

"And I want to make sure you stay that way. But I'll say

this. Two episodes in two days. That tells me you're not completely fine. We'll talk tomorrow."

She left, and Mila dropped her head, rubbing her face. "Well, I didn't expect that."

"Me either," I admitted. "But she seems surprisingly cool with it."

"We'll talk more in private. She'll warn me about all the dangers of being involved with you."

"And will you listen?" I asked, my voice tight.

Mila turned to me, her eyes soft in the light. "Yes, but I'll make up my own mind."

I touched her cheek. "Thank you."

I frowned. "You're still pale. And she's right. That's twice I've made you faint. Maybe you should listen to Andi and stay away."

"Maybe you should stop worrying about that."

I smiled and leaned closer, kissing her. "I don't think that's an option anymore."

"For me either."

"Then we're stuck," I observed.

She sighed as I kissed her again. "I guess so."

I left her in her room. Neither of us mentioned the pool. She needed her rest, and I needed to think. In my room, I brought up my contract with MJ on my laptop. I had scanned in the dog-eared pages, the original in my safe-deposit box along with some other important items.

I went through it again, shaking my head. I had signed it when I was young and stupid. When MJ and I were both new to the acting world. I thought we were a great team and she was all I needed. And for a while, we were. Then her ego grew, and my problems started.

Both became too much to handle.

I rubbed my eyes, staring out into the darkness from the seat on the balcony. I needed to tell Mila the truth. She shouldn't be involved with me unless she knew. Unless she could accept my limitations. I wasn't sure Mila was an affair sort of girl. She was the kind you fell in love with, married, and planned a lifetime around.

I had no lifetime to offer. No stability. All I could offer her was a few weeks on set. Some passion and my attention for a short time. Invariably, I would drift away, and she would go back to her life.

I hung my head, rotating my shoulders. I was a bastard. A selfish bastard. Even though all of that was true, even though I knew she was a virgin, inexperienced, shy, and sweet, I still wanted to pursue this. I knew I would walk away, or that she would get tired of me and leave, but I still wanted this. Wanted her. Even for a short while.

Because when I was in her company, forever didn't seem impossible. The future wasn't empty. I wasn't alone.

Being Nicholas Scott wasn't awful because she liked me.

And even though I knew that, too, would change, I also knew I was selfish enough not to stop it.

And that right there was the reason I should.

CHAPTER ELEVEN

MILA

"Sammy," I breathed out. "Really?"

"The man is an animal in bed. Plus, he is so incredible," my sister sighed. "He was hurt badly, Mila. He hides so much of himself. But he shows me."

"Sounds like you're in love with him."

"No, we both agreed it's just for now."

"Uh-huh. Agreements can change."

"I don't think Luke wants that."

"What do you want?" I asked.

She was silent for a moment, and when she spoke, her voice was low. "I'm not sure anymore."

Then she changed the subject, injecting a bright note into her voice.

"Dad and some of the cousins are coming to help with rebuilds. I'm so excited to show them the ranch."

"I know," I hummed, walking out to the balcony and looking outside. "Mom told me when I talked to her earlier.

She said Dad was pumped about the project. She said he was thrilled about the thought of tackling all the work."

"Of course he is. He loves working and building. Mom says he's been dying for a project."

"He loves to stay busy, and we have no new houses to build in the complex."

"What about you?" she asked. "How is the infamous Nicholas Scott?"

Just then, I saw him, walking across the center courtyard. He stopped, looking up in my direction. We were hundreds of feet apart. Lots of people between us, but I swore I felt his gaze observing me, assessing me. Not seeing anyone else but me, just as my focus was zeroed in on him. He tilted his head, then touched his mouth briefly and kept walking. I swore I felt that touch on my own mouth.

A woman rushed up behind him, talking rapidly. He shook his head and walked faster. She hurried after him, obviously not pleased. I had seen enough pictures of her to know it was his agent, and neither of them looked happy. She was furious, and he looked anxious.

"I'm sorry, what?" I asked, realizing Sammy was trying to get my attention. "Oh, ah, Nick. He is great. Exactly what the role needs."

"Nick?"

"Oh, ah, people call him that. I guess I picked up on it."

"What is he like in real life?"

The word was out before I could prevent it. "Amazing. He is simply amazing. Last night—" I stopped talking abruptly.

"Last night?" Sammy questioned. "What about last night? Mila, is something going on?"

"No," I replied too quickly. "Nothing."

"You forget how well I know you, little sister. That is your 'I am trying to cover something up' voice."

I sighed. "We had dinner together. Well, a picnic. He took me out to see the sunset to a place we could be private."

"And why do you need to be in a private place with a drug-addict movie star?"

"He is not a drug addict."

"Alcoholic, then. Mila, what are you doing?"

"Stop judging him. You don't know him."

"And you do? After a few days?"

The anger I had been tamping down for days exploded. "And what about you, Sammy? Sleeping with a client? You were on him a couple days after you met. Why is it okay for you and not for me?"

"Luke doesn't have addiction problems," she snapped. "And I have experience. I'm not acting on a secret crush I've harbored for years."

"I'm done with this conversation."

"Don't you dare hang up, Mila Morrison. I swear—"

I disconnected the call.

"She's right, you know," Andi said behind me. I whirled around to see her standing at the door to the balcony, a cup of coffee in hand. "I knocked and came in. You were on the phone."

"Don't start." I walked past her to the table and poured a coffee, stirring the cream in too vigorously, splashing the coffee onto the white cloth.

"Dammit," I muttered, mopping up the spill with the napkin I had been using.

Andi sat down, placing her hand on mine. "I'm not starting anything, kiddo. I'm just worried."

My anger deflated, and I sat down. I met her worried gaze.

"I like him, Andi. He likes me. We have some sort of weird connection."

"Your connection is the character. You are both reacting to that. I've seen it before."

"No, it's more."

She drained her coffee and sat forward, earnest. "You're a grown woman and can make up your own mind, Mila. But use caution. Have you asked him about his addictions? I noticed a drink in his hand a few times. I assume, with rehab, he shouldn't be drinking. His eyes looked red yesterday—is he using again? You need to know what you're dealing with." She looked sad. "I don't want you to lose your heart to someone who can't love you back. Addicts love themselves the most. Love their drugs or alcohol more than anyone else. I know." She shook her head. "I went through that with my brother. He refused to admit or commit to a new life. He was in and out of rehab so often and never truly believed he had a problem. Until it killed him. I don't want that for you."

I stared at her. "You never told me that."

She shrugged. "I've never gotten over losing him. I don't talk about it." She met my eyes. "Please be careful, Mila. Don't get involved with someone who is going to drain you dry of all the good emotions and leave you with a broken heart and trust issues. Remember what I said before. He is an actor. He can make you believe what he wants you to believe. Tread carefully. Ask him outright about his addictions." She studied me. "If you can't, then walk away. I'll wrap up our time here, and you can go home. Zoom with the actors if needed. Get away from him. Don't make me regret asking you to come here."

I saw the worry and sincerity in her eyes. I knew she was only trying to protect me. But I was convinced she was wrong about Nick. That they all were. Something in his eyes held me captive. Something told me I needed to be the one to break whatever cycle he was caught in. I didn't want to go home. I wanted to stay here with him. I looked down at my hands. Did that make me part of his cycle? Was I lying to myself?

There was only one way to find out.

"I'll talk to Nick tonight."

She nodded. "Listen carefully to his words, Mila. My brother was an expert at getting me to believe his denials. There were times he got me to believe it was everyone else, not him. I loved him too much. I wish I had been harder on him. Pushed more."

"Do you think it would have made a difference?"

"I don't know. I think he was too far gone. His doctor told me the bottom line was, he didn't want to change, and nothing I said or did would have made him. But I regret it some days."

"Maybe Nick is different."

She stood and bent to kiss my cheek. "For your sake, kiddo, I hope so. I really hope so."

━━━━━━

NICHOLAS

I had a headache already, and the day had barely begun. I leaned my head back on the leather and tried to shut out the annoying voice beside me. But MJ wouldn't shut up.

"You can't give me the silent treatment forever."

I sighed, knowing she was right. We had a lot of shit to discuss. I opened my eyes and turned my head to look at her. She was unapologetic, haughty, and angry.

Never a good combination with MJ.

I cast a glance over her with a frown. Her hair was brassier than usual. She was wearing more makeup, and her outfit was better suited to a younger woman. She was revealing far too much chest and leg. She always used to wear suits. When did that change?

I realized she was waiting for a response, but I had no idea what her question was. I didn't care much either.

"You had no right to tell them where I was. You know how much I hate the paps. How much they love to taunt me. Why the hell would you do that to me?"

"You need to be out there more."

"Then hook me up with a charity or a hospital visit. Something positive," I snapped. "Don't fucking throw me to the wolves."

She laughed, the sound unpleasant to my ears. When Mila laughed, it was soft and sweet. Or loud and full. Honest. It made me smile, not want to cringe and wonder where the cauldron was hidden.

"You are so overdramatic. No wonder you love acting. It's publicity. It won't kill you to feed them something." She snapped her fingers. "You and Lacey should pretend to date."

"She's married."

"You and Bradley, then."

I gaped at her, and she waved her hand. "Okay, too much. I'll find another actress who needs some PR. You two can be seen on cozy dates." She loved to do that—feed the rumors. Get my name out there, no matter the consequences.

"No."

"I think—"

I cut her off. "I don't give a fuck. I said no. And I mean no."

"You're being difficult. Is the stress getting to you already?"

"The only thing causing me stress is you, MJ."

The car pulled up to the gates of the studio, and I breathed a sigh of relief. I waited until we'd arrived at the building, and I put my hand on the door handle, not opening it just yet.

"In fact, I'm starting to rethink this relationship."

"We have a contract. An exclusive, unbreakable contract." She smirked when she reminded me of that.

I shrugged. "Maybe I don't care anymore. You can't get blood from a stone."

I felt the thrill of smug satisfaction when I saw the shocked look on her face. I stepped from the car and leaned down. "I mean it, MJ. Tread carefully right now."

I slammed the door and headed into the building, not looking back.

* * *

Mila was different this morning. I couldn't put my finger on it. She was friendly and cordial but withdrawn. She arrived last, frustrating me when she sat on the opposite side of the conference room table where I couldn't touch her. My fingers itched to feel her skin under mine again. She somehow calmed me simply with her presence, but now, I felt a wall between us. I wondered if last night had been too much for her. It had been intense and intimate as hell.

Was she regretting it? Regretting me? My heart hammered simply at the thought of her withdrawal. Our character discussions were winding down. Bradley didn't come to the meeting, and Lacey's questions were sparse. She told Mila how much she appreciated her time and was grateful for all the insights.

"You'll be around still?" she asked.

I waited anxiously for Mila's response. Andi spoke for her. "For a bit."

I didn't like that reply.

Andi looked my way, a direct challenge in her gaze. "Any other questions, Nick?"

"Nicholas," I corrected.

One eyebrow rose slowly, and she pursed her lips. "Nicholas," she repeated. "Any other questions for my client?"

I barked out a laugh. "Your *client*? Am I on trial here?"

"Of course not," Mila chided her agent with a shake of her head. "I know you had the most questions, Nick. Are you good, or do you have more?" she asked, her voice gentle. It soothed the ragged edges of my nerves, helping to calm me.

I saw Andi wait for me to correct Mila on the shortened form of my name. I allowed very few people to use it. But I didn't. Mila could call me anything she wanted. I preferred *Nicky baby*, whispered in her breathless voice, but I would settle for Nick from her.

For now.

"I have a few. One big one, though."

Lacey stood. "I'm out. I need a snack."

Bradley was already gone, leaving Andi, Mila, and me. Amber was busy setting up the shoot today.

"What is your question?"

Andi's phone rang, and she glanced at the screen, frowning. "I have to take this." She stood and left the room, standing outside the door. Silence fell between Mila and me. Outside the door, I could make out the muffled conversation involving Andi. The muted sounds of shouts and voices prepping the set.

Mila's eyes locked on mine, the beautiful irises all at once tender, worried, and anxious. I wondered what was causing the turmoil. It concerned me. I had read up on her disorder, and I knew anxiety could push it over the edge.

"Are you all right?" we both asked at the same time, breaking the silence.

"I saw you with MJ. You didn't look happy."

I shook my head. "We're arguing. Nothing new. But I'm worried about you."

"I'm fine."

"Why are you so far away, then, Mila?"

"I was trying to maintain a professional image, Nick."

I studied her. She was a lousy liar.

"You'd make a terrible actress, Shortcake."

She sighed. "We need to talk."

"Now?"

"No. Not here. Tonight."

"Fine. Dinner. My room or yours?"

She paused. "Mine."

"Are you breaking this off?"

"No."

I heaved a long exhale of relief. "But you want to talk?"

"Yes."

I glanced over my shoulder, then swiftly changed chairs so I was closer to Mila. I reached out and grasped her fingers that were restlessly drumming on the tabletop. I liked the fact that as soon as our digits became entwined, we both relaxed. "Was last night too much, Shortcake?"

"Last night was incredible."

"You don't regret it? Regret me?"

"No."

"Okay. Then tonight, we'll talk about us."

She nodded.

"In the meantime, I have a couple more questions."

"Okay, shoot."

"You said I was your muse. Why?"

"You kept coming to mind when I wrote Duncan. You have—" she swallowed and paused "—you have emotions in your eyes I don't think anyone sees. Anyone but me."

"Anyone but you?" I repeated.

"They see the actor. The performance."

"And what do you see?"

"I see the pain you hide from the world. The way Roxie could see Duncan's pain." She frowned. "I wrote him using your description because when I saw him, I always saw you. I saw your pain. Your turmoil. It's part of the performance, yes, but it's part of you. It lives in you. You bear it alone." She hesitated. "Don't you?"

I stared at her. No one had ever said anything that profound to me. No one knew, saw, or cared about my private pain. In fact, they did everything they could to cover it up. The image they created of me was as false as the parts I played. All a mirage. Believed by the world to be true.

Except to her. Mila.

I felt raw sitting across from her. It was as if she had laid my soul bare. Her simple, honest words rang in my head, and I didn't know how to respond to them.

The conference room door opened, and MJ walked in. "Nicky boy, you're wanted on set. Playtime is over." She glanced at Mila. "So, you're the author?" She rubbed her lips. "Interesting."

I rose to my feet, the need to protect and shield Mila from MJ tangible. I glared at her. "What are you doing here?"

"We have a conversation to finish."

I shook my head. "I'm done with you today. I need to concentrate on my scenes."

She crossed her arms. "I say when we're done. We can talk tonight since I don't want to disrupt your *acting*." She spat the word as though it left a bad taste in her mouth.

"I'm busy."

"Doing what?"

Mila stood. "Nicholas kindly agreed to have dinner with me to finish his character discussion. I have another deadline to attend to, so I can't remain on set to answer any more questions."

"Is that right?" MJ drawled. "Dinner—how cozy."

Mila laughed, the sound light. "Hardly cozy with the crew I have around tonight. But I can spare a little time for the star."

MJ blinked. I hid my smile, reassessing my earlier opinion. Mila could act if needed. At least, I hoped she was acting.

Andi came in, and Mila smiled at her. "I'm almost ready to go."

Andi and MJ introduced themselves. It was chilly to say the least. They sized each other up and found the other's deficiencies. Andi was at least cordial. MJ was…well, MJ.

She tossed a script at me. "I want you to read this between takes. You're up for an audition before you leave for Canada." She sniffed, her words dripping with derision. "It's a real film. Meaty and gritty. You are far more suited to that sort of role than fluff."

Then she walked out.

I met Mila's eyes. "Sorry."

To my surprise, she laughed. "Wow. Judged and found lacking by the devil herself."

I wanted to kiss her. Wrap my arms around her and hold her, but I held back.

Andi glanced at the script. "I read that book. Heavy stuff."

"Yeah, not interested. MJ has other ideas. I have yet another fight on my hands." I ran a hand through my hair.

"If you ever decide to stop fighting, call me. I have some names for you," Andi offered.

"You won't take me on?" I teased.

"I do authors, not actors. But I know some good, honest agents and managers who will work with you. Not against you."

"I'm sort of locked in."

She smirked. "I employ a lawyer who can find a loophole in the most ironclad of contracts. If you're interested, let me know." She glanced at Mila as she left. "I'll meet you outside in twenty."

"You really aren't staying?" I asked.

"Maybe tomorrow. We have a bunch of things to work through," she said sadly. "I want to see you work your magic."

"Today isn't exciting. We'll start the real stuff tomorrow." I stepped closer. "And I'll show you magic anytime, pretty lady. Just like last night."

"We have to talk first."

"We will. But if I don't kiss you in the next ten seconds, I am going to explode."

She looked behind me and must have been satisfied with what she saw. She lunged, gripping my shoulders and rolling up on her toes. I caught her around the waist and kissed her, dipping my tongue inside her sweet mouth and tasting her. I groaned, holding her tight, knowing it had to be fast. I was breathing hard when I pulled away, smiling at her rosy cheeks and wet mouth.

"Now, I'll go be Duncan."

I left before I changed my mind, dragged her into the kitchen area, set her on the counter, and lost myself in her for a while.

It was hard to walk away from her, but she was right. We had to talk.

She deserved to know the man I was so she could decide if I was the man she wanted to be with.

Christ, I hoped so.

CHAPTER TWELVE

MILA

I spent the afternoon researching addiction. What happened in rehab. Why so often it failed. The struggle the person faced daily to make it work. It was intense. Sammy texted me in the afternoon, her words simple but heartfelt.

SAMMY

> Mila, I'm sorry. You're right, I shouldn't judge. I just worry about you because I love you.

> You can't stay mad at me. I'm your favorite big sister.

I stared at the screen, my thumb tracing over her words. It was rare I was ever on the outs with anyone in my family. Or anyone I cared about. Today, I had managed to upset two people I loved. Sammy and Andi. I sighed and replied.

ME

Not mad. I'm sorry I got upset. I care about him. I love you.

I have to live and make my own mistakes too, you know?

Her reply was swift.

SAMMY

I know. I just don't want to see you hurt.

I sent back a heart emoji, not sure how to reply.

ME

Talk soon.

I tossed my phone to the side, walking out onto the balcony. It was hot today, the breeze nonexistent. I lifted my face to the sun for a few moments, letting it warm my skin. I was restless and edgy. The pool was deserted, and I was certain the adults-only one would be empty this time of day. I thought about going down and doing some laps to help get rid of my energy, then dismissed the idea. I wasn't in the mood.

I wasn't sure what I was in the mood for. Even writing held no appeal.

Deciding a walk might be good, I gathered up my hat and glasses, heading to the door. Andi was on the other side and jumped a little as I pulled open the door.

"Hey, kiddo. Where you off to?"

"Just a walk. Feeling restless." I stepped back. "Come in. I'll go in a bit."

She followed me in and sat at the table, glancing at my

notes. "Research," she mused. "I should have known you'd be looking into addiction."

"I need to know what I'm fighting against."

"Are you prepared to fight this?" she asked quietly. "Does Nicholas already mean that much to you that you want to take on this fight? It can be painful. In fact, it *is* painful."

"Yes."

"I was afraid you'd say that." She sat back. "He's been in rehab four times in three years. Erratic behavior is a standard for him on set. It's a slippery slope, Mila."

"I want to hear his side of the story. There's more than we know, Andi. I'm convinced of it."

"Not everyone who is broken can be fixed." She met my gaze. "Not everyone wants to be fixed."

My heart thudded hard in my chest. "I know."

"I don't want you hurt, kiddo."

"I have to make my own mistakes, Andi. I need to talk to Nick."

A ghost of a smile crossed her face. "You get to call him that."

"Better than Nicky boy. He hates that."

"His agent is a piece of work," she scoffed. "I did some checking. Quite the ballbuster. He's been her client since he started. She has a few others, but he is her main focus. She has a reputation for bulldozing."

I frowned. "I get the feeling she is behind some of his problems. Can you really sign a contract that locks you in permanently?"

"They are rare. I would really love to see the wording. I bet Jacob could find a way to break it." Andi paused. "But then again, he'd have to want that."

I nodded. I had no idea what Nicholas wanted. What he

was thinking. What he would say tonight. I only hoped I was strong enough to listen and to accept.

Nicholas appeared around seven. He had let me know he was on his way, and I waited anxiously. He looked apprehensive when I let him into the room.

"How was filming?" I asked.

He shrugged. "Making a movie is a lot of hurry up and wait sort of thing. I was only in a couple shots, but it was a whole day of sitting around."

"What do you do to fill in the time?"

"I like to draw. I keep a sketchbook handy. Lacey knits. Bradley works out a lot. And he writes poetry."

"You draw?"

He nodded. "Yeah."

"Would you show me one day?"

He smiled, looking pleased. "If you want."

For a moment, there was silence. "I wasn't sure what to get for dinner."

"How about something simple?" he suggested. "Sandwiches and salad?"

"Sounds good."

"I'll order." He winked, trying to lighten the tension between us. "I'm good at ordering room service."

I smiled. "Sure."

While he was ordering, I wandered back to the balcony. The sun was low in the sky, the colors beginning to gather. I felt him come up behind me. He leaned close, resting his hands on the balcony rail, dropping his chin onto my shoulder. "Pretty," he murmured.

"Yes."

He slid one arm around me, pulling me to his chest. With a sigh, he kissed my neck. "You feel so far away."

"I'm right here."

"You're holding yourself back."

"I'm worried."

"About what I'm going to tell you?"

"Yes."

"So am I," he confessed.

Then he spun me in his arms, covering my mouth with his. I wrapped my arms around his neck, whimpering as he kissed me. His tongue twisted with mine, and he explored me. He pulled me closer, kissing me deeper. Harder. Every doubt, every worry I had, faded away in his arms. I felt as if I was exactly where I should be. Where I wanted to be. I hummed in satisfaction as he slid his hands under my shirt, ghosting up my back, his long fingers gentle. I slid my hands into his thick hair, tugging on the curls. He wrapped one hand around my long hair, fisting the strands. He moved, sitting down, and I straddled him, gasping at the feel of his hardness trapped between us. He broke from my mouth, kissing and licking his way up and down my neck, murmuring and praising me. "You feel so good, Mila. It's all I thought about today. How you felt. Your taste. Needing to have you close."

Then his mouth was back on mine. He cupped my ass, guiding me, the friction between us feeling so good. His touch unlocked something inside me. An emotion, a desire I never knew I possessed. I gripped his hair harder, and he groaned.

The loud knock at the door pulled us apart. We stared at each other.

"Cockblocked by sandwiches," he muttered.

He stood, setting me on my feet.

"I'll go to the door," I offered. "Not sure you should right now." I brushed past him, feeling him still hard.

I signed for the tray and handed the waiter a tip. He smiled at me, flirty and cute. "That's a lot of food for such a small woman," he quipped.

"Good thing I'm here with her, then." Nicholas appeared at my elbow, glaring.

"Oh yeah, right. Have a good night." He turned and hurried down the hallway.

"Keep walking, asshole," Nicholas snarled under his breath, making me laugh.

"He was being friendly."

"He was hitting on you."

"You're being silly."

"And you're being blind. Now, come sit with me."

We sat at the table, the tray of sandwiches and cut-up veggies and cheese between us. He poured some wine, taking a long sip before picking up a sandwich and eating.

I watched his movements, suddenly worried.

Should he be drinking that wine? I racked my brain, recalling I had seen him drink several things. Scotch, wine, a martini.

Maybe alcohol wasn't his problem. Perhaps it was drugs. But didn't addicts often switch out one vice for another? Was I encouraging his behavior? Oh God, what if he was addicted to both? What if Andi was right?

Was I strong enough for this?

"Hey." His voice interrupted my thoughts. "What's wrong?" He stroked my cheek. "You've gone pale." He became concerned. "Are you okay? Your eyebrow isn't twitching. Are you feeling faint?"

"No, I'm fine. It's nothing."

"Eat, then. You need to eat."

I picked up a sandwich, not at all hungry but doing it to make him happy. I tried not to watch him drink the wine, but he noticed.

"Liquor is not a vice," he said, setting down his glass. "That's what you're thinking, isn't it?"

"I'm sorry," I said.

He smiled, the expression on his face tight. "It's fine."

"Drugs?" I whispered.

He set down his sandwich. "No."

I was confused.

He sat back, wiping his fingers. "I'm not addicted to liquor, sex, opioids, or pharmaceuticals. I'm not addicted to anything."

My heart sank. Andi was right—he was in total denial.

"If you can't admit it, you can't get well."

He shook his head. "I will never get well, Mila."

"Won't you even try?" I whispered, tears already beginning to well in my eyes.

He laughed, the sound bitter and sad all at the same time. "I am trying, Shortcake. No one knows how hard I try."

"Tell me."

He stood and paced around the room. I covered the food, knowing neither of us would touch it. I moved to the sofa, unsure what to do. I wanted to touch him, to stop his restless movements, but I wasn't sure if I should.

He turned and looked at me. "Do you know why I kissed you earlier?"

I shook my head.

"Because I wasn't sure if you would let me kiss you again, and I wanted to feel your mouth under mine one last time."

"We can fight this together," I whispered.

"I want to believe that."

He sat across from me, and I dared to reach out for his hand. He grasped mine, staring down at our entwined fingers. He lifted them to his mouth, kissing my knuckles and pressing my palm to his face. He met my gaze, and I saw his pain. His fear. No longer hidden, the emotions bled from his eyes. He was in agony, and I had no idea how to soothe him.

"I'm here. I'm listening."

He leaned forward and pressed his mouth to mine. Softly. I grasped the back of his head, kissing him back, trying to make him understand I would listen. I would help.

As long as he would allow it.

"I'm not addicted to any substance," he reiterated. "I drink, but not to excess. I avoid pills unless they are prescribed. I don't do any sort of recreational drugs."

"The rehab?" I asked. "Why?"

"I have never been to rehab."

"What?"

He took in a deep breath. "Hollywood can handle drug abusers and alcoholics. The business is full of them. It's almost accepted. Sex addicts are common. Fetishes run rampant. They are catered to. Hidden, usually, but still acceptable." He was quiet for a moment, rubbing his thumb over my hand, staring down at our entwined fingers.

"What *still* isn't acceptable, what is *still* hidden a lot, is mental illness."

"Mental illness?" I repeated.

He looked up, shame on his face. "I'm mentally ill, Mila. I suffer from Bipolar II. The other studio I'm contracted to and MJ do everything they can to cover it up. It doesn't go with the image they've created for me. The whole alpha hero sort of thing." He swallowed. "It feels odd to say it out loud."

"Because they make you hide it?"

"Yes. And I'm never comfortable with the subject, but I want you to know me. The real me." He glanced down at our hands again. "It doesn't feel wrong telling you."

"It isn't wrong. I think you're incredibly brave to tell me."

He laughed, the sound bitter. "The studio wouldn't agree. Neither would MJ. They make me feel ashamed of it."

"But you can't help having a disorder," I protested, my mind racing a hundred miles an hour.

"They don't like it. They hide it. I'm not allowed to discuss it. It's an ironclad rule in my contract. Just telling you could give the studio grounds to dismiss me."

"They would rather the world think you're an out-of-control addict?"

He nodded. "Like I said, it's acceptable." He shrugged. "I have three more films in the franchise I'm attached to at the other studio, and then I'm done. I'll figure it out after."

"Nicholas," I said, aghast. "That is so wrong."

"I know. I live with it every single day."

"Do you have any help?"

"I have prescribed drugs I take. I don't want to be this way. I don't want to have meltdowns. Still, they happen. And when they do, the story comes out I've gone off the deep end again and am in rehab. The press eats it up."

"You said Bipolar II. What is the difference?"

"I'm not manic. I have what are called hypomanic episodes."

"Which are?"

"I get restless, irritable. My emotions run high and low, sometimes very quickly. I'm often so energetic and happy, you can't tell I'm having an episode. Because I can't shut down my thoughts, I talk more and I require little sleep. I get sort of wired—like too much caffeine." He shrugged. "Because I get so involved in a character, I forget my meds. It sets off an episode, and things escalate. Sometimes I fall into a deep depression after."

"So you go back on your meds, and things are okay again?"

He smiled ruefully. "Not quite that simple, but yes, I get straightened out. I lose myself for a while. It's frightening, and it takes its toll. My life goes on. Such as it is. Sometimes it takes me longer to mend and find myself again. I recover from the episode. I'll never recover from the disorder."

"And they cover it up by saying you're in rehab."

"Yes."

"Do you get counseling? See a doctor?"

"I had a therapist I saw regularly. He retired. I got someone else, and frankly, I don't like her. She doesn't like me either, I don't think. We Zoom so I stay on track, but I want to find someone else. Someone I trust more."

I leaned forward. "Then you need to find someone else. Someone you trust. You can't do this alone, Nicholas. Mental illness is just that. An illness. Without treatment, it will fester, get worse. You have to look after you."

"You sound like you're speaking from experience."

"One of my friends has bipolar. She gets depressed a lot. Her parents watch over her carefully. Her partner does. She has so much support, and she still struggles at times. You're trying to do this on your own. The people who should be protecting you, helping you, are covering it up. It's so wrong. You need help, not to be hidden! Those *bastards*," I seethed.

He blinked at my vehemence.

"I don't know a lot about the different forms of the condition," I admitted. "My friend was diagnosed in her teens, and she was always a private person. But she told me, and I used to sit with her when she was down. Some of the newer treatments have helped her a lot, and she leads a fairly normal life. But it still affects her. She says she couldn't cope if it weren't for all the support." I stared at him, aghast. "You're trying to do this on your own."

He shrugged. "I have no choice."

I couldn't stay away from him. I launched myself off the sofa, and he caught me, holding me close. "You're not alone, Nicholas. I'm here."

He tightened his arms. "I thought you'd walk away."

"No."

"Thank fuck," he murmured.

NICHOLAS

I held Mila tight, not wanting to release her from my embrace. She let me draw strength from her closeness, and I finally loosened my hold enough she could ease back and look at me. I met her eyes, buoyed by what I saw in them. There was no judgment, no disdain. Only understanding, gentleness, and worry.

For me.

The last person who truly worried about me was my mother. No one had looked at me with such gentle emotions since the day she died.

I hadn't thought anyone would ever look at me that way again.

I shook my head in wonder. "How do you do that?" I asked quietly.

"Do what?"

"Calm me, center me by simply being close. Make me feel as if I'm okay just by looking at me?"

"You are okay, Nick. You have a disorder you have to live with. It doesn't change who you are."

I barked out a laugh. "It does to MJ and the studio execs."

She made a face. "They need to get their heads out of their asses. Mental illness needs a light shone on it, not to be hidden. They should be ashamed of themselves."

"I'm not the only one in this situation."

"It's so frustrating. They should allow celebs to speak out, talk about it. It would help so many people. Have they learned nothing from history?"

"I know. And some celebs do speak out, but not enough."

"No, it's not. The studio looks like the hero keeping you around, and you're labeled as a substance abuser. That isn't right."

I shrugged, unable to keep my eyes off her. Her cheeks were flushed in anger, her eyes flashing. She was furious on my behalf. Worried about my reputation. Concerned for me.

She huffed a sigh. "I hate that your agent doesn't do more to help you, rather than hide your disorder."

"MJ's concern is for her payday. Her reputation. Not my personal mental well-being." I stopped speaking, lost in memories for a moment. "It wasn't always like that."

"You've known her a long time, you said?"

"We grew up together. We were best friends. We both had dreams. We worked together in those early days, supporting each other. We struggled together. She fought for me back then, and we were a real team. Then something changed. I grew one way, she grew another. She was a good agent and worked hard to get me noticed, but now, all that happens is we argue. Constantly. Nothing I do pleases her, it seems. Then suddenly, she becomes the MJ I first knew, and we're good for a while." I lifted one shoulder in confusion. "I'm never sure which MJ I'll deal with some days."

"That must be difficult."

"It is. Some days more than others."

"Still, you're very loyal to her."

"I remember how we were. How much we cared for each other. Looked after each other."

"And you've paid her back many times over."

I shrugged, knowing she was right. "I'm not sure anyone else would take me on with the rep I have now."

She fiddled with my collar, looking unsure.

"Ask me, Shortcake," I murmured affectionately.

"When were you diagnosed?"

"Later than some. My mid-twenties. My first bad episode was after my mom died. I spiraled pretty hard. MJ had known she was dying and didn't tell me. My mom knew it and hid it from me. I was furious, and not long after she passed, I had a breakdown. A bad one. It was the scariest thing I had ever experienced. I couldn't control myself. My body. My thoughts."

"Oh, Nick," Mila whispered, framing my face with her palms. "How awful."

"MJ covered it up, saying it was grief. The doctors the studio had me see were happy to write it off. The next time wasn't long after, and I admitted myself to the hospital. Got different opinions. Those doctors said the word bipolar. I realized how often I had covered up my depression. Pushed it aside, losing myself in the characters I played. It was almost a relief hearing why I felt the way I did so much of the time. MJ was horrified. So was the studio. They put it all under wraps. I was on a huge upswing in my career—but falling apart in private. I agreed to their terms so I could keep acting, and I hid my personal life. I stayed on the meds and with therapy, but with no support from them." I let out a long breath. "When I had another episode, they did the whole rehab thing. Once it was out there, it was too late to object, and frankly, I didn't care. I had no one to worry about, and it was such an accepted thing in Hollywood, no one paid it much attention. Except now, I had a reputation." I grimaced. "I am known for my short temper at times too, so that doesn't help. It only adds to the list. The whole bad-boy rep."

"One you need to break."

I smiled at her fierceness. "One I can't break unless I walk away from this life, Mila."

She frowned. "Is it really life if you have to hide?"

Her words stopped me cold.

"It's the only one I know."

"Then I'll have to show you a different one."

We stayed close the rest of the night, neither of us wanting to leave the small bubble we'd created. Mila asked me other questions, and I answered them as best I could. I felt no anxiety with her or her queries. I knew they were coming from a place of concern and nothing else.

We sat back at the table to eat the sandwiches we'd abandoned. I noticed a script on the corner of the table. "What is that?"

"Oh." She picked it up. "You left it in the conference room earlier."

"Oh, right." I grimaced, taking it. "The one MJ wants me to audition for."

"You shouldn't do it."

"Why?"

She glanced away, and I leaned forward, sliding a finger under her chin and urging her head in my direction. "Tell me why."

She inhaled. "I read it. It's a horrible, dark role."

"I know. She likes the gritty ones."

"This one is beyond gritty. You told me your episodes often happen when you lose yourself in a role. Forget to take your meds. This afternoon after I looked through that script, I did a little research."

"Writers are good at that." I winked at her, wondering where this was going.

"Your last two stints at 'rehab'"—she used her fingers for air quotations—"happened when the roles you had taken on were very intense, dark characters. I think they're too much for you to handle. They trigger a spiral."

"Are you a doctor now?" I asked, feeling a little uncomfortable. "You think I can't handle the roles? Tell what is real from acting?"

"No, that isn't what I'm saying. You lose yourself in your acting, Nick. You become the character. You admit you forget your meds sometimes. I think the darkness takes over. I think there is a correlation."

I glanced between her and the script. Was she right? Could one trigger the other? I could recall the feeling of being weighed down the longer we filmed the last dark role I had accepted. It was one of the reasons I had wanted to do this film. The character was intense, but in a different way. He was broody and gruff. But he loved as intensely as he brooded. He wasn't dark. Mila was correct—the role MJ was so intent on my getting would be very emotionally draining.

And somehow, on some level, I knew that. I didn't want to do that role.

The clever mind Mila possessed zeroed in on that fact instantly.

"You are pretty smart," I said quietly.

She smiled. "I see things differently."

"I like how you see things. I like how you see me. I was afraid that would change once you knew the truth."

She scoffed. "I can deal with you being bipolar. Your condition doesn't define you. That your agent, the person who should have your back and protect you, can't do that speaks volumes."

Once again, this woman rendered me speechless.

I stood and bent over her, kissing her. I hauled her to her feet, holding her close as I ravished her mouth.

"What was that for?" she asked.

"Because I can."

She beamed up at me. "Yes. Yes, you can. Anytime you want."

"Good."

CHAPTER THIRTEEN

NICHOLAS

"Can I stay?" I asked against her mouth. Her sweet, addictive mouth. The only thing I wanted to be addicted to in this life.

She moaned softly, wrapping her arms tighter around my neck. "Nick," she whispered.

"I just don't want to be alone. Let me hold you." I buried my face in her neck, breathing her in. "Please."

"Yes," she replied.

I carried her to the bedroom, setting her on her feet. "You, ah, need to do your thing?" I indicated the bathroom.

She laughed, the sound sweet and warm. "I'm pretty simple. I have an extra toothbrush," she offered. I followed her into the room, taking it, surprised when she indicated the second sink. It felt oddly right, brushing our teeth side by side. I watched her wash her face, strangely fascinated by the way she smoothed lotion onto her face and then her hands and arms. I used the other washroom down the hall to give her some privacy, and I stripped off my shirt and jeans, leaving on my boxers. I hoped that wouldn't make her uncomfortable, but she was surprisingly relaxed as I slipped into bed beside her. After she turned off the light, I pulled her into my arms and lay back with her head on my chest. I stroked through her hair, smiling as she sighed in pleasure.

"That feels so nice."

"You have such beautiful hair."

She hummed and lifted her head, meeting my eyes in the dim light spilling in from the hall.

"Thank you. I'm glad you think so."

"You are so beautiful, Mila. Inside and out."

"I think the same way about you."

I smiled, cupping her cheek. "God, I adore you."

She looked shocked. "I don't think anyone outside my family has ever adored me."

"Then I'm glad I'm your first." I pulled her closer and kissed her.

I only meant to show her my adoration. Let her feel my emotions. But as soon as our lips touched, it was as if a match had been lit. The fire grew from a small flame to an inferno instantly. The instant our mouths connected, it felt as if our souls did as well. I didn't care how over the top that sounded. I felt it.

I pulled her tight, devouring her. She returned my desire with a passion that both shocked and delighted me. In seconds, I was over her, our bodies aligned. She wore a set of shorts and a tank top, the thin material not hiding the way her nipples hardened and rubbed on my bare chest. She dug her fingers into my skin, trailing them up and down my back in long, sensuous passes. She made the most erotic little noises in her throat. She tangled her legs with mine, her skin like silk against my coarser texture. I groaned at the feeling of her wrapped around me. I kissed her harder. Deeper. I sat up, dragging her tank over her head and going back to her mouth immediately. I cupped her breasts, the feel of them full and heavy in my hands, and she whimpered as I stroked her nipples, then lowered my head and took one in my mouth.

She gasped, bucking against me, and it took all I had not to push her back and strip her completely bare. Bury myself in her.

But she deserved so much more.

I gentled my mouth, laying her back and stretching out beside her. I kept kissing her, caressing her, but I refused to take her tonight. Not this way.

She opened her eyes, frowning. "You're stopping."

"Just for now. I have an early call time, and once I've had you, Mila, I won't want to leave you that quickly. It will take hours for me to get my fill of you."

"Oh," she breathed out.

What I said was true, but still, I couldn't resist her. I trailed a finger down her sternum. "Are you achy, baby? Do you need me to ease that ache so you can sleep?"

She bit her lip and nodded.

"Tell me what you want."

"Touch me."

"Yes," I groaned. I covered her mouth with mine and gave her exactly what she wanted.

Twice.

MILA

It was still dark when Nick slipped out of bed. He bent and kissed my temple. "I'll see you on set. Come find me." His voice was full of laughter. "Bring me coffee, Shortcake."

A while later, I had breakfast while talking to my dad and telling him how well things were going. He informed me how much he loved the ranch.

"Your sister is involved with this Luke fellow," he muttered. "Great guy, but I'm not sure there is a future."

"She's a grown woman, Dad."

"Still." He sighed. "Mom likes him and says I'm being overprotective."

"You?" I gasped in an overdramatic fashion. "I am shocked."

"Sarcasm doesn't suit you, Pumpkin."

I laughed. "I wonder where I got that from? Three guesses, and the first two aren't Mom."

"Liv," he called to the background. "When did our girls get so lippy?"

"Never noticed," she called back. "They're always sweet."

"All of you," he chuckled. "All of you like to give me a hard time."

"Would you have it any other way?" I asked.

"No."

I was still smiling as I hung up. Andi looked at me across the table.

"You're in a good mood."

"Not really. But Dad makes me smile."

"How did last night go?"

I wasn't sure what I should share with her. Nick hadn't told me not to tell her, but he had mentioned he shouldn't be telling me. I made a decision, and I told her everything after getting her promise to stay silent.

Her expression ranged from sorrow to anger as she listened.

"He needs new representation."

"I know."

"I'll talk to him."

"But he'll know I told you."

"He's pretty smart, and I think he'll figure that out anyway. I want to see his contract with that bitch. He's on loan from the studio in charge of that franchise. They allowed him to make this movie, but he has three more he is scheduled to make for them. I know this from our negotiations. He needs a break from them as well. They need to get their heads out of their asses and into this century. Mental illness is not a stigma."

"I know."

She studied me. "It didn't change how you feel about him."

"Not at all."

"It is a tough condition to live with."

"Let's not get ahead of ourselves. We're pretty new. I have no idea where this is going."

She drained her coffee and got to her feet. "I know you. I know that look. You're already in, both feet to the fire, and you don't care about getting burned." She sighed. "Sammy and a rancher, you and an actor. Who knew? Your dad is going to have a meltdown." Then she shrugged. "I need to talk to the boy. Get your stuff, and we'll head to the set."

The thought of seeing Nick again this morning gave me butterflies. He had brought me to orgasm twice last night using his talented fingers. He refused to let me reciprocate. I was anxious to see him, longed to touch him, and wanted to be alone with him again. I hoped I could accomplish all three in a short span of time.

"Okay."

It was fascinating to watch a film be made. I saw what Nick meant about "hurry up and wait." There was a lot of downtime. I sat in the director's chair I'd discovered with my name on it, gazing around in awe. So many people scurried around. There were sounds and voices calling, sets being shifted, cast members conversing. The scent of food and coffee lingered in the air. The lights were hot, and wires and cables were running all over the place. I tried to stay out of the way. My gaze followed Nick everywhere. The instant they marked a scene, he became Duncan. Broody, sexy, and tormented. Fighting the love he had for Roxie.

I waited until there was a break and went over to the table and got him a coffee. I headed his way, and he glanced up, a smile breaking out on his face when he saw me.

"Shortcake," he said, taking the cup from my hand with an appreciative sip. "Finally."

"You were amazing." I indicated the set. "A perfect Duncan."

He smiled again, the gesture fading as he looked over my shoulder. "Fuck," he muttered.

MJ appeared, practically elbowing me out of the way and ignoring my presence. "Where the hell were you last night? You didn't return my calls. I went to your room this morning, and you never came to the door."

"I, ah, wasn't there."

She rolled her eyes. "Too busy screwing a new piece of ass, Nicky boy? Too important to call your agent back?"

"Stop it," he hissed, glancing in my direction.

"Oh, I think your little smut writer is hardly shocked at your behavior. All your experience will come in handy for the sex scenes, tawdry as they are."

I felt my eyebrows rise at her level of rudeness.

He glared at her. "Shut up, MJ. Just *shut up*."

"And what is this BS I just heard? Arlene called and said you canceled your audition. I assured her that was a mistake and rebooked it."

"It's not a mistake. I don't want that role."

My hopes soared. He was listening to me. Every instinct inside me told me that role would shroud him in negativity and darkness.

"You need a meaty, gritty role after this drivel," she argued. "If it weren't for the positive exposure, I wouldn't have allowed you to take it on."

I couldn't stay quiet any longer.

"You could at least pretend to show me a little respect," I said dryly. "Considering how long the book was on the *New York Times* best-selling list, I hardly think drivel is the appropriate word."

She looked at me, disdain written on her face. "Oh, the author has an opinion. I didn't know you were still wanted around here."

"Yep. Here I am. On set as per the request of the director, the producer—" I looked pointedly at Nick "—and the cast."

Nick shook his head, silently warning me not to keep goading her.

"Seriously," she muttered. "I wish I hadn't agreed. But

with the stunts you keep pulling, Nicky, I had no choice. The next role will suit you far more."

I saw red. Pure, angry, brilliant red. *Stunts* he pulled? She made it sound like his condition was something he did for fun. She had no empathy.

"Excuse me," I snapped. "Stop talking to him like he is five years old and stepped in the mud. He's a grown man capable of making his own decisions. I read that script, and I agree with him. That role isn't good for him. For his career or his peace of mind."

Nick's eyebrows shot up, and he looked shocked. And upset. He rose out of his chair, and without thinking, I took a step closer.

MJ's eyes narrowed, and she looked between us. Her voice lowered when she spoke. "His peace of mind? What do you know about his *peace of mind?*"

I refused to back down, even though I knew Nick wanted me to. I felt his hand slide over mine, holding me close to his side.

"I know enough to know his talent extends far beyond violence. Darkness. That's where you like to put him so you can keep him there."

She looked between us. Glanced down and saw how Nick was holding my hand. Her gaze flew up, and she glared. "Ah. I think I know where you were and who you were with last night, Nicky boy. Giving the author a private performance, were you? Spilling all your secrets?"

"Keep your voice down," he said, his tone low and furious. "Stop embarrassing yourself."

"Myself or you?" She began to laugh. "Oh, this is rich. You and the smut author."

He stepped closer, almost hissing in his anger. "I told you

to shut up, MJ."

"Oh, don't worry. I'll keep your secret. Just like I keep *all* your secrets, Nicky boy."

His grip on my hand tightened, and I saw the color drain from his face.

She leaned toward me, dropping her voice even more. "Don't get used to his company, sweetheart. He comes and goes pretty fast. That is one thing he is good at."

She turned and stormed away.

***

Nick tugged me into the director's chair beside him, and we sat in silence for a moment. I looked around, surprised no one seemed to be looking in our direction.

"There's too much going on for people to worry about a squabble between an actor and his agent," Nick assured me. "It happens on set all the time." He scrubbed a hand over his face. "I thought you were shy, Mila? You were fearless."

"She provoked me. I wasn't going to let her disparage you or me."

"I wish you hadn't goaded her."

"I wasn't going to let her talk to you or me that way." I sat back. "Why do you let her be so disrespectful?"

"MJ is always spouting off. I don't listen to most of what she says when she's in a mood. I didn't want to push her and make you her focus." He shook his head sadly. "Now she has you in her sights too."

I shrugged, surprisingly not caring. "She is nothing to me, Nick. If she causes me any trouble, I'll get Andi to sort her out." I smiled. "Or my lawyer."

He stared at me in wonder. "You're pretty brave under that shy exterior."

"I'm not good with big groups or meeting new people, but I cannot abide bullies. And she is one."

He didn't say anything, his expression anxious. I slipped my hand into his, and he looked down at our entwined fingers. "How is it, Shortcake, that your touch calms me in a way nothing else does?"

"Magic," I whispered.

He smiled. "You are that."

I looked up to see Andi and Amber strolling toward us. "Oh no, what now?" I wondered out loud.

Amber heard me because she was laughing when they stopped in front of us. I saw Andi take in our clasped hands, but she didn't comment.

"The production schedule has changed."

"Oh?" Nick asked.

"We're canceling BC and heading right to Ontario. Between Toronto and Port Albany, we have everything we need for exterior and interior filming. We'll finish up these scenes and move the production there. It helps on the budget and streamlines the filming. Win-win situation." She flashed me a smile. "You get to go home sooner than you thought. But Andi assured me you'd hang around the set some, if needed."

Nick squeezed my hand. "Of course," I replied.

"The winery and that building in your complex—the Hub? Your uncles agreed to let us film there. The town has exactly the look we need. And your uncles own a bunch of buildings they'll let us use for exterior shots, plus the corporate office Roxie works at. They've been amazing."

"Did Uncle Aiden get his walk-on?"

She laughed. "All of them did. They'll be extras in the

wedding scene we'll shoot at the winery. I can't believe how beautiful all that is. How perfect it is for the film." Then she paused. "I guess since you wrote it, it must have inspired you."

"It's a lovely town," I agreed. "When do you plan on being there?"

"Three weeks or so. All the permits will be in place, and we'll have it all organized. We'll wrap here as soon as possible, then head that way. We'll be ready to go when the actors show up."

"Great."

I met Andi's eyes. "We'll talk, kiddo," she assured me. "In fact, I have some new offers to discuss with you."

"Sure. I'll be ready to leave in a few minutes. I don't think I'm needed any more today."

"Okay."

She and Amber moved away, and Nick looked at me. "You're wrong."

"Oh?"

"I need you, Shortcake."

I laughed. "I think you can do without me for a few hours. Surely the coffee is not that bad when someone else makes it. Or, you know," I teased, "you've seen me make it several times. You could get off your butt and make it yourself, movie star."

He chuckled. "How do you feel about having the filming done so close to home?"

"I like it. I can be in my own place where I'm most comfortable."

"I guess you'll be leaving soon, then," he said softly.

"A few days, I imagine."

"I want to take you out."

"On another picnic?" I asked.

"No, a proper date. There's a place I go—it's out of the

way, the owner knows me, so I can sneak in the back way. It's about an hour's drive from here. You could see some of the coast, we can dress up and have dinner. No one will bother us, so your privacy is intact. It will take a couple of days, but if I can arrange it, may I take you out to dinner, Mila?" His expression was serious, his gaze intense and worried. "If you're still here."

I met his gaze with mine, hoping he saw what I was feeling. I didn't want to leave him. The thought of it made my chest ache. I didn't understand how quickly he'd become important to me; I just knew that he had.

"I'm sure I will be. And I'd love that."

"Okay, I'll make some calls." He glanced around, then leaned close and kissed me. "I'll see you tonight?"

"Yes. Tonight."

CHAPTER FOURTEEN

MILA

"You're awfully quiet, kiddo."

I glanced up at Andi. We were back at the hotel, and she was going through some foreign rights offers. "Sorry. Just thinking."

"The offers are all good."

"Oh, I know. You wouldn't encourage them if they weren't. I'm good with them."

She sat back, contemplating me. "So, what's on your mind? Or, should I say, who?"

I felt the heat in my cheeks. "Am I that obvious?"

"To me, you are. You forget how well I know you." She took a sip of coffee. "What's going on with you and Nicholas? I certainly felt the flow between you. And I heard you defending him to MJ. Not all of it, but what I overheard, you were fierce."

"She's awful."

"I know. Stay away from her. But we're discussing Nick, not his choice of representation."

"I don't know. He's…important."

"How important?"

I met her gaze. "More than I expected him to be."

"Kiddo—" she began, but I held up my hand, stopping her.

"I know. I've only known him a short time. I'm sure you'll tell me I don't know him at all."

She set down her coffee mug, placing her elbow on the table and resting her chin in her palm. "It's been just over a week. You can't possibly have developed deep feelings for him." When I didn't reply, her eyebrows rose. "Mila?"

"I write about soul mates and love all the time."

"Writing and living it are two different things. One is a fantasy, and the other is based in reality."

"My dad said he knew he loved my mom right away. Reid and Becca were in love before their first real date. Even Bentley knew how important Emmy was going to be to him. It happens."

"They lived in the same city," she pointed out. "They had common interests."

"Nick and I are similar in many ways."

"He lives in California. You live in Canada. You write fictional characters. He plays them."

"So you think what I feel isn't real?"

She sighed and leaned back. "I think you've met a man you've crushed on for a long time. He is playing a character you invented. I think it might be easy to mix up reality and fantasy."

I thought about what she said. It didn't come from a place of malice, but one of concern.

"When Nick and I are together, it's us, not my characters."

"I don't want to see you hurt."

"Maybe I won't be hurt. Maybe all I want is an affair."

She shook her head. "You aren't built that way, Mila." She paused. "Have you slept with him?"

"No."

"Why not?"

"He says he won't take something I've saved unless I'm a hundred percent sure."

She pursed her lips. "My opinion of him has grown a little."

"He sees me differently than other guys, Andi. He sees Mila. He likes my quirks. I like how I feel when I'm with him."

"Which is?"

"Not poor little Mila, the bullied kid. The delicate flower everyone watches out for. He makes me stronger, and I think I'm good for him. And he makes me braver. I don't understand it, but it's true."

"For how long?"

"I don't know."

"How will you feel when this bubble bursts? When the filming in Ontario is closer to home and things change? When the filming wraps up? Do you see him flying back and forth? Would you move to LA?"

I knew I couldn't move here—even for Nick. I shrugged.

"Maybe he'd move."

"And what about when he has his next episode?" she asked quietly. "When you see the disorder and not the man?"

"I can help him."

She shook her head. "That is a huge burden to take on. Mental illness takes a toll on the person and those around them."

"He is not a burden," I protested.

"But it's true, kiddo. It affects those they love. It drains you. I know."

"I know you do."

"You know if you got serious, your identity would eventually come out, right?"

I paused. I hadn't thought about that completely. I supposed it was naïve to think it wouldn't be discovered.

She stood. "I'll be honest, Mila. I don't know if you're looking at the whole picture. Relationships are hard. Long-distance ones, especially so. Plus, his celebrity status and reputation? And his issues? Your privacy? His agent? The world he lives in—that's a shit-ton of problems to handle. You need to think long and hard about it." She held up her hand before I could protest. "I know you're a grown woman and you can make your own decisions. Just be sure they're based in reality. Not fiction. Imagine a life with Nicholas outside of this world. With your family. With the demands on him. I know you want kids. Does he? Bipolar is thought to be genetic. Would you want to risk that? Would he? Is that something you can live with? Be honest with yourself."

Then she walked away.

I gave up waiting for Nick by ten. I went down to the pool, needing the physical release. I did lap after lap, finally stopping and treading water in the deep end. I huffed out a long exhale of air, my thoughts still chaotic and jumbled.

"Something on your mind, Mila?" Nick asked from the shadows. He sat forward, into the faint light reflected off the pool. I could see the exhaustion written on his face as he contemplated me. "You'd think you were being chased by a shark the way you were swimming."

I shook my head. "Just doing my laps."

"Sorry. Amber kept us on set late. Since they're dropping BC and moving up Ontario, she wants all the garage scenes done."

"I assumed so."

He sat back, crossing his ankle over his knee. "You didn't assume I was with another woman or out carousing?"

"Were you?"

"No."

"Good. I didn't think so."

"I was surprised by your lack of texts and calls."

I laughed dryly, drifting toward him. "Sorry, do you want me to play the jealous, suspicious type?"

"No. It was a pleasant surprise. MJ blew up my phone. That was enough."

"No doubt messages filled with love and encouragement."

He barked a laugh. "Yeah, something like that."

I rolled my eyes, pretty sure of what the messages would contain.

"I assumed you were on set and busy. I also thought you would call me when you got back if it wasn't too late. I heard Amber say something to Andi about filming late and that tomorrow is a closed set, so I knew you were working." I chose my next words carefully. "I'm also aware you don't owe me any explanations about your whereabouts, Nicholas."

He tilted his head, narrowing his eyes. He stood and pulled his shirt over his head, kicked off his shoes, and pushed his shorts off his hips, leaving him in black boxers. I swallowed at how sexy he was in the dim light, the way it played over his tight muscles and torso. He stepped into the pool and headed my way. He reached through the water and dragged me into his arms. He stared down at me. "You can ask me anything, Shortcake. I'll tell you."

The words were out before I could stop them. "Do you want kids?"

He blinked. "Well, I'd like to have sex with you first, if I'm being honest. In fact, to have kids, we need to have sex."

I slapped his chest, and he bent his head, nuzzling my neck. "Someday I want kids, Mila. With the right person. Someday I would like to lead a normal, healthy lifestyle without all this craziness," he murmured in my ear. "Someday I want a home, a wife, and to know where I belong."

I clutched at his shoulders and held him close. His words felt sad. Reflective. As if they were an unattainable dream for him.

"Why?" he whispered.

"I was wondering."

"Can you tell me why you were wondering that question?"

"It was one of several I was thinking about."

"You want to share the others?"

"Not right now."

"Okay, Shortcake." I felt his lips press against my temple. "When you're ready, ask away."

"Why is tomorrow a closed set?"

"Oh, ah…" He trailed off, then chuckled. "I can't believe I have to say this to you. Tomorrow is the scene where Roxie and Duncan throw down in the garage. Amber always has as few people around as possible so we're more comfortable."

It was my turn to say it. "Oh, ah…right. I'll stay away, then."

He chuckled. "It's part of the job, Mila. You wrote the scene. You should know it has to be filmed."

"I guess I never thought of it on the screen. Or that I would know the man acting out that part."

"Remember that word. *Acting*."

"How do you do that?" I asked. "I mean, you're almost naked and Lacey is so pretty and you kiss her. You don't get, ah, turned on?"

He stepped back and cupped my face, kissing me. "I am usually too busy worrying that my modesty pouch will slip or how hot the lights are. Or if I remembered to eat a mint. Or worried she didn't. Sometimes I'm so busy thinking about the choreography we practiced so it looks natural, I forget my lines and we have to do it again. Or she does. We rehearse this shit so much, trust me, Mila. There is nothing romantic about it. It's a scene. We act. Neither of us enjoys it or gets cranked up over it."

"Ah."

"Now, if you were playing Roxie, we'd have a big problem." He pulled me close, lifting me so I had to wrap my legs around him. His stare was dark and intense. He flexed his hips. "A big one, baby. I'd probably get so into the scene I'd fuck you raw, the way Duncan fucks Roxie. I wouldn't be able to stop even if we were being watched."

I whimpered and he bent, covering my mouth with his. He slid his tongue inside and kissed me deeply. Hard. Wet. Passionate. He kissed me until I was breathless. Until my chest was heaving, my body shaking, and I wanted him to show me how he would fuck me. I felt his cock pressed between us. His breathing was ragged, his voice raspy, and his hands clutched me possessively.

Then the gate opened, and we broke apart. He swam to the edge of the pool in the shadows, and I slid back to the deep end.

A staff member called out his greeting and filled up the towel rack, taking the empty basket with him.

Nick and I stared at each other across the water. "I should go and get some sleep," he said, his sentence coming out more like a question.

"Yes, I guess so."

There was no mistaking his disappointment. "What's going on, Shortcake?" he asked. "Something spook you? MJ frighten you off?"

"No. I just know you have an early call."

"I would happily give up the whole night for you."

"I know."

"Is it the fact that you're headed home soon? The shine has faded from our illicit little meetings?"

"Don't say that."

He smiled and climbed from the pool, grabbing a towel and drying himself off. He pulled up his shorts and grabbed his shoes and shirt, draping the damp towel around his shoulders.

He stopped by the gate.

"You didn't deny it, though."

The click of the gate shutting behind him sounded like a gunshot.

Yet I didn't stop him.

* * *

The next day seemed endless. I stayed away from the set, not wanting to watch the sex scene being filmed. Despite what Nick had said, the thought of watching him touch Lacey— even acting as though he was enjoying himself with her—was too overwhelming. I did more research on bipolar disorder, shocked to discover the high divorce rate when one of the partners had the condition. I read about genetics, noting some theories that the disorder was thought to be inherited from the mother. Another site stated it was believed bipolar disorder could skip a generation. I researched the differences between Bipolar I and Bipolar II. Many of them talked about how to deal with episodes, how the condition could trigger overly aggressive sexual appetites, deep depressions, angry outbursts, or, in the case of Bipolar II, the patient was almost euphoric, hardly requiring sleep, yet upbeat and energetic all the time. There were so many theories, thoughts, and interpretations. The information was vast, and after a while, I had to shut down my computer. It was overwhelming. The one definitive thing I found was there seemed to be varying degrees of how the disorder affected each individual. Some were high-functioning. Others suffered terribly. Medication, therapy, and support were all essential interventions.

I was certain of only one thing when it came to Nicholas Scott. He didn't have the essentials needed to fight this on his own.

I didn't hear from him in the evening, and although I swam late that night, he never appeared. I tried to assure myself it was because he would be tired, but I feared I had hurt him with my withdrawal the night before.

I ached not seeing him. It felt as if a small part of me was missing. I told myself that was crazy. I barely knew him. It wasn't as if he was an essential part of my life.

But still, the sensation continued.

The next morning, Andi mentioned flying home. "I have some things cropping up I hadn't expected. If they're going to wrap here soon, I thought we could head back. If they need you, they can Zoom. Or they'll see you back home."

It made sense. I had no desire to go back to the set today. Andi said the filming hadn't gone well yesterday, but when she spoke with Amber, the director was sure today would be better.

"What happened?" I asked.

"I don't know. Nicholas wasn't at his best, I gathered."

"Oh."

"Much like you were off yesterday."

I shrugged, not replying.

"Should I book us the flights home?" she asked.

I looked over her shoulder. "Yes."

The rest of the day I spent pretending to write. The words were stilted, and the ones that came out were sad and twisted. Soaked in emotion that changed the entire story. In the end, I saved the work in a different file, already knowing it would be part of another book. But today, I didn't have it in me to write the lighthearted rom-com that had been flowing so well.

Today, I felt anything but lighthearted.

I felt weary. Sad. Disheartened.

I took a walk, sending scathing glares at the paps hanging around the hotel from behind my sunglasses. I spoke to Sammy and my mom at the ranch, forcing a smile into my voice as I listened to them talk about the project being done and how much my mom loved the ranch.

"We're all going to come for a girls' weekend," she said enthusiastically. *"Rachel is going to reserve the cabins and all the experiences for us!"* Then she lowered her voice. *"I think your sister may end up staying here, Mila."*

"Really?"

"She and Luke…well, suffice it to say, I have never seen her like this. I think this is serious. He is quite wonderful. Your dad and I like him a lot."

I wondered if they would feel that way if I brought Nick home and told them what he meant to me.

Not that the chances of that happening were high.

She was pleased to hear I'd be home soon and assured me everyone was excited about the filming. I managed to inject enough false happiness into my voice, so she had no idea how I was feeling.

But once I hung up, I walked out to the balcony, sitting down and letting my shoulders drop. I hadn't slept well the night before, and I was tired. I felt Nick's silence even more today, and half a dozen times, I picked up my phone to text him, only to stop. Twice, I was tempted to call the driver to take me to the set, but I didn't. I wasn't sure Nick wanted to see me. I wasn't sure I was strong enough to see him.

Because, despite everything I read, every fear I had, the one thing that kept coming back to me was the fact that somehow, Nicholas Scott had become extremely important to me. I felt his need for me as acutely as I thought he knew mine for him. And it wasn't a silly crush. From the moment we met, we'd felt the draw to each other. On some level, we recognized the other person's hidden pain, and we eased that.

Darkness fell and I sat there, not moving. I knew I should pack or write. Go for a swim. But that wasn't what I wanted to do. Finally, I got up and poured a bath. Soaked for a while in the lavender-scented water, the steam and scent soothing. I brushed my teeth and pulled on a robe. There was a text from Andi saying she'd booked our flights home, and I stared at the words, fresh pain hitting me.

Would I have the chance to say goodbye to Nick? Dinner was off the table now, but I hoped at least we could be… friends. Tears filled my eyes. He was more than a friend.

My phone buzzed again, and my eyes widened at the simple message.

NICHOLAS

I miss you, Shortcake.

My fingers shook as I replied.

ME

I miss you too. I'm sorry.

NICHOLAS

Do you want to see me?

ME

Yes.

NICHOLAS

Open your door.

CHAPTER FIFTEEN

MILA

I flew across the room, tearing open the door. Nicholas stood on the other side, looking as anxious as I was. He stepped in, looping an arm around my waist and pulling me tight to his chest as his head descended, his mouth covering mine. With a sob, I flung my arms around his neck, kissing him back. Somewhere in my mind, I heard the door shut, felt him pick me up and carry me to the bedroom.

He deposited me on the bed, his body following mine to the mattress. "Not again, Shortcake. Don't leave me alone again," he commanded in between kisses.

"No," I vowed.

"I need you. For tonight, tomorrow. However long you'll have me."

"Forever," I promised.

He hovered over me, the light playing off his face. He had circles under his eyes, the brown irises almost black. His scruff was thick, his voice raspy. "How can I need you so much?" he wondered out loud. "How can you be so important?"

"I feel the same."

"Tell me what you want."

"You, Nicholas. I want you."

"Are you certain?"

"Yes."

He kissed me again, and this time, it felt different. I tasted his want and need. His gentleness. His lips were full and soft on mine, his tongue seeking and exploring. He reached between us, tugging on the sash of my robe and pulling it open. The cooler air hit my skin, and I gasped as he trailed his fingers over my torso. I pushed at his shoulders, and he sat back, yanking his shirt over his head. I traced the taut skin over his muscles, smiling as he shuddered. I tugged on his waistband and he plucked at the arms of my robe, and moments later, we were naked and pressed into each other.

I swam in the sensations. His skin on mine. His tongue in my mouth. On my neck. Licking at me. The nip of his teeth and the soothing sensation of his kiss that followed. He explored my mouth thoroughly. Tasted me everywhere. I had never known how erotic it was to have the scrape of a man's scruff on my thighs. How it felt to have my nipples sucked and played with or the sensation of a soft tongue on my clit bringing me to a shattering orgasm. He gave it all to me.

I explored him and the wonders that his clothing hid. The tattoo over his heart that I kissed. How he groaned when I played with his nipples. The way his muscles bunched as I stroked him. His hiss of satisfaction when I took him in my mouth, my fumbling attempts met only with whispered words of praise and adoration. He was long and hard, sweet and salty, velvet and steel. He loved it when I caressed along his shoulders or gripped his back with my blunt nails. He smiled in satisfaction as I cried out his name when he slid one, then two fingers inside me, pumping in tandem with his thumb rubbing circles on my needy clit. I came again, our eyes locked while I succumbed.

Then he hovered over me, his face intense.

"I'm on birth control," I whispered.

"I haven't been with anyone for months, and I was tested. I'm negative," he assured me.

"Please," I murmured, arching my back as he touched me again.

"Are you sure?" he asked.

"Yes."

"This will change everything."

"It doesn't have to."

"Yes, my love," he whispered. "It does."

He framed my face with his hands and kissed me. Long, slow, and sweet. He settled between my legs, his hard cock pressing on my tight entrance. He bent one leg against my chest, opening me farther, and carefully, he notched himself inside me.

My eyes flew open, my body already tight with pain. He apologized against my lips. "I'm sorry, baby. It'll get better. I promise."

He moved, and I felt more pain. I gasped at the feeling. I was full. Too full. The pressure was incredible, and I tensed around him. "I'll stop," he murmured. "Right now."

"No. Just give me a minute."

He held himself still. I felt his body tremble from holding back. I knew he wouldn't move until I told him to, no matter the effort it cost him. The pain receded a little, and I nodded.

He moved again, and this time, the pain wasn't as bad. A

small, dull ache I could ignore. As he withdrew, I shivered, a moan escaping my mouth.

"Shh," he soothed, gliding a hand down my torso and sliding it between us. "I'll help you forget." His touch on my clit was light, soft, and indulgent. It relaxed me, and I took in a deep breath.

"That's my good girl," he praised. "Open for me."

I let out a shuddering breath, and I felt him slide in deeper. My gasp was more about pleasure than pain. My body began to respond, and I whimpered his name. He kissed me again. "I'm sorry," he whispered. "I have to move."

"Slow," I begged.

He pulled back, thrusting forward gently. It felt better this time, and I eased my grip on his shoulders. He did it again, and I felt the flicker of pleasure. I looked up at him with wide eyes.

"Again," I pleaded. "Oh God, please, Nick."

"Fuck, baby, yes," he replied and kissed me again. This time, he was hungry, devouring my lips and mouth ferociously. The pain was diminished but the pleasure built as he began to move, and I held on for dear life, unsure if I would survive.

But what a way to go.

NICHOLAS

Inside Mila was extraordinary. The heat and tightness that surrounded my cock was unlike anything I had ever experienced.

I had been miserable without her the past two days. Nothing felt right. My mind was everywhere but where it should be, and it had reflected in my performance. Amber had pulled me aside, asking me what was going on.

"You're as stiff as a board. Where is your head?"

Desperate, I shut out everything else and became Duncan. I lost myself in the role, but as usual, when the lights went out and the camera stopped rolling, I was left adrift. My thoughts immediately went back to Mila. Her subtle rejection at the pool haunted me. It shouldn't. I had no expectations of her. She owed me nothing. She certainly didn't owe me her virginity. She had been saving herself for the right man, and we both knew I wasn't him.

Except, dammit, I wanted to be.

Everything about that small woman called to me. Her voice and her laughter. Her teasing. Her stubbornness. The way she had gone toe-to-toe with MJ had shocked me. Delighted me. Appalled me. The last thing I wanted was for her to be on MJ's radar, yet the fact that she had stuck up for me was incredibly touching.

How quickly she had gotten under my skin was astounding. The protectiveness she made me feel for her was new and unusual. I had never experienced that with another woman I had dated. The desire I felt for her was strong. The need to be close to her was intense.

The sadness at the thought of not seeing her was overwhelming.

I had given up the fight when I got back to the hotel. I showered and planned to go to bed, but I knew I couldn't. I had gone up to her room, standing outside her door, texting her like the coward I was. Giving her the chance to say no without having to look in my eyes. Desperately praying she would open the door for me.

The need on her face when she did was the straw that

broke the camel's back. I couldn't keep my hands to myself anymore. I couldn't get close enough to her. Kiss her deeply enough to satisfy me. Touch or taste her enough to ease the ache I felt.

And now, buried inside her, the emotion ran rampant. I never wanted to be separated from her again. I never wanted a day to pass without kissing her. Touching her.

I moved inside her, feeling the way she gripped me. Listened to her little noises. Experienced this with her. Felt that male pride, knowing I was the only one who ever had. The only one who ever would.

Our gazes locked in the soft light. Her wondrous eyes were wide and filled with the same emotions I was feeling. Her mouth was open, little gasps escaping as I pumped steadily into her. Her lips were wet and swollen from mine. Her abraded nipples rubbed on my chest as I hovered over her, our skin gliding together. She was slick and hot, tight and perfect around me. I felt her muscles fluttering, and I knew I could make her come. I needed her to come. I was frantic for her release. I kissed her, our tongues mating the same way our bodies were, and I slipped my fingers between us and rubbed light circles on her clit.

She cried out, tightening around me, clutching my back, scoring me with her blunt nails as she spasmed. I rode it out, finally giving in and orgasming. It blasted through my body, skyrocketing me fifty thousand feet in the air, tumbling and groaning as I floated back to earth.

I collapsed, pushing her into the mattress, breathing heavily. She wrapped her arms around me, holding me close. For a moment, I bathed in the afterglow, then rolled to the side and gathered her into my arms.

For a moment, there was silence. I wasn't sure what to say after such a profound experience. Mila turned her head and pressed a kiss to my damp skin.

"So that is what all the fuss is about."

I began to laugh, holding her tight.

"It only gets better, Shortcake."

"Holy shit," she muttered. "I'll probably expire."

"I'll save you."

She snuggled closer. "I think you already have."

I pressed a kiss to her head. "No, you have that wrong. I think you saved me."

I tucked an arm under my head, still holding her. "But where do we go from here, Mila?"

"Forward."

"Together?"

She was quiet. "Do you want that?"

"Yes. But I think the bigger question is if you want that." I sighed. "I know I'm a lot to take on."

"I did a bunch of research again. Some of the stats are scary."

"I know."

She slid a finger under my chin, turning my face. "But sometimes the risks are worth it. They bring the sweetest rewards. I think you're worth it."

I lowered my head and nuzzled her lips. "Thank you."

She yawned and I smiled. "Get some sleep. We'll talk in the morning. I'm not due on set until twelve."

"You won't leave?" she asked, drowsy and soft.

"No, baby. Not until you tell me to."

"Okay. I guess you're stuck with me forever, then."

Forever. I could live with that.

I woke up the next morning alone. I slid my hand across the still-warm sheets, but Mila was gone. I sat up, relaxing when I heard the water running in the shower. I got up, stopping in the doorway, watching her. Her hair was wet, streaming down her back, the color darkened by the water, reminding me of the first time I saw her in the pool. Unable to help myself, I stepped in behind her, wrapping my arms around her and dropping my head to her neck, nuzzling the skin.

She jumped, then relaxed back into my embrace. "Hi," she whispered.

I spun her in my arms and covered her mouth with mine, kissing her until she was breathless. "Hey, Shortcake."

She snuggled into me, and I kissed her head. "Okay this morning?"

She leaned back, the water sluicing through her hair. "Last night was amazing."

"You don't regret it?" I asked, my words quiet, my eyes beseeching hers.

Please don't regret me.

"No. You—we—were everything I dreamed of and more."

"Yeah, we were."

She slid her arms around my neck, rolling up on her toes. "Can I wash your back?"

"You can wash anything you want." I waggled my eyebrows at her, and she laughed, the sound warm and sweet.

"You seem to be poking me with something."

"Ignore it."

She pressed her mouth to mine. "What if I don't want to?"

I had her pressed against the tile in a second. "You're not too sore?"

"No."

That was all I needed.

We ate on the balcony, my appetite ferocious. Mila watched me eat, her gaze indulgent. She laughed when I snuck the bacon off her plate, slapping my hands away.

"Mine," she protested.

I leaned forward, grasping the back of her neck and kissing her deeply. "*Mine,*" I growled.

A throat clearing broke us apart, and I tried not to smirk as Andi walked outside and sat down. She looked between us and shook her head as she poured her coffee and picked up a muffin.

"I see you two made some decisions."

Mila blushed but straightened her shoulders. "We did."

Andi met my eyes. "Her identity is private. That is not an option."

"I understand."

"I love her like a sister."

"I'm glad."

"I'll do everything I can to help you, but God help you if you hurt her."

Her words and quiet support surprised me. MJ would have already gone off the rails.

"I don't plan to."

She sat back. "How is this playing out, kids? We're supposed to leave, Mila. Is this just a scratch-the-itch sort of thing, or are we attempting a long run?"

We had already talked about it in the night. Mila looked at Andi, leaning her elbows on the table as she spoke.

"I'm going to stay for a few more days, Andi."

"On your own?"

"I'll be here," I interjected.

Andi flashed me a "duh" look and focused on Mila. "Is that a good idea, kiddo?"

"It's what I want. I'm not ready to leave just yet."

"How long?"

"A week. Then I'll come home and get ready for when the crew arrives for filming."

Andi nodded. "And has accommodation been discussed for Port Albany?"

"Not yet." Mila glanced my way. "Nick can stay with me or at the hotel with the crew. Whatever he prefers."

"For propriety's sake, I'll stay at the hotel," I said, secretly thrilled that Mila wanted me with her. "But I might not be there a lot." I lifted her hand and kissed it. "We'll see how that plays out."

"Your dad?" Andi asked her.

"I'll talk to my parents."

"What about *your* agent?" Andi asked me pointedly.

"She never goes on shoots unless I request it. And I will not be. She hates travel and being inconvenienced. She'll stay in touch via Zoom and cell phone."

"She won't be happy about this development between you. Her opinion of Mila—"

I cut her off. "Doesn't matter to me. She has no say in who I am involved with. I'll make that clear to her today. I won't let her near Mila."

Mila's phone rang from the other room, and she jumped up. "That'll be Sammy. I'll just be a minute."

Andi tilted her head, studying me. "She'll never move to LA, Nicholas. She would die here."

"I know. I wouldn't ask her to."

"Where do you see this going then, if I can ask? She isn't a fling kind of girl, no matter what she might think. And she's not an elixir."

"I already know that. My disorder can't be cured, only controlled. I have no idea what the future holds for us, but she makes me feel something I haven't felt in a long time. *Hope.* I don't have to hide anything with her. She accepts me for me. Disorder and all. She makes my world better. She makes me want to be better. Do better."

"And when MJ interferes?"

I leaned forward, my voice low. "Could you look over my contract, Andi? Let your lawyer friend see it? I think I might be ready for a complete change. But before I discuss it with Mila, I need to know my options."

She smiled. A real, honest smile. "You're serious about her."

"I am. I only want what is best for her. And I want that to be me."

I saw her skeptical expression.

"I know it's fast, Andi. I know you think she could do so much better than me. And you're right. She could. But there is something between us. We both feel it. We both want it. I'm asking you to keep an open mind." I dropped my voice. "To help me."

For a moment, she said nothing. She searched my expression then made a decision.

"I know an agent. Big in the business, but lives and works out of Toronto. I am good friends with him and his wife. I could ask him to meet with you while you're in Toronto. Privately, of course."

I sat back. "I'd like that. Thank you."

"If you hurt her, I'll make you regret it."

"If I hurt her, it will be the biggest regret of my life."

She nodded. "Then we understand each other."

CHAPTER SIXTEEN

NICHOLAS

"**I**'m not going to Canada."

I rested my arm on the back of the director's chair, looking around the set, hoping to appear casual. "I don't expect you to. You rarely travel when I go on location."

"I suppose your new little obsession will be there?"

I shut my eyes and turned to face MJ. "She is not an obsession."

It was a lie; I was totally obsessed with her, but not the way MJ thought. Mila brought a warmth to my life, a quiet acceptance and sweetness I had been missing. One I didn't want to give up.

"She lives there, and she'll be on set on occasion, I imagine."

"And you'll fuck her every chance you get. I'm warning you, Nicky boy. She's a clinger."

"Christ's sake, stop calling me Nicky boy. You know I hate it. And she is anything but." I met MJ's eyes, noticing how cold and distant they were. "Stop disparaging her. Show a little respect."

She laughed, the sound unpleasant. "Respect? For what? Your latest attempt at a relationship we both know is doomed to fail?"

"Jesus," I muttered. "You make me sound like a manwhore. I barely even date. It's all **PR** shit, MJ. Shit *you* create. Stop it."

"Does she know?" she asked. "Does she know you're not what everyone thinks? That you'll never be normal?"

Her words were a punch to my gut. "She knows and accepts it."

She rolled her eyes. "Wait until she experiences one of your episodes."

"I'm being very careful with my meds. I'm exercising, watching my alcohol intake, sleeping well, and looking after myself."

"You fall off the wagon all the time."

"Mila pointed out all my episodes the past three years correlate to the darker roles I play. The way I tend to stay in character and probably do forget my meds. I'm being extra cautious. She added some more reminders on my phone."

"Mila, Mila, Mila. God's gift to you, isn't she?" The sarcasm in her voice was evident.

I bit back my retort. Mila was a gift to me, but I didn't want to push MJ anymore.

"Watch your tone, MJ. I swear to God—"

She glared at me, cutting off my words. "What, Nicky? You'll fire me? You'll walk away? We both know I own you. You have obligations left to the studio they won't let you out of either. You're stuck. You owe them three more movies in the franchise."

I was tired of her threats. Of her talons dug so deeply into my skin I could feel her pull even when she was elsewhere. MJ had talked me into the franchise. I hated that role. I'd never expected it to skyrocket the way it did and trap me into such a long commitment. I should have listened to my gut.

I stood, matching her glare. She was tall for a woman, with a steely determination, and she could break a man's balls without chipping a nail. A force to be reckoned with. Once, it worked for my benefit, but now, I was exhausted being caught up in her orbit.

"You are going to push me too far one day, MJ. Despite our history, everything we've been through together, my loyalty isn't endless. I have no idea why you're so threatened by Mila, but I'm warning you. She is off-limits. You hurt her, you hurt me. And I will not hesitate to hurt you back."

"I'll break you," she hissed. "You'll never work again."

"If I have to walk away and leave this life to get away from you, I'll do it."

Her cackle made the hairs on the back of my neck rise. "You wouldn't last two weeks without me. You forget who is always there when you break. I clean up the messes and get you back on your feet. Your precious little author has no clue what happens when you hit the wall. And you will. I guarantee it. And when she walks and you're all alone, drowning in your sorrow and not even sure what your name is? You'll come crawling back."

She stepped away, fury dripping from her eyes, her voice like ice. "I'll see you around, Nicky boy. I'll check in before you leave for the land of maple syrup and snow."

She turned and walked away.

MILA

I was out for a walk when Nick called me. I sat on a nearby bench and answered the call, happy to hear his voice.

"Hi."

"Hey, Shortcake."

"How's it going?"

"The worst is over." He chuckled. "We have two more scenes Amber wants for today. But my friend called, and he has everything arranged for tonight if you still want to have dinner with me."

"You have the time?"

"Yeah, tomorrow is another early call, but I have tonight."

"I'd love to go out to dinner with you." I glanced toward the hotel. "What about your friends?"

"I have a plan. I'll pick you up at seven, okay?"

"Sounds good."

"Wear something pretty, Mila. And leave your hair down. I love it when you wear your hair down."

I shivered at the possessive tone in his voice.

"Okay."

I hung up and headed back to the hotel. I opened the closet, staring between the lovely dress Cami picked out and the pretty yellow one I had bought. I heard a knock on my door, and I called out to Andi to come in. I carried both dresses with me.

"Which should I wear tonight…" I trailed off at the sight of MJ standing in my hotel room, looking around with a sneer on her face. I had left the door ajar for Andi, not expecting anyone else.

Our eyes met, hers cold and unfeeling. I tried not to show my discomfort and instead straightened my shoulders.

"MJ," I said coolly, pleased my voice didn't tremble. "Andi's not here. Neither is Nick."

"I didn't come to see either of them." She flicked her fingers at the dresses in my hand. "Date with Nicky boy? He's going all out to impress you, isn't he?"

"What can I do for you?" I asked, draping the dresses over the sofa.

"I came to give you a piece of friendly advice."

I had to laugh. "I doubt anything you do is considered friendly, MJ. Especially when it comes to me."

"Nicky's on a high right now. You're his newest obsession. His"—she rolled her eyes—"light. Once he gets over the high and realizes everything is the same, he'll be done with you."

"Everything is the same?" I questioned.

"He thinks he can beat the disease. Find a cure. You make him feel good. So right now, that cure is you."

I frowned. "I disagree with you. I think Nick accepts his *condition* and is simply trying to fit his life around it. I don't think he thinks of me as a cure."

"Look, Mia—"

"Mila," I corrected.

"Whatever. You seem like a nice little girl. Do yourself a favor. Walk away before he destroys you. Before he takes the light he's found and drags it into the darkness."

I barked a laugh. "You can't give someone bipolar disorder. It's not a cold you can catch."

She crossed her arms and glared at me. "He'll drain you."

"That's my business and not yours." I mimicked her stance. "Why do I scare you so much?"

"You don't scare me," she scoffed.

"I think I do. You're worried I might have more influence on Nick than you do. That he might see how you really don't have his best interests at heart. That he might actually have other options."

For a moment, she said nothing. Hate blazed from her eyes, and I knew I'd struck close to home.

"Nicky and I have been through too much together. He would never leave me. And if you push him to, you might find yourself the one being left," she spat.

The door opened, and Andi walked in, looking shocked at seeing MJ there. "Problem?" she drawled, walking my way and standing next to me.

"No. MJ was just leaving."

MJ tossed her hair, the brassy color bright under the lights. "Trying to save your client some heartache, Andi. I know Nicky better than anyone, and I know what he can be like. Once the shine wears off, she'll have a lot of shit to deal with."

I felt a tremor go through me. "I know what Nick is capable of. He has a lot of strength inside. Despite how he's handled, he is the most amazing man I have ever met."

"I think Mila has made her decision. Thanks for dropping by," Andi finished for me, gripping my elbow. "Don't let the door hit you on the way out."

MJ spun on her heel, grabbing the door handle. "Have fun playing house. It won't last." She paused. "And he hates yellow," she snapped and flounced from the room, slamming the door behind her.

I sat down, my legs shaking. I took in some deep breaths, and Andi slipped a glass of water into my hand.

"You didn't pass out," she said. "You stood up to her."

"My God, she is vile," I muttered.

"She certainly has balls."

"Is she in love with him?" I asked Andi.

"Fixated for sure. Possessive. Not sure if she knows how to

love." Andi frowned. "Please be careful, Mila." She rubbed her head. "I told your dad I would watch out for you. You fall for the lead who has issues, and you anger his psycho agent. And you're bringing home that same man who might be a bit obsessed with you. Van is going to kill me."

"Not quite the bore you thought I was, am I?" I couldn't help but quip.

She began to laugh. "Nope. So, you're wearing the yellow, right?"

"Yep."

"Okay. Let's get you ready."

At seven, Nick arrived. He came in, carrying a small bunch of flowers. He stopped when he saw me, and he stared. Swallowed. Stared again. Twirled his finger, silently asking me to do the same.

He came closer and kissed me. "You are breathtaking," he murmured. "My God, Mila. You are stunning."

"Thank you." Feeling shy, I patted his lapel. "I like you in a suit."

"I clean up well."

"You both look nice, kids," Andi said, a slight touch of sarcasm in her voice. "How are you getting to prom exactly?"

I laughed at her, taking the flowers from Nick and putting them in a large glass I took from the bar. I touched the petals of the flowers with a smile. I couldn't recall the last time I had been given flowers by anyone outside my family.

"Downstairs in a nondescript black van waiting by the back door. I sat in the third row, and we went right past the paps coming in. They had no idea I was in there. The driver will take us to the restaurant and drop us off. Another car is already waiting there, and I'll bring us home in it. I've already tipped the guard at the front, and I'll text him as we approach so the gate will be open and I can drive right in. It's not my car, so they won't be looking for it."

"You've done this before."

"Too many times." He scrubbed his face. "Not for dates, simply to live. See some friends. Grab a pizza. Go for a run. I have no idea what is so exciting about me walking or having dinner that they need to be so intrusive."

"People are curious."

"I wish they were more curious about curing cancer or listening about climate change. Not what I put on my plate or who I share a meal with."

Andi nodded. "Still, going out is risky. For both of you."

I picked up my shawl, and Nick hurried over to help me drape it around my shoulders.

"I just want to take Mila to my favorite place and have a meal with her. It shouldn't have to be so difficult," he said.

"It's part of your life," Andi replied.

"Thanks to MJ," he snapped. "Her freaking love of notoriety. Wanting press all the time."

Andi and I shared a glance. I begged her with my eyes not to say anything about MJ's visit earlier. I didn't want to tell Nick right now. I just wanted to enjoy a night with him.

"Shall we go?"

"Have fun," Andi said with a smirk. "Don't stay out too late."

Nick held out his hand. "You ready?"

I slid my palm against his. "Yes."

———

"It's so pretty here," I murmured, looking around the restaurant. We were tucked into a back room, the window overlooking the water. The sunset cast its brilliance on the waves, and the sky was lit with beautiful colors.

"Not as pretty as the woman I'm sitting with."

I smiled at him. He was relaxed and handsome. Leaving the hotel was easy, the paps not even looking our way. The drive was quiet, although more than once, his mouth covered mine, devouring my lips and holding me close. I'd been pleased to discover my lipstick stood up to its name and was smudge-proof, even though Nick seemed determined to prove otherwise.

"I'm a little overdressed."

He shook his head. "No. I love your dress."

"You don't hate yellow?"

He frowned. "No. It's one of my favorite colors. So is red." He touched my cheek. "And lately, gold."

I felt the color flood my cheeks. He constantly told me how my eyes fascinated him.

He smiled, stroking my cheek. "I love how you react to my words, Mila. You make me feel so incredible."

Unbidden, MJ's words from earlier popped into my head. "You don't think I can cure you, do you?" I asked. "That I'm some sort of therapy that will heal you?"

He sat back, looking shocked.

"Why would you ask that?" Then he frowned. "*MJ*. That sounds like the kind of shit she would spout."

"She dropped by today."

"Oh, you too?" he asked. "Spreading her joy everywhere." He took a sip of his drink. "Tell me what she said. Let's get this discussion over with so we can enjoy our night."

I repeated the conversation, and his face darkened. "You

aren't a *medicine*, Mila. You stir something inside me. Feelings and emotions. You make me feel better because you make me feel better about myself. MJ is constantly telling me what is wrong with me. What I do that is incorrect. I think her favorite thing is to belittle me. You do the opposite. You point out what I do right. You bolster me." He picked up my hand and kissed it. "Your touch soothes me, I admit. Being close to you makes me calmer. Knowing you're around, I'm happier. But it was that way for my parents. I remember my dad telling my mom she was his center. She focused him."

"What happened to your dad?" I asked.

"He died of a heart attack when I was in my teens."

"I'm sorry."

"Thank you." He frowned. "You help focus me, Mila. You make me stronger, but I don't think you're *curing* me. You're making me happier than I can recall ever feeling, but isn't that what love is supposed to do?"

I felt my eyes widen. "Love?" I whispered.

He shook his head. "Too much?"

I had to look away from the intensity in his eyes. "No," I whispered. "I feel it too."

"You threaten her."

"That's what Andi says."

"MJ likes—needs—to be the center of attention, no matter what. She wants the focus on her. She lives for the spotlight." He laughed dryly. "Way more than I do. I love the work. She loves the hype. She craves it."

"She should have been the actor."

He lifted one shoulder. "In many ways, I think she is."

"It would be hard to live that way," I mused. "She must be exhausted all the time."

He shook his head. "You are so incredible. She's been nothing but awful to you, yet you show her grace."

"That's how I was raised by my parents."

"They did an outstanding job." He blew out a breath. "I'm glad you're heading home soon and away from her. I'll be anxious to join you."

"What did she say to you?"

He told me, and it was my turn to be affronted.

"We have lots of maple syrup, but snow is only in the winter. You'll be there during the heat of the summer. We don't live in a frozen tundra twelve months of the year."

"I'll let her think that. She hates the cold, so she'll never show up." He chuckled. "Now, can we stop talking about her and talk about us? About what you're going to show me in Canada?" He leaned close. "About how I'm supposed to survive once you leave?"

"It's only for a couple of weeks. Maybe less if filming wraps up."

He leaned forward and kissed me. "Then I am going to do my best to speed things along. My performances will be perfect." He winked. "The best incentive I know will be having you in my arms again."

"Okay, then."

He laughed. "Ready to order?"

"Yes."

CHAPTER SEVENTEEN

NICHOLAS

Mila sat back, wiping her lips. "That was incredible."

I grinned. "I know. Manny's food is fabulous. I love it here. Great meals, I never get bothered, and the margaritas are delicious."

"And powerful."

"That's why I only had a small one. Yours was full size."

"Aiden would go crazy. He loves Mexican, and this fusion is out of this world. How did you find it?"

"He used to have a food truck close to where I lived. His dad is Mexican, and his mom is Asian. He combined both for some of his dishes, and I was addicted. I think I lived on his ginger beef tacos for a month once. I ate there all the time. Cheap and delicious. We got to be friends. When he found this place, I fronted him the money to buy it. I'd had my break, and I thought he deserved his. I have never regretted it. He is always busy, but he fits me in anytime I want."

I saw the look that passed over her face, and I chuckled.

"Not other women, Shortcake. I usually come alone and often eat in the kitchen. He has a big family table in there. I brought MJ here once early on. She hated it."

"What is to hate?"

"She likes fine dining. Or, in other words, expensive. Places she can be seen."

"Ah."

Our waitress, Manny's daughter, came to the table. She grinned at the empty plates. "Good, right?"

I laughed. "Amazing as always, Carmen. Our compliments to the kitchen."

"Dad is bringing dessert."

"Great."

A few moments later, Manny appeared, sliding his deep-fried ice cream and homemade churros onto the table. I eyed the pots of chocolate and the dulce de leche, already knowing Mila would love both. I introduced them, and he smiled, sitting beside me.

"You are too pretty and smart to be an actress," he said with a droll wink. "What are you doing with this guy?"

"I heard he knew the best Mexican-Asian fusion restaurant in the state," she replied. "I'm done with him now."

Manny laughed and I grinned.

"I'm working with Mila right now. But you're right. She isn't an actress." I smiled at her fondly. "She is the most real person I know."

Manny smiled. "Good. You deserve real, my friend."

We chatted for a few minutes, and he clapped me on the shoulder and left after kissing Mila's hand. She hummed in delight after tasting the desserts, and we polished off the platter. I loved watching her eat. Enjoy the food. Most of the women I knew nibbled on salad. Sipped their wine as if they had to make it last a month. Mila relished her food. Delighted in the tastes and textures. I liked how her delight made her look. Soft, rounded—a pleasure to touch. Not flat.

"Aiden and my dad would fly to California just to eat here. My whole family would."

"Will I meet them?" I asked, strangely nervous. "Your family, I mean."

She looked at me over the rim of her glass. "I expect so since you'll be in the complex."

"How will I meet them?" I asked.

"How? I don't understand."

"Will I meet them as 'this is Nicholas Scott, the actor,' or —" I swallowed the sudden thickness in my throat "—'this is Nick, my, ah…'" I flicked my fingers, unsure how to complete the sentence.

She smiled and took my hand. "I will introduce you however you're comfortable with, Nick."

"I'm yours."

"Then I'll introduce you like that. 'This is my Nick. My boyfriend.'"

A word shouldn't make me smile so hard, but that one did.

"That works." I leaned forward, suddenly worried. "What if they don't like me?"

"My mom will want to take care of you, and my dad will quiz you, then talk to you man-to-man. My uncles will test you, and my aunts will love you up. My cousins will tease you to death, so tease them right back. You'll be fine. I think they'll like you a lot."

"Yeah?"

She smiled. "Yeah."

Again, I smiled so hard, my cheeks hurt. I wanted to meet

her family and get to know them. I hoped they gave me a chance.

Carmen came over, and I handed her my credit card. "Put it through before your dad knows," I warned.

She smiled, and I settled the bill. Manny never wanted to take my money, but this was a date and I wanted to pay for it.

We headed for the door, pausing as another customer came in, shaking his head.

"Holy shit, what a circus," he muttered, looking at me. I saw the recognition in his eyes, but he didn't react. Men usually didn't. The women, though—they often screamed. I hated it when they screamed. It made me want to run.

"If they're waiting for you, I'm sorry, man." He brushed by me, and I peered out the side window, cursing.

"What?" Mila asked.

"We're surrounded. Paps everywhere. *Fuck.*"

Manny came from the kitchen. "They're out back too, Nick. I have no idea how they found out."

I had a pretty good idea, although I never recalled telling MJ where I was going. But this had her written all over it. She'd anger me and out Mila at the same time.

I wasn't going to allow that to happen.

"We'll just stay inside until they get tired of waiting," Mila suggested.

"They never get tired," I snapped.

"Oh."

She was quiet for a moment as I fumed, internally cursing MJ, this life, and everything else.

Carmen joined us. "I'm off now. I could run over a few with my car."

Mila looked at her. "Oh, I have an idea!"

"What?"

"If you loan me a uniform, I could go out with you. They'll think I'm just a waitress and not look twice. Nick can wait a bit and walk out on his own."

"They'll follow me." I protested, even though I saw how she was thinking. My car was parked around back close to the door, so they'd only get a few snaps of me and I would be alone.

Carmen waved her hand. "I'm headed into the city to meet some friends. I'll drop Mila off wherever she needs to go, and you can head to your place."

Mila smiled at me. "I'll meet you at the hotel."

"This isn't how I wanted our night out to go."

She squeezed my arm. "We won't let them spoil it. We'll have fun at their expense."

I couldn't resist her smile. "Okay."

***

Ten minutes later, Mila and Carmen headed out the door, casually strolling, ignoring the muffled shouts I could hear. Mila wore one of the simple uniforms Manny had loaned her. She'd put her hair up under a bandanna and donned a pair of glasses she'd borrowed from the lost and found. She didn't appear upset or worried, instead offering me a mischievous smile and a fast kiss.

"See you at the hotel."

I watched anxiously as she and Carmen walked through the throng of photographers. They threw questions and yelled at the girls, but neither reacted, although Carmen flipped them the bird once. Then they got in Carmen's car and drove off.

"Jesus," I breathed out. "It worked."

"Your woman is clever. Cool under pressure too."

She had been cool. She hadn't panicked like I had or gotten mad. And she hadn't passed out. She simply came up with an idea and went with it. Now I had to do the same.

"I'll wait fifteen minutes and head out."

Manny handed me a bag. "This has her dress. I put a towel around it and some food on top so it looks like you're taking a doggie bag. They'll think you ate here alone." He grinned. "No story."

"Perfect."

I drank a cup of coffee, then texted Mila. Except her phone chirped from inside the bag, and I realized she'd left her purse behind. With her phone. Now I couldn't get hold of her. My anxiety crept up a little, but I pushed it down and got ready to head out.

"Go through the back. There are fewer of them," Manny advised. "I told them I was calling the cops, so some left."

I squared my shoulders. "Okay. I'm out."

I walked out the back door and headed to my car. Some had moved across the street, but the real assholes, the ones who liked to give me a hard time, came closer, ignoring Manny's threats of trespassing. There were shouts and flashes as the throng descended, yelling and trying to get me to react.

Where's your date?

How much have you had to drink, Nick?

Should you be driving?

Who were you meeting?

What are you working on?

Why are you hiding?

The one group I detested more than anything were a little more personal.

Here to get some drugs, Nick?

How long until your next stint in rehab?

What? Food and a fast fuck and you're off?

What's in the bag? Alcohol for later?

I wanted to shout back something equally as rude, like, "*No! Your mother's underwear I took as a souvenir.*" It would amuse Mila when I told her later, but I knew better than to engage.

I got to the car and slid inside, gunning the engine and pulling out of the parking lot as quickly as I could. I shielded my eyes from the flashes and kept the car moving forward, grateful I didn't hit any of them. I wouldn't have minded running some of them over, but I really just wanted to get to the hotel and make sure Mila was okay. It upset me that she didn't have a phone. What if she got into some trouble? My heart raced at the thought.

Finally out of the lot, I floored it and drove away, looking in my rearview to see a couple cars coming after me. I headed toward the highway, determined to lose them. Or at least get back to the hotel before they had a chance to descend again.

I managed to beat them, and security opened the gate quickly for me. I hopped from the car, feeling my anxiety growing. MJ hadn't answered her phone, coward that she was, and my scathing voice message would let her know she'd crossed the line this time. The front desk informed me they hadn't seen Mila, and there was no answer in the suite. The elevator took forever, and I pounded on her door, turning when Andi called to me from across the hall. "Nicholas?"

"Where is she?"

Andi looked confused. "Isn't she with you?"

I threw out my arms. "Does it look like she's with me?" I snapped.

She frowned and grabbed another keycard from her pocket. "Calm yourself down, Nick. Why isn't Mila with you?"

I explained what had happened, pacing and getting more upset by the moment when we saw the suite was still empty.

"*Fuck*, what if she had a car accident? What if Carmen let her out somewhere, and she got lost trying to get here? What if she's downstairs getting harassed even now?"

"I'm sure there is a reasonable explanation. Did you call Carmen's phone?"

"Manny said she'd forgotten it. Neither of them has a phone." I pulled on my hair, my mind racing, my imagination running overtime. "She's out there…" I exploded. "Goddamn MJ—this is her. I don't know where Mila is, I can't reach her, and I don't know how to fucking find her!"

Andi grabbed my arm. "Stop it. You're overreacting, Nick."

I pushed her away, and I headed for the door, flinging it open, startling Mila, who was on the other side. She gasped, stumbling back, and I reached out, grabbing her arms and dragging her into my embrace.

"Oh, thank fuck, you're safe. You're here," I muttered into her neck. I stepped back into the room, bringing her with me. "You left your phone. I couldn't call you. You should have been here when I arrived." I pulled back. "Where were you, dammit?"

She blinked at my vehement tone, and she winced. "You're hurting me."

I released her, stepping aside.

"Don't yell at me," she said.

"I'm-I'm sorry. I was worried. Upset."

She cupped my cheek, and I turned my face, kissing her palm. "I'm sorry," I repeated.

"Carmen had to go home and change before going out. Then we got a little lost. It took us a bit to find the hotel." Mila smiled ruefully. "I wasn't much help with directions, and her car is older. No navigation system. We had to ask a few people, and we got turned around. But I'm here now. I'm fine."

I pulled her into my arms again. "Good. That's good."

She let me hold her. "Breathe, Nick. Just breathe with me."

I realized I was holding her too tightly. Reacting too strongly. I managed to loosen my embrace, and I took in some calming breaths. She pushed at my chest and I let her go, but I was glad when she took my hand.

"What a night," Andi commented. "I was just going to go grab a drink when Nicholas showed up. He got me worried."

"I'm fine," Mila insisted. "Carmen was great. I'm going to send her some signed books."

I handed her the bag Manny had given me. "I think he put some snacks in for you."

"Awesome. Andi, the food was incredible."

"Save me some." She walked past me. "Try to relax now, Nicholas. I'll see you in the morning, kiddo."

She left, and Mila and I stood, staring at each other. I was still anxious, my heart beating fast. I was angry at MJ, frustrated the evening ended the way it had, and strangely annoyed at Mila for being so calm.

"You couldn't have called from Carmen's?" I asked. "You didn't think I'd be worried?"

"She doesn't have a landline, Nick." She studied me. "Please calm down. Don't let this ruin what was a lovely evening."

"Oh, it's ruined, thanks to MJ and the paps."

"No, it took a detour. You're the one ruining it now," she said softly. "I'm here and I'm fine. You're here. We could go for a swim or have a shower and relax."

"I don't want to go for a goddamn shower. Or a swim."

"Maybe you should go back to your room, then."

I barked out a laugh. "I see. The first time you see the other side of me, you push me away. I guess MJ was right."

She shook her head. "I'm not pushing you away, Nick. And I'm not seeing your disorder. You're upset. I just think you need some time to collect yourself. I don't like being yelled at. You're taking your anger at the situation and MJ out on me. I know the evening went awry. I wasn't happy either, but it's over. Can't we just move past it and keep going?"

Everything she said was right. Made sense. And I was yelling. I shouldn't; I knew that. I also knew she didn't deserve my anger, and she was correct on that too. I was taking it out on her.

And I wasn't sure I could stop. I had to get out of there.

I walked past her, ignoring the way she reached out. Pretending not to hear her dismayed gasp to my shrugging off her touch that I usually craved. Still craved, but was too angry to admit it. I heard the hurt in her voice when she murmured my name. Or her plea of "Don't go, Nick."

I kept walking.

Because that was what I did best.

I swore I could hear MJ laughing in my head.

CHAPTER EIGHTEEN

MILA

I flung back the blanket and pushed myself off the mattress. I couldn't sleep, and pretending I would was getting me nowhere—fast.

I headed to the living room and out onto the balcony. The grounds of the hotel were quiet, the pool's surface smooth and still. A few lights shone through drawn curtains, and I could hear the distant sound of traffic—that seemed to be a normal thing here constantly, no matter the time of day.

I felt a tug on my chest, and suddenly, I was homesick. I'd had enough of LA. Enough of all of it. I wanted to sleep in my own bed. Wander around the streets of the complex, knowing I was safe and able to do so. Andi would freak if I tried to go for a walk this time of night in LA.

So would Nick.

Nick.

His overreaction to what occurred had taken me back. His anger, his raised voice—all of it. It was as if he had lost the ability to think rationally for a few moments. His accusation that I was sending him away because of his disorder. It hadn't even occurred to me that was the cause of his anger, but I wondered if it was. He had been under a lot of stress lately. Maybe he was spiraling?

Then I shook my head. He wasn't manic. He was angry. The same way Reed got angry with Heather when she didn't look after herself, or Dad got angry with Sammy when she ran herself ragged. They got upset because the person they loved wasn't taking care of themselves.

My thoughts stopped me. Earlier, Nick had mentioned love. He'd dropped the subject almost immediately, but he was the one who'd put it out there.

Was it possible that Nick was falling for me?

I already knew I was falling for him.

I sat down heavily, my body anxious, my mind troubled. I glanced toward my laptop, but it held no draw for me. My thoughts were too jumbled to write. I glanced down at the pool, suddenly wanting to feel the cool water rush over my body as I dove in. I wanted to have the weightlessness the water provided and float.

I peered across the grounds toward the adult pool. It was 3:30 in the morning. The pool was closed. I chewed my lip, wondering if the lock had been fixed on the gate. I'd been able to simply push the gate open last time.

I shook my head. I was being silly. I couldn't go swimming on my own at this time of the night. It was foolish and reckless.

Except, then I decided I felt like being exactly that. Foolish and reckless.

I was going swimming.

The gate opened without my pass. I had stuck to the shadows and made sure no one saw me coming this way. I didn't want to be stopped. I looked around, checking the corners, but I was the only one there. No Nick lurking in the darkness. No one to distract me. I had glanced toward his room, but the windows were black. I wondered if he was asleep or, like me, awake and upset. Then I pushed those thoughts from my mind.

I undid my robe and slipped into the water, the coolness hitting my skin like a lover's caress. I dove under, gliding through the water and coming up at the other end. I did that over and over again, the complete silence under the water soothing my frayed nerves. Finally, I stopped, sitting on the steps, letting the night air caress my skin. A sound met my ears, and somehow I wasn't surprised when I heard the pad of footsteps behind me and felt Nick's intensity approach.

"Swimming alone this late at night is dangerous," he said. "And foolish. Neither of which you usually are, Mila."

"I guess tonight I felt differently."

He sighed and sat beside me on the steps, extending his legs in front of himself. "You know, the hotel could kick you out for breaking the rules."

"You're doing it as well."

"I guess we'll be getting kicked out together," he said.

I didn't respond. My throat felt thick and full. Instead, I drew my legs up to my chest, wrapping my arms around them.

Silence fell for a moment.

"Mila," he said quietly. "Look at me."

I blinked away the stupid moisture building in my eyes and turned my head, meeting his dark gaze.

"I'm sorry, Shortcake. You're right. I overreacted, and I was a fucking jerk."

"I wasn't telling you to leave because you have bipolar."

"I know. Again—jerk."

"I thought it was 'a fucking jerk.'"

"That too." He tucked a piece of hair behind my ear. "I wanted you to have a wonderful night. Then it all went to hell. I was upset and worried—and angry. Not a good combination." He sighed. "MJ called and insisted it wasn't her. She said I never told her my plans, and she had no idea where I was going."

"Do you believe her?"

"I don't know. I want to. I just don't think I can anymore." He leaned closer. "But what I want is for you to accept my apology and let me hold you and say I'm sorry properly."

"How does one do that?" I asked.

"Like this."

He pulled me onto his lap and crashed his mouth to mine.

I felt his apology. Sensed his worry. Knew he was contrite and anxious. I felt it in the tightness of his embrace and the way he devoured my mouth. When I kissed him back, his shoulders relaxed, his mouth gentled, and his body molded to mine.

He pulled away, burying his face into my neck. "Forgive me, Mila. I was so worried about you. I haven't worried about anyone since my mom. I was terrified that because of me you might be hurt or scared. I hated that thought, and you're right. I overreacted."

I stroked along the back of his neck. "I'm sorry you were so worried. It all went bad so fast."

"I know. I wanted the date to be perfect for you."

I pulled back and cupped his face. "You can try again. At home. No one will bother you there. We can go out for supper, go bowling, make out by the water, all sorts of silly things."

"I like the making-out part." He smiled and touched my

lips. "But I think we should practice here with more making up."

"Oh." I felt his erection grow between us.

"I have a lot to make up for," he whispered against my ear, licking and sucking at the lobe.

"Yes," I gasped as he drifted his fingers across my thighs. "Yes, you do."

"Then let me show you how *hard* I want to make up."

I swallowed my groan as he touched me. "Yes."

NICHOLAS

Days later, I sat in my chair, sipping my terrible coffee and feeling melancholy. The set seemed empty without Mila around. Which sounded crazy, given the number of people here on any given day. But they weren't *her*. I had gotten used to seeing her sitting and watching the filming, asking endless questions. Observing the wonder on her face as she watched her words become immortalized on film. The coffee was awful without her special touch, and I missed her smile. Her touch. Her laughter and teasing. She offered her affection easily, and I hadn't realized how much I needed that until she was gone and I was alone again. I had sketched her a few times, and she loved them, often looking over my shoulder as I began a new drawing or shaded in another one. I teased her over her historical romance books she brought with her to stay busy between takes.

She loved the genre, explaining it was so different from her own that it was easier to read. "I don't compare them to my own books then," she said. "I can get lost in that world."

It made sense.

She had told me one day the character in the Millionaire Marquess *reminded her of me.*

"He loves to draw and paint. He hides parts of himself away, but he is a wonderful character. Caring and loving, even when he tries to hide it," she enthused. "Scarlett Scott writes the best rogues."

I lifted an eyebrow. "I'm a rogue now?"

She grinned. "A bit."

I took her to my trailer and showed her what a rogue I was.

Now I couldn't walk into it without seeing her there.

I saw her everywhere.

Filming was going well. I arrived early every day and stayed late, looking over the daily rushes and learning more about the art of making a film from Amber and her crew. It was fascinating and something I hoped to do one day. Actors faded as their looks waned, and I wasn't sure how much longer I could do this.

How much longer I wanted to do this.

I hated going back to the hotel, knowing she wouldn't be there. The swimming pool felt wrong when I'd go to burn off some excess energy.

I missed her everywhere.

We'd made up—more than once—but I still felt terrible about my anger. I'd spent every moment I could with her until she left. Her forgiveness was complete. She never threw my behavior in my face or reminded me of my angry words. She simply let it go. It was refreshing. I wasn't used to such benevolence. MJ liked to rub my nose in my mistakes every chance she got.

Our goodbyes had been ridiculously over the top. I felt as if she was leaving me forever, rather than a couple of weeks.

Holding her before she left for the airport, I had kissed her until she was clutching my shoulders and breathing hard.

"I have to go," she whispered. *"Andi is waiting."*

"Call me," I demanded. *"Promise me you'll call."*

"I will."

She stepped back, then slipped a slender gold chain from her neck. She always wore it, the metal glinting in the light. She placed it in my palm, wrapping my fingers around it. "You keep this and think of me."

I opened my hand and looked at the necklace, then put it around my neck. On her, it hung down low on her clavicle. For me, it hugged my neck, but I liked the feeling. It was still warm from her skin.

Aside from filming, I hadn't taken it off.

We called and texted every day. She told me about the advance crew, who were busy with exterior shots and setting up for our arrival. She sent me funny memes and pictures. Her voice was the last thing I heard every night, and she woke me every day.

I could hardly wait to wake beside her again. I wasn't sleeping as well, and for the first time ever, I found very little solace on set. Everything reminded me of her.

The paps were relentless, and I gave up my car and let the studio drive me to and from the hotel. It was wearing on me as it always did, and I looked forward to leaving.

MJ stayed away, our communication conducted through texts and phone calls. I remained civil, not wanting to provoke her. I was anxious to meet with Andi and the people she was going to put me in touch with. I felt a flicker of hope, thinking perhaps they could help me break out of this pattern. Find a loophole to help me start fresh.

I scrubbed my face and headed to my trailer. I had a few things to pack up, and I needed to head to my place and grab some items before leaving. I hadn't been there since filming started. It was far easier to stay at the hotel. I lived an hour outside of LA, so not only was it closer, but the security level was also better.

I stayed busy until a knock on the door brought me out of my musings. I was surprised when MJ came in.

"Hi," I said coolly, adding a few things to my bag.

"Getting ready for your adventure to the land of snow?" she quipped.

"I am."

She tossed a bag on the sofa. "I went to your place and packed you some things to save you a trip. Your favorites. You don't own sweaters, so you'll have to buy some, plus whatever else you need."

"It's not cold there right now," I told her, surprised by her thoughtfulness.

"Ah."

I sat down, facing her. "Thanks."

She dug in her purse and handed me a bag. "I got your prescription refilled. I was worried you'd forget."

I took it, nodding. It was on my list to do later, but I was grateful she had done it. "Thanks," I repeated. "I thought I had more pills left than I do, and I meant to take care of it."

"Part of my job," she said.

"Haven't seen you in a while." I had thought I'd seen her on set a few days prior, but I must have been mistaken. Or if she'd been there, she'd avoided me.

"Been busy. Leaving you to do what you do best, Nicky boy. You don't need me around to act."

"I suppose not."

I looked at her, meeting her eyes. She didn't look angry today. Or cold. She looked like the MJ I remembered.

"You have time to have dinner tonight?" she asked. "I know you leave tomorrow night."

"Oh, I already told Amber I wanted to look over the rushes," I lied. I was leaving early, but I didn't want MJ to know and risk a crowd at LAX. I'd be on the red-eye flight and in Toronto by morning with the time change.

"Yeah, I heard you've been hanging around here a lot."

"Keeps me busy and focused."

She nodded, looking disappointed, but she didn't argue.

"You didn't go to your audition."

I shut my eyes, preparing for a fight. "I don't want the part, MJ."

"Shame. It would be a great role."

I shook my head. "I can't. It feels all wrong."

She sighed but, to my shock, let it go. "Okay, I'll let you get to it. Safe travels, Nicky."

"Thanks, MJ. For the packing, and these." I held up the bag. "I appreciate it."

She smiled. "Be safe. Call me if you need something or if they're mistreating you. Don't let any of the polar bears eat you."

"I'm pretty sure they stay away from the cities," I responded with a smile.

"Well, don't go looking for them. And don't do anything foolish. Like fall in love."

Her statement took me by surprise, and I had no words to respond. No denial.

Our eyes met, hers searching, mine shocked. The look on her face changed with whatever she saw in my expression. It hardened, along with her gaze.

"I guess it's too late for that."

She slammed the door behind her.

***

It was the longest flight of my life. I knew there would be a driver waiting for me when I arrived, and he would take me to the hotel in Port Albany. Amber had been in heaven when she'd told me the town was a gold mine for the film shoot. There was a building they could use for corporate interiors, a house for Roxie, one for Duncan.

"So much scope, Nicholas," she enthused. "Never mind the place they all live. It's incredible." She had laughed. "Mila's family is so big, we can use a bunch of them for extras. It's cutting costs. We'll only have to do a short time in Toronto for some exteriors and a couple street scenes. I might come in under budget." She winked. "Then I get a bonus."

I had laughed with her. I was looking forward to seeing where Mila spent her time. I was also incredibly nervous about meeting her family but, at the same time, looking forward to it as well.

I had gotten through LAX without an issue, keeping my head down and my glasses firmly on my face. I barely slept on the flight, wishing I had told Mila I was coming early so she would be there. I would call her from the hotel and arrange to see her as soon as possible.

The terminal was busy, and I was pleased to see the driver's sign with the code I'd been given. In the back seat of the car, I sat back, watching the scenery. It was a busy road, reminding me of LA, but the vista was different. Slightly overcast today, Toronto was definitely cooler than California. To my surprise, I fell asleep, waking when the car stopped. I blinked in confusion at the sight of the pretty two-story house in front of me. The driver turned and handed me an envelope, and I opened it as he slid from the car, getting my suitcase out.

You have two days—it's all I could arrange.
Enjoy,
Andi

Bewildered, I stepped from the car. "Are you sure this is right?" I asked.

He nodded. "Those were my instructions. Have a good day."

He reversed and I stood, gazing around. It was a nice subdivision. Well-placed houses, wide streets, and I swore I could hear water somewhere close.

Had Andi arranged a house for me and Mila? Was that why I was here?

A voice calling out startled me, and I stepped back as a huge-looking man came closer. Beside him was a small woman, and their hands were clasped. He stopped in front of me, eyeing me up and down. I had a feeling he found me lacking.

"Can I help you, son? You lost?" He frowned, his voice deep and not happy. "How did you get in here?"

Another man appeared, equally as large, waving at him. "It's all good," he called. "I got this."

A noise behind the first giant drew my attention, and my heart stuttered at the sight of the person standing on the steps of the house.

Dressed in sweats and a loose shirt, her hair pulled up on her head in a messy ponytail, glasses perched on the end of her nose, and looking as confused as me, was Mila.

She was breathtaking.

"Nick?" she asked, her hands covering her mouth.

"Shortcake," I breathed.

Then I was moving. Darting around the huge man and rushing toward her. I caught her as she launched herself off the bottom step, dragging her into my arms and kissing her with utter abandon.

I didn't care who was watching. Who the man cursing behind me was. All that mattered was Mila was back where she belonged. In my arms.

She tasted of coffee and Mila. Felt perfect against my body. All the anxiety I had been feeling, all the worry that with time and space between us she would reconsider us, fell away. She was here. I had her. That was all I cared about.

Except I heard a throat clearing to my left.

"You know," a deep voice mused. "I'm getting pretty tired of seeing strange men playing tonsil tag with my daughters before we're even properly introduced."

I opened my eyes, meeting Mila's golden irises. I pulled back a little. "Your dad?" I murmured against her mouth.

"Yes," she whispered.

"Shit. I'm a dead man."

Since I was about to expire, I had to kiss her again. Mila had no objections, flinging her arms around my neck and returning my affections wholeheartedly.

"Damn, boy, you really need to step away," another voice said.

With a sigh, I let Mila go, setting her on her feet. I framed her face and pressed a kiss to her head. "It's been awesome, Shortcake."

Then I turned and met the dark navy eyes of her father. Up close, he was even bigger. He stared at me, unrelenting and stern, his arms crossed over his massive chest. The woman next to him was no doubt Mila's mother, but unlike her husband, she regarded me with a slightly bemused expression and a smile playing on her lips. She had a small hand resting on his large bicep, as if holding him back. Another man, tall and big, stood to one side. His grin was wide, his eyes dancing.

"Now this wasn't the behavior I was expecting from you, Mila."

Mila laughed, the sound nervous. She slid her hand into mine. "Mom, Dad, this is Nicholas Scott." She pointed behind her dad. "That's my uncle Aiden."

I held out my hand. "Mr. Morrison. A pleasure to meet you, sir."

He looked at my hand, then at me. I held my ground. Aiden chuckled. "You might wanna wipe Mila's lip gloss off your mouth before you shake her father's hand, Nick." Then he grasped my hand, shaking it vigorously. "I'm happy to meet you. Big fan."

I felt my eyes widen, and I turned my head slightly, meeting Mila's gaze. She bit her lip and nodded, and I tried to be inconspicuous as I wiped the pink gloss away, wondering why today of all days she'd chosen to wear it. I attempted to signal to her to do the same, and with a giggle, she brushed her smudged lips as well. I wiped my hand on my pants and turned back to the small group. Aiden was still smiling, waiting for me to speak.

"Nice to meet you, Aiden."

When he let go of my hand, I smiled at Mila's mom. "And you must be her sister," I said with a wink.

She began to laugh. "Oh, I see why she likes you." Then she shocked me, pulling me in for a hug. She was small and warm, and she smelled like cookies. I shocked myself and hugged her back, then stepped away and met her father's eyes. "Sir," I said. "I meant no disrespect. I just missed Shortcake so much, I forgot."

"Shortcake?" he asked.

"She's little and sweet," I replied.

His wife sighed and nudged his arm. "Isn't that lovely, Van? He has a nickname for her. Just like you have for all of us."

"Pumpkin," I said. "You call her Pumpkin."

"You know that?" he questioned, looking between us.

"Daddy," Mila warned. "Don't make me mad. You know I'm scary when I'm mad."

We both snorted at the same time. "Scary, right," we muttered together. Then we began to laugh. Our eyes met, and something clicked. He held out his hand. "Nicholas. Welcome to Port Albany."

I shook his hand in gratitude. "Thank you, sir."

"It's Liv and Van," her mom insisted.

"I kinda like sir," Van mused, rubbing his chin.

"Is that what Liv calls you in bed?" Aiden quipped.

Van narrowed his eyes, and Aiden began to run. Van chased after him, and I started to laugh again at their antics. They acted as if they were six, not sixty-plus. Aiden turned as he ran. "Come for drinks later at the Hub! I need to talk about my back story for my character!" he shouted before disappearing around the corner.

"Isn't he in the background scenes?" I asked.

Everyone laughed. "That's Aiden. Before you know it, he'll be a waiter or something and have lines."

Liv smiled at Mila. "We were coming to get you for pie and coffee."

"We'll put Nick's luggage inside and be there in a few moments," Mila promised.

"All right." Liv smiled as she walked toward where the men disappeared.

I picked up my suitcase, following Mila. "Please tell me that means we have some time alone," I begged quietly.

She let me follow her into the house, shutting the door and locking it behind me. A second later, she had me pressed against it, rolling up on her toes and dragging my mouth down to hers. "Yes."

CHAPTER NINETEEN

NICHOLAS

I was lost to her. Her taste, her touch, her scent. All my senses were on overdrive. Except, apparently, my hearing.

"Well, look at that," a feminine voice said behind us. "Tonsil hockey in the late spring."

I pulled away from Mila's sweet mouth, startled. The sudden movement caused my head to smack into the hard wooden door.

"Ouch," I muttered. "Motherfucker, that hurt."

"Tsk, tsk, you kiss my sister with that mouth?"

"Do people regularly pop up out of nowhere around here? Interrupting private time?" I asked Mila, who was looking up at me with the most adorable smile on her face.

"That's Sammy," she explained. "I forgot she was here."

"Nice," Sammy sniffed. "Replaced by the actor and left behind."

But I heard the affection in her voice and saw the smile on her face. I met her eyes. "Hi, Sammy. I'm Nick."

"I've gathered."

Mila continued to look up at me, and I smiled, tracing my finger down her cheek. "Hey, Shortcake. I've missed this face," I murmured, lost in her gaze.

She smiled again, looking delighted.

Sammy cleared her throat. "I'm still here."

"Don't you have a cowboy you can sext? Or call him and wind him up?" Mila asked, not looking away.

"I dunno. This is awfully interesting. Besides, I heard Mom say something about pie."

"You should go get a piece," Mila instructed, crowding against me. She flexed her hips. "We'll come in a minute."

Sammy snorted. "Keep that up, and I'm sure you will."

I shut my eyes, trying not to laugh. This was not at all how I saw my reunion with Mila going.

"You're blocking the door, you know," Sammy said.

"Use the back one."

Again, Sammy started to laugh. "That's what she said."

She headed toward the rear of the house. "See you kids soon."

I gave up and let my amusement out. Mila giggled, her eyes wide and luminous.

"So you've met some of my family."

"They're certainly vocal."

"Brace yourself. News travels fast here. And you have fans. They've been waiting to meet you."

I gave up on my plans of her and me naked. Or even alone. "Take me to your parents' place, Mila. I have a feeling your father is timing us. And I don't want to keep my fans waiting."

She pouted, and I kissed her mouth. "I am going to get a headache in about an hour. I always do when I travel. I'll need to lie down, alone and in the dark. You'll need to write something and watch over me."

"How closely will I be watching?"

"Close enough you'll feel every inch of me, baby."

"Okay, then. Let's go. I need you in pain soon."

"Great."

I looked around in wonder as we walked to her parents' house. This community was an amazing place, well laid out, open, and peaceful. Mila pointed out the various houses and the family members who lived in them. "That's the Hub," she said. "Amber wants to do some filming there."

"This is incredible."

She squeezed my arm. "I can't believe you came early."

"I was going to surprise you. Andi surprised me."

"She knows how much I've missed you."

I pressed a kiss to her head. "I've missed you, Shortcake. I stayed busy, but it's been endless." I winked at her. "I haven't had a decent coffee since you left."

Her laughter made me smile. "I'll have to make up for that."

"Yes, you will."

She paused at the door to her parents'. "Are you ready?"

"As I'll ever be."

Except, I wasn't.

Three hours later, I sat at the Hub, surrounded by uncles, aunts, cousins, her nan and pops, and whoever else they managed to find at the last minute. Coffee flowed, pie was consumed, and I was peppered with questions. It was like a press conference.

Yet, I felt nothing but welcomed. The women fussed over me, the men asked a lot of technical questions, and Mila sat beside me, her hand in mine, only moving on occasion to get more coffee. The building was remarkable, and I knew Amber would be thrilled. The views, the vast rooms, and the people. I wasn't sure there were this many naturally good-looking people in Hollywood.

Coffee and pie led into Chinese food and wine. Some of the best scotch I'd ever tasted. More people showed up, and I was surrounded. There were babies to meet, more cousins to try to keep track of. The laughter was constant.

"Is it always like this?" I asked Mila, leaning close.

"No." She grinned. "Usually, it's worse. Wait until Sundays."

"Sundays?"

"Family brunch. We get a big crowd."

I looked around. "You mean there're more?"

She nodded. "This is mostly everyone who lives here. Richard and Katy arrive this week, and all the cousins who live in Toronto or locally will show up. It gets loud."

"This isn't loud?" I asked with a laugh.

"No, trust me. It's crazy. And the food? When all the triplets are here, it's frightening."

"If they eat like Aiden and Ronan, I imagine so."

"Wait until you see what Liam can pack away. He's working on a project right now, but you'll meet him on the weekend. He's even bigger than Aiden."

"Holy fuck," I muttered. They grew them big here.

"It's a lot of fun. If… I mean, if you want to come, that is."

I took it all in. The people. The relaxed atmosphere. The unexpected welcome. The incredible building and the scenery. The sense of family and home that permeated the air. The intense feeling of contentment being here with Mila. I had never experienced anything like it. Normally one to shun large crowds, I found myself smiling at the thought of another gathering with these people.

"Yeah, I do, Shortcake."

"Yeah?" she replied, looking pleased.

I bent close to her ear. "But I need you alone soon."

She leaned up, murmuring into my ear. "Sammy is spending the night with Ronan and Beth."

I turned, meeting her gaze. "Then we need to leave."

"Follow my lead."

***

"I think you're hiding your true talent behind your writing," I mused as we strolled toward her house. I had her tucked tight to my side, my arm wrapped around her. She fit perfectly there, as if meant to do so.

"What do you mean?"

"You should be an actress. You even convinced me I was exhausted and felt a headache coming on."

She laughed. "You do look tired, Nick. It didn't take a lot of convincing. My family travels a lot, so they understand jet lag."

"I didn't sleep well after you left," I confessed. "It seemed odd. You were the first person I ever shared a bed with more than once, yet it felt wrong to be alone."

"You didn't do the overnight thing?"

We stopped walking, and I looked down at her. "Contrary to my reputation, I rarely dated. I had some casual relationships. Dating a celebrity isn't easy. There are some women who want to be seen with you. I figured that out early on in my career. There are others who have a fantasy about you." I shook my head. "I rarely lived up to the expectation, and they walked. There was one woman early on…" I took in a deep breath. "It didn't work out."

"Why?"

I ran a hand through my hair. "I was diagnosed in my mid-twenties, not long after I made it big. I was with Gwen, and we both had a hard time with the result. There are often side effects with the meds, Mila. I experienced a lot of them when I first went on them."

She looked at me with a frown. "Gwen didn't like that?"

I barked out a laugh. "Neither of us did. I had problems —sexually."

Mila's eyebrows shot up. "I see."

"Gwen informed me it was hard enough to put up with me, but if I couldn't give her what she wanted in bed, she wasn't sticking around."

"That was selfish."

"It was for the best. We wouldn't have made it in the long run. I know that now, but it hurt like a bitch at the time."

"Obviously, things changed in that area."

"Yes. I got the right meds, the right dosage, and things improved. But it shook me. I really cared about her, and she walked." I touched her cheek. "And how I felt about her is nothing compared to how I feel about you, Mila. I don't think I'd survive it if you left me."

"I'm not walking."

"What if I had to have my meds adjusted and it did happen, Mila?"

"Well, there is more to intimacy than sex."

"But sex is important."

"Yes. But your tongue and fingers still work. We'd figure it out."

I blinked at her.

"I survived thirty-odd years without sex, Nick. If we had to be inventive while you found what you needed to be healthy, I could handle it."

"Has anyone ever told you how amazing you are?" I breathed out.

"I'd like it if you showed me."

I swept her up in my arms. "I'm going to show you. Several times."

She laughed softly. "Hurry, Nick."

I tripped over my suitcase I had placed in her room earlier. I cursed as I stumbled and fell onto her bed, with her pinned underneath me.

"Oommph," she gasped. "Slow down, Nick. Don't kill me."

"Hurry, slow, which way, baby?" I groaned, laughing as I pulled away, only for her to yank me back down.

"Every way," she whispered. "I've missed you. I've missed us." She paused. "I love you, Nick."

I stared at her. "Say it again."

"I know it's fast, but I love you."

"Fuck being fast," I growled. "I love you too, Shortcake. So fucking much."

I covered her mouth with mine, relearning her sweetness. We rolled and twisted, pulling at our clothing, tugging on the material that separated us until we were bare and our skin touched, her softness melding into my harder planes.

"God, you feel so good," I moaned. "You're so soft, Mila. So beautiful."

I pulled on her ponytail, letting the thick tresses flow over my hands. "I love your hair." I kissed the juncture of her neck. "How you smell right here. So fucking sweet."

She cried out as I sucked her nipples, mumbling how flawlessly they fit into my hands. I kissed my way down her body, settling between her legs. I looked up, meeting her gaze. "And how you taste here, baby. Musk, honey, and you. The perfect combination." I licked at her clit, smiling at her whimper as her head fell back. I teased her, stroking the velvet heat and wetness I had missed so much. I kissed her pussy the way I kissed her mouth, stroking deeply with my tongue, tasting her. I slid my fingers in, groaning at how tight she still was, the way she gripped my digits, knowing in a few moments she would grip my cock and hold me inside her body. I played with her until she cried out, gasping my name and coming around my mouth and fingers. I kept at her until she was boneless and limp, then I sat up, pressing her thighs open, wrapping her legs around my waist.

"My turn, Mila."

I slid into her, savoring the moment. Inch by inch, I sank into her, feeling her pull. Her desire. When I was fully seated, I ran my hand down her sternum. "You ready, baby?"

"Yes," she whispered, our gazes locking.

"It's gonna be hard. I've been waiting."

"Give it to me."

I wrapped my arms around her, lifting her to my lap. She

gasped at the feel of me lodged so deep inside her. I groaned at the intense sensation of how she squeezed around me.

"Hold tight."

I began to move, thrusting up into her heat. She buried her face into my neck, her arms holding me tight. I was surrounded by her. Her hair tickled my thighs and my chin. Her scent drifted into my nose. She dug her nails into my skin. I held her tight, cupping her ass with one hand, working the plump flesh. I rocked into her hard, and she rode with me, our bodies in perfect sync. I felt the stirring of my orgasm, the tendrils of the pleasure beginning to wrap around my spine. I shouted her name as I succumbed. The heat of my release washed over me as I spilled inside her. My nerves were on overload, the sweat pouring down my back. I hissed and groaned, held her tightly and exploded. Ecstasy I'd never experienced enveloped me, and for a few moments, I was mindless, floating in a sea of intense pleasure. Mila cried out as another orgasm hit her, and she clutched at me, sobbing my name and milking me dry.

We stilled, our bodies locked in a tight embrace, the room around us still. My chest rose and fell rapidly, pushing into hers. She lifted her face, her cheeks damp and flushed, her mouth red. I captured her lips and kissed her, pouring all the emotion I felt into that kiss. She returned it with the same passion. I carefully laid her back and untangled our limbs, stretching out next to her and gathering her close.

"Wow," she whispered. "You really missed me."

I began to laugh. Somehow this woman always found a way to make me smile, even in the most serious, profound moments with her.

I pressed a kiss to her temple. "Yeah, baby, I did."

She traced a pattern on my chest, her fingers soft and lazy.

We didn't talk, we didn't separate, we simply enjoyed the peacefulness and tranquility of the moment.

"Nick?" she whispered.

"Yeah?" I hummed.

"I'm glad you're here."

"Me too, Mila." I paused. "Tell me again."

"I love you."

I pressed a kiss to her head. "I love you too."

MILA

Nick slept, keeping me close. I still couldn't believe he was here. He wasn't supposed to arrive for another few days. Now we had time to be together. Just us, without all the distractions.

I watched him slumber, smiling at the way he nuzzled into me and murmured my name. I had missed him so much. Leaving LA was easy. Leaving him wasn't. I was grateful to be home, back among familiar things. The sights and sounds of Port Albany. The peaceful water, the scent of the flowers and gentle sunshine. All different to the wildness and heat of LA.

But lacking the intense, warm presence of Nicholas Scott.

I was happy to see everyone. Feel the love in their hugs and the proclamations of the fact that they'd missed me. Their desire to hear all about the movie. The general excitement that some of it would be filmed here. When I was finally alone in my room, Sammy and I sat and talked for hours. I heard all about Luke, their tumultuous relationship, and his grand gesture.

"You're moving to the ranch, Sammy?" I asked. *"Marrying Luke?"*

"Yes." She laid her hand on her heart. *"I love that grumpy man so much, Mila. I feel as if part of me is missing with him not here."*

I nodded in understanding, and she tilted her head. "You have the same look on your face, baby sister. What's happened?"

I told her everything, not holding anything back. She listened as the evening waned and the shadows stole the light, darkness descending around us. We had moved to the kitchen, where all our big talks happened, and an empty bottle of wine sat between us, along with the remnants of a frozen pizza we'd heated up.

"You love him?" she asked.

"Yes. I do. I know it. I feel it so deeply. He's—" I paused, unable to come up with the right words "—he's inside me, Sammy. Everywhere."

"But LA?"

I shook my head. "I know there are obstacles. I don't even know if he loves me back, but I think he does."

"And the bipolar situation? That is a lot to take on, Mila," Sammy said with a frown.

"Yes, but if you love someone, you accept them for what they are. Who they are. Mom and Dad always taught us that. They loved Reed even with his stutter. They loved me even though I pushed them away. You fight for the people you love."

She smiled and grasped my hand. "You have the biggest heart, Mila. I just don't want to see you hurt. Or get involved in something you can't handle."

"I have researched it. Thoroughly. Nick is high-functioning. He hates hiding what he is. I think if he had better management and someone in his corner, he would do even better."

"His agent sounds like a walking nightmare."

"She is something."

Sammy pulled her leg up to her chest and looked at me as she rested her chin on her knee. "Dad is going to go crazy. Both his girls fall in love with men who are going to take them away from the nest. He is already upset about Luke, even if he does like him."

"I don't know what my future holds," I admitted. "I only hope it holds Nick."

I smiled, thinking of our conversation. Of all the texts and calls from Nick that happened daily. They helped the days not be so lonely. I told my mom about my relationship with Nick, at least the PG version. She laughed over the gofer parts and smiled at the toned-down account of the swimming pool meetups. She was concerned about the distance, my inexperience, and Nick's reputation. She became more so when I told her the truth.

"That is something you need to consider hard," she advised.

"I have. I am. Nick and I have discussed it a lot."

"Are you certain about this?" she asked. "Your feelings are that strong?" She paused. "They aren't simply some sort of fantasy come to life?"

I shook my head. "The real man is better than any fantasy." I leaned forward, earnest. "He researched my condition as much as I did his. He wanted to know all about it. What he could do." I grabbed her hand. "Mom, when he's around, I'm calmer. Stronger. Twice, I was in situations I am sure I would have had an attack over, but I didn't."

"I don't want you hurt."

"He is worth the risk."

"Your dad—"

"I need to know you're on my side. I want him to meet Nick and judge him on the person he is, not his disorder. That is such a small part of him. His heart is what matters."

"I've never known you to feel this way about someone," she mused.

"I never have."

"I'll meet him and make up my mind."

"Thanks, Mom."

Nick stirred and opened his eyes. He met my gaze with one of his wide smiles. He kissed my temple, then my cheeks, dragging his mouth across my skin to my lips. "I've missed waking up with you."

"You only slept a short time."

"Really? I feel wide awake." He pulled me tight to his chest. "Whatever will we do all alone in an empty house and in the dark?" He cupped my ass, grinding into me. "How will you help me get back to sleep, Shortcake?"

"You wanna play cards?" I asked. "Go Fish or something?"

He began to laugh, rolling over so I was under him. "I'll happily drop my line in, Mila. See what I can catch."

"I hope your rod is strong," I murmured, opening my legs so he could settle between them. He shifted, the head of his cock slipping in, teasing me.

"Strong and thick, baby," he groaned, flexing his hips and sliding in farther.

"Then reel me in."

CHAPTER TWENTY

MILA

By two the next day, I was exhausted. Nick kept me up most of the night, and he was out for a run by six. I did some writing, but once he got back, he'd wanted to spend time with me, and we had gone nonstop all day. I showed him everything. We went to the beach, the cliffs, the town, and even the Hub again. He loved the entire scope of it. We walked the streets, and I pointed out which house belonged to whom. Since it was a nice day, lots of my relatives were out in the gardens or on their balconies and porches. He met more people and chatted with the ones from the impromptu dinner the night before. Everyone was friendly and happy to see us. He was endlessly curious, asking questions, seemingly delighted in my answers, given the number of replies he found amusing.

"This place is amazing," he enthused. *"I've never known such great people. Your family..."* He trailed off and shook his head. *"I can't describe them."*

"Nosy is one word," I said dryly. *"Starstruck and curious are a couple of others."*

He laughed, slinging his arm around my shoulders. "Welcoming and nonjudgmental are two more. Friendly and loving."

I had to agree. And I was thrilled how well he seemed to fit in and how they accepted him just as Nick.

"Did you tell your parents about us before I got here?"

"I told my mom more. She talked to Dad, then he and I talked. I told him we had a relationship and I wanted him to give you a fair shot. I think I told him to stay calm."

"He was great."

I had smiled. "He is."

I poured a cup of coffee and sat down, hearing Nick and Sammy talking. She came into the kitchen. "Oh good, I thought I smelled a fresh pot."

"Yeah, I need it."

She grinned as she filled a travel mug and carried it to the table. I knew she was leaving soon to head into the production studio to work on her piece.

"Where is Nick?" I asked, surprised he hadn't followed her.

"He went for a run."

"Again?"

"Energizer bunny." She winked. "Lucky girl." She chuckled. "You look exhausted, though."

"We, ah, were up most of the night. I have no idea how he is still going."

"And chatty. So exuberant about being here. About the movie—everything really. Very upbeat."

I nodded, something twigging in my brain, but I couldn't place it.

"He certainly loved Mom's pie yesterday. And the Chinese food. He said it was the best he ever tasted."

"He said everything smelled better here too," I mused.

"Yes, he said that to me as well." She grinned. "I'm going to spend the rest of the day working at the studio. I'll probably stay overnight in Toronto since it'll be late and I want to work on Luke's piece tomorrow."

"Thanks, Sammy."

She smiled. "At least I won't have to keep the volume down when I video-call him naked this time."

"You didn't last time either," I said with an exaggerated grimace. "Thank God for headphones."

She laughed. "Oops, my bad."

Then she left, and the house was quiet.

When Nick returned, I was sure he'd be tired, except he was anything but. By the time ten rolled around, I couldn't keep my eyes open. I headed upstairs, getting ready for bed. Nick followed, a book in hand.

"That's one of mine," I said.

"I know. I haven't read this one."

"How many have you read?"

"All but two."

"Wow. I had no idea."

He smiled. "I fell in love with your words and imagination, Shortcake. I think somehow my heart fell in love before we ever met you. I think we were waiting for you."

I felt tears fill my eyes. "Nick," I whispered.

He cupped my face. "I fell in love with your heart once we met. With all of you."

"Me too."

Then I yawned. Wide and loud. He chuckled. "Let's get you to bed. You look ready to fall over."

"You should too. You ran twice today."

"Not being on set, I have lots of restless energy."

We moved around, getting ready. It was incredible how comfortable we were with each other. How easily he fit into my space. I liked seeing his things around. His shirts hanging in the closet, his toothbrush beside mine in the holder.

I crawled into bed, and he wrapped himself around me. I kissed the tattoo over his heart. A beautiful rose with one red drop of blood caught on one of its thorns.

"What is this for?"

"In memory of my mom. Her name was Rose."

I traced the ink. "It's beautiful."

"MJ was furious when I had it done. She didn't want me marring my skin."

"None of her business."

He chuckled. "That's what I told her. Plus, I reminded her that is why there are makeup artists on set. So far, it has never been an issue. I wouldn't remove it even if it were."

I felt his sadness and wanted to make him smile.

"I wanted to get another tattoo, but I was never brave enough after what happened to the first one."

He looked surprised. "You have a tattoo?"

"I did."

"What? Where?"

I tapped the crease of my thigh. "Here."

"What happened?"

"I don't know. It was a little mouse. So cute. I loved it. It was there one night, gone the next day." I paused. "I think my pussy ate it."

He blinked, then he began to laugh. He gathered me in his arms. "Fuck, Mila, you make me happy."

"Good."

He pressed a kiss to my head. "Go to sleep."

"You don't want to look for the mouse?"

He drifted his fingers over my center, his voice teasing. "I dunno. This thing safe? I mean if it devoured a mouse, what's it going to do to my cock?"

"It only likes wild game. Not chicken."

He rolled us, hovering over me, laughing, kissing, and talking all at the same time. "Then I'm gonna let your pussy choke my chicken. Hard. He'll fight and survive."

It was my turn to laugh. Until he made me scream.

Twice.

***

The next morning, I eyed Nick with worry. "You barely slept again, and you've already been for a run? How are you not exhausted?"

"I'm good," he replied. "Raring to go."

I bit my lip. "Um, did you take your meds last night?"

He frowned. "Damn. I forgot. With the whole game hunt we had going on, it slipped my mind. Thanks for reminding me."

He reached over me into his toiletry bag, pulling out a bottle. He shook out two pills and swallowed them with a gulp of water from the tap. He picked up his toothbrush and stretched over to grab the toothpaste. He knocked the bottle and it fell, the pills spilling out onto the floor and the bottle rolling under the cabinet.

"Dammit," he muttered.

"I'll get them," I offered, bending and scooping up the pills. I set them in a pile on the counter and located the bottle.

I stood, noticing another bottle in his bag. I pulled it out. I read the label to make sure it was the same prescription and held it up. "Do you want me to combine these?" I asked.

"Sure," he said with a shrug. "Knock yourself out. I just take from whichever bottle I grab."

I poured the last few pills from the one bottle into my hand then noticed a slight difference between the ones I was holding and the pile on the counter. I picked up one of the pills on the counter and studied it, comparing the two. Both were the same shape, but one was a slightly dissimilar color and a touch smaller. One contained a logo and had a number stamped on it; the other pill had a logo, but it was slightly altered. I double-checked the label to make sure they were the same drug, then I glanced at Nick. "These pills look different," I said.

"How so?" he asked.

I showed him the variations. He frowned.

"MJ picked them up for me. I never noticed the difference." He scratched his head. "Could they be generic?"

"The label would indicate that."

"I have no idea," he said. "Does it really matter?"

The niggling thought from yesterday returned. "I think it does," I said slowly. "How many of these new pills have you taken?"

"I don't know."

I looked at the pills in my hand, eight total. Three of them were different from the others. I had no idea how to ask Nick what I wanted to ask him without him getting upset.

"Um, does MJ have access to your meds?"

"If she was in my trailer, yes. But she wasn't around…" He trailed off.

"What?"

"I thought I saw her one day, but she never came to see me. Maybe she was in my trailer. But why?"

I swallowed. "The running," I whispered. "Your excess energy. Everyone commented on how chatty you were the other day. Sammy mentioned it last night too. And you're so…" I stopped speaking.

He looked at the meds, then at me. "Happy. I'm overly happy. You think she did something to my meds? Why the hell would MJ do that?"

"To push you into an episode. I think—" I swallowed "—I think it's starting."

He stared at me. Then at the pills. He didn't deny my accusation. "To push you away," he said slowly. "To make me fail."

"To keep you close. Dependent on her."

"Jesus," he muttered, grabbing the back of his neck. "Not even MJ would stoop to that, Mila. There has to be another explanation. They're just different-looking pills."

"We need to find out."

"How?"

"I have an idea."

"Then tell me."

My pharmacist, Ash, smiled at me across the desk. I had introduced him to Nick, and he took us to his small office in the back of the drugstore. I had known him since I was a kid—my entire family knew and trusted him.

I showed him the pills and explained my worry. "Can you tell what kind of pill it is?"

"Not without proper testing." He indicated the pills. "With your permission?"

I nodded, and he crushed each pill, testing the dust with something, then with his tongue.

"I don't know what it is, but I know what it is not. They are not the same pills," he said, holding up the bottle. "There is no fentanyl, thank goodness, but I believe these are fake. They are very chalky, so that is probably a large part of their makeup." He looked at me. "Very clever of you to notice the difference."

"Can they be tested?"

"Yes. I will send them off for you."

"What can I do?" Nick hissed. "I need more pills. Real ones." I heard a touch of panic to his voice. "I can't go without those meds."

"I know. There is a doctor I know at the clinic down the street. I'll call him and explain. I'm sure he will help," he assured us. "I will be right back."

He left, and I turned to Nick. He was pale, his pain and confusion evident. "How could she?" he asked.

"She's desperate. You're getting too strong for her to hold you much longer."

"What would have…" He stopped talking and swallowed. "Fuck, you would have had to deal with an episode. A full-blown one. It would have stopped production. Your family would have seen. Christ, I can't even think about it."

I captured his hand. "And we would have made it through together, Nick. But we caught it. She didn't win."

"I need to cut ties."

"You need to press charges," I muttered. "She was endangering you."

He didn't respond to my comment. He was too busy thinking. "I would have lost you."

"No," I said firmly. "I am not going anywhere, Nick. I love you." I framed his face with my hands so he had to look at me. "I love you," I repeated. "That is not going to change. And when you have an episode, I will be there. When I faint, you'll be there. Together."

He pulled me into his arms. "Thank God."

CHAPTER TWENTY-ONE

MILA

We went back to the compound, a new bottle of pills with us. The doctor in the clinic had been helpful and had confirmed Nick couldn't be without his meds, and he'd agreed to give him a new prescription.

At the house, I was surprised when Nick called Andi. He hung up, telling me she was coming to Port Albany that afternoon.

He paced and raged, his euphoria of the past few days gone. His anger had taken over. He was livid. He stopped pacing at one point, looking at me. "Can you call your dad?"

"My dad?"

"Yes."

"And ask him…?"

"To come over. I want to talk to him." Then he shook his head. "No, I'll go see him."

Before I could stop him, he left. I wasn't sure what to do. *Go after him? Stay? Why did he want to talk to my father?*

My mom showed up about ten minutes later and came into the kitchen. I was at the table, busy on my laptop, trying to find out as much information as I could on counterfeit pills, how much Nick might have been affected by them, and what to expect over the next while until his meds kicked in again. I liked having as much intel as I could get.

Mom got a coffee and sat down.

"What's going on with Nick and Dad?"

"He asked to speak to your dad in private. And I heard him ask Van if he could call Halton." She shook her head. "What's going on?"

I told her everything. She looked horrified. "Poor Nick," she murmured. "How dreadful." She paused. "How much of what we saw was Nick?"

I shook my head. "Most of it. Aside from the talking. He is usually a bit quieter. It was the start of an episode. The running, the energy, the euphoria. It's hard to see, but I noticed a few things. He is a wonderful man, though, Mom. He was still Nick, just a little more animated."

She nodded. "I read up on it. That woman needs to be arrested."

"I agree."

She stood. "I don't know how long they'll be, but we should stay busy. Cookies?"

I nodded. "I'll get the mixer."

We had just pulled out the last tray of baked cookies when Dad, Nick, and Halton walked in. I looked between them, anxious and curious. Dad picked up a cookie, munching it and sitting down. "Any chance of coffee?"

Mom grabbed some mugs, and I put a plate of cookies on the table. I looked at Nick, who smiled and took my hand. He looked as exhausted as I felt. He tugged on my hand, pulling me to his lap, wrapping his arm around me. He nuzzled into my neck with a sigh.

"I needed that."

"What did you talk about?" I asked.

"I told your dad everything. And Halton. Asked their advice."

"Everything?"

Dad nodded, taking a sip of coffee. "He shared his truth, I gave him mine."

I blinked. "Have you been reading new age books again, Dad? His truth?"

He chuckled, breaking the tension. "No, but we were both honest. Which you should have been with me, Pumpkin."

"I wanted you to know him first, not his disorder."

He shrugged. "It is part of him."

"Part, not all."

He held up his hand. "I hear you. But now I know, and I know what has happened."

Halton spoke. "I gave him some advice. And the name of a good lawyer who deals with the entertainment industry. I'm pretty sure it's the same lawyer Andi was talking about. I got them together a few years ago. They'll look after your boy." He snagged another cookie. "I'll leave you to it."

"What's the plan?"

"Talk to Andi and this lawyer. Break my contracts—whatever the cost. Get away from MJ. Start fresh."

"Can you do that?"

He sighed. "If I never worked another day, I am set for life. I love acting, but the reasons for it aren't the right ones. When I work, I become someone else. I never wanted to be Nick."

"And now?"

"I want to be me. I like the me I am when I'm with you," he confessed.

"Nick," I whispered, cupping his cheek.

He turned his head, pressing a kiss to my palm. "I want to direct. I've been spending a lot of time with Amber, learning. I want to keep learning. Make my own mark."

"I think you'd be brilliant."

"I would be with you by my side."

A throat clearing startled me, and I met my dad's amused gaze. "We're still here, Pumpkin. As much as I'm trying to be supportive, can you save the lovey stuff for after we're gone?"

"Sorry."

There was a knock, and Andi walked in, followed by two men. We all stood as she looked around. She grinned at Nick. "You ready to do this?"

"Absolutely."

<hr>

NICHOLAS

"Are you sure?" I asked, my mind reeling. When Halton and Andi told me this guy was a shark, they weren't kidding. And he'd found a drop of blood in the contracts, and he was poised to attack.

I met his gaze. Shrewd and intelligent. Jacob Marks was a man of few words, but when he spoke, you listened. He was in his sixties, his white hair trimmed and gleaming. He was short and rotund, but he was intimidating.

"The studio broke its own contract," he said. "Page twenty-four of this ridiculous piece of garbage. So did your so-called agent. In subsection C of clause seventy-six, it states neither party can knowingly cause harm or inflict damage. They caused you mental and physical distress. They knew your condition and hid it. Damaged your reputation by putting that rehab story out there. Insinuating you had an addiction to drugs and/or alcohol. I have all the press shit around it. The statements, the so-called 'supportive' messaging. All bullshit." He sat back, looking pleased. "If you want, we can press charges if we can prove she swapped out those pills." He gave me a meaningful look. "And if she did it once, she's done it before."

I thought back to the last couple of episodes. I had been so sure I had taken my meds. MJ had picked up my prescriptions before. I couldn't recall if the dates lined up, but since she often was in and out of my trailer, she could have switched them anytime. I never studied my meds or suspected anything—I simply took them. But she'd insinuated I had forgotten, and I was so used to doubting myself, I accepted it. Assumed she was right—that I was so deep into my character I forgot.

I had accepted so many of her opinions, I had disregarded some of my own.

"I just want her out of my life. I don't want her making decisions for me anymore." I leaned forward. "Can you help me with that?"

"If you hire me, yes." He flashed his smile. "And pay my retainer."

I glanced at Mila, who nodded. Andi looked pleased. "Done."

"Then let's get that witch out of your hair." He stood. "I'll be in touch."

The second guy with Andi was the exact opposite of Jacob. He was tall, lean, dressed casually in jeans and a Henley. His dark hair was perfectly combed, and he wasn't much older than I was. He exuded a calm strength and quiet demeanor. Tom Jeffries was a name I recognized as a sought-after agent in Canada. He represented a lot of well-known celebrities, and I had heard it was difficult to get a meeting with him.

But he was friends with Andi, which gave me an in.

He had been quiet, talking to Andi or Mila in a low voice, listening to what Jacob and I discussed. He met my gaze with his intelligent one. "You'll be looking for new representation. Someone, ah, different this time. Someone who actually has your best interests in mind."

"Yes. You know my story? All of it?"

He leaned his elbows on his knees, bending forward. "That you have bipolar? News flash, Nick. So do thousands of other high-functioning people. It's nothing to be ashamed of. And not everyone is determined to hide that fact. Even Hollywood —the right side of Hollywood—is coming around to seeing that mental illness needs to be addressed openly. Help and support those who need it. But until people are brave enough to speak out, it stays in the dark."

"You want me to do that—speak out."

"Yes."

I considered his words and what they meant. The thought of not hiding, being able to speak the truth was freeing. Still, I worried.

"MJ has always been in the same city as me," I said. "Does it work as well with you elsewhere?"

He laughed. "Zoom, Skype, whatever you want. Video calls. I fly there, you fly here. I meet up with you on set. It's easily done, Nick. If you want to hear my ideas and thoughts, I'm happy to sit and discuss them with you."

"You'd take me on?"

He chuckled. "You sound surprised."

"Ah, sort of. I've been told I am high-maintenance."

All levity left him, and I saw the sharp businessman emerge. "Your so-called agent is a snake. She has used and abused what should be a trusted agreement. From what I know, what I've heard today, she is out for one person—herself. She is a manipulative, narcissistic bitch, interested in only one thing. Her own agenda. Forget all the shit she has drummed into your head. Forget feeling like you owe her. She owes you so much, you could never collect it in two lifetimes. If you're ready to make a change, if you're willing to listen and work with me, not for me, I'll show you what an agent can do. I can guarantee this—you say no, it's no. You want a role? I'll help you get it. Once I'm finished wiping her from your career, you get the power back. And you keep it. You're the captain. I'm just the rudder keeping you on course." He sat back, once again calm and relaxed. "For my percentage, of course."

I had to laugh. "Of course."

"Should I set up a meeting at my office? You can meet the team."

I glanced at Mila, who was talking to Andi. Our eyes met and locked, and I knew she had heard him.

"I don't want to do anything to jeopardize this movie."

"It won't. This will take time and planning. I'll work with Jacob and Andi. Mila will be protected, and so will you."

I looked back, and Mila nodded, looking anxious.

"Set it up."

He followed my gaze with a smile. "You know," he said quietly. "Lots of actors don't live in LA. Canada is a great country. This little town seems ideal for a place to live and have a normal life. You can have them both." He winked. "You might want to think about that."

I sat on the front steps, looking around at the quiet streets. I drew in a long breath, enjoying the fresh, crisp air. I could hear the water a short distance away. It wasn't like the ocean in California with its wildness and vast, open vistas. There was a lazy rhythm to the water, the same as there was to this little community. I had never known such peace.

Mila came out, sitting beside me. Everyone had left a short time ago, and I had wandered out here, sitting down, my head filled with so many thoughts. One, in particular, stood out, the implications of it even more prominent than the thought of what, no doubt, would be an ugly parting from MJ.

"This little town seems ideal for a place to live and have a normal life. You can have them both. You might want to think about that."

Those words echoed in my head on repeat. Was it possible to have a life here with Mila and still have my career? I had never considered it before, but now that the idea was in my head, I couldn't shake it.

I slid my arm around her waist, drawing her close. She rested her head on my shoulder.

"You okay?" she asked.

"Overwhelmed," I admitted.

She lifted her head and turned into me. "What can I do?" she asked. "What do you need?"

I kissed her sweet mouth. "Right now, I have everything I need. You."

"You must need something else."

I smiled. "Until they figure everything out, it's business as usual. Filming starts in a couple of days. I'm going to go and see Amber and be honest with her. Tom thought of a cover story since MJ will be expecting me to fall apart, so that's taken care of. I'm going to concentrate on my role, enjoying my time here—and you."

"Stay here. With me. Please."

I kissed her again. "Yes."

"How are you feeling about MJ?" she asked.

"Deceived, angry. Over it. I have been loyal for too long. My mom was so fond of her, it felt as if I was betraying her if I cut ties with MJ, so I always found excuses for her. Accepted her behavior. Forgave constantly because she always made me feel it was my fault. No matter what happened, it was my doing. But she lied. Constantly lied. She shook my belief in myself. She made me feel less." I shook my head. "No more. What she has done is unforgivable. My mom would feel the same way. She would be shocked by this. Horrified at the way MJ has behaved."

"She'll deny it."

"I know. But there is no other explanation. She switched the pills. I will never trust her again. I hope once this is over, her reputation is in tatters. The only thing she can manage will be a 7-Eleven store."

"I love you," she whispered. "And you're not less. You're everything to me."

I bent and captured her mouth. She was sweetness and light. The exact opposite of the darkness that had surrounded me for so long.

A voice interrupted us, and I looked up to see Aiden walking up to us. "Enough of that," he scoffed. "Pizza, wings, and board games at the Hub." He rubbed his hands. "And I'm calling dibs on the top hat for Monopoly." He grinned. "I look great in a top hat."

Mila began to protest. "Oh, Aiden, I'm not sure—"

I cut her off, the idea of games and pizza, surrounded by her family, suddenly appealing. "I get the race car."

"You'll have to arm-wrestle Mad Dog for it."

I sniffed. "I can take him."

"We start in half an hour."

"We'll be there."

"That's twelve hundred bucks for rent," I said to Aiden.

He growled, sliding me the cash. "You know, if you get tired of being an actor, a slumlord would work for you."

I waved my hand. "I'll make improvements to the property when needed. You just keep landing on my places and paying me the money you owe."

Bentley chuckled, lifting the dice to take his turn. When I had met him the other night, I'd thought he would be aloof and cool. He was anything but. All of Mila's family was the same. Loving, caring, and fun. Tonight had been exactly what I needed. Pizza, beer, and games. Laughter and teasing. There weren't as many people as usual, but it was perfect. Maddox had whipped my ass at pool; Bentley and I took him and Aiden at darts. Van and I went head-to-head at ping-pong, and we called a draw. Reid and I talked computers and games.

Bentley landed on his own property and smiled, sitting back and crossing his arms, satisfied. Mad Dog landed on Chance and turned up a "Get out of jail free" card.

Mila sat down beside me, laughing when she saw the piles of money in front of me. I waited until Aiden shook the dice, once again landing on one of my properties. "Ah, a good one. Fifteen K, my friend."

"I don't have it."

I sat back, tapping a finger to my lips. "Perhaps we can work out a deal."

"Oh yeah?" he grinned, running a hand over his torso. "You want a piece of this?"

Bentley barked out a laugh, and Mad Dog grinned widely.

I blinked. "I meant some training. In the gym."

"Oh. Well, we could do that too." He batted his eyes. "You don't think I'm pretty enough for you?"

I winked at Mila and grinned. "Sure, big boy. You wanna go a round with me? They'll be peeling you off the walls. I promise you that."

He looked shocked as everyone else laughed. "We'll do the gym thing," he muttered.

"Sounds good."

He looked at Mila. "Rein him in, Mila."

She kissed my cheek. "Nope. He's doing just fine on his own."

I kissed her back. She was right.

* * *

We strolled home in the inky dark. "Will you sleep tonight?" she asked.

"I hope so. I'm not feeling as restless, but it will take a bit for the meds to even out. I need to see my doctor when I get back to LA."

She hummed, but I felt the way she tensed.

I pulled her closer. "That's not for a while, Mila." I pressed a kiss to her head. "And I was thinking about what Tom said earlier."

"Which part?"

"Living somewhere other than LA."

"Ohh…" she breathed out. "Anywhere in particular?"

"Wherever you are," I said honestly.

"Here?" she whispered.

"Well, with Sammy marrying Luke, you'll need a roommate. I can give you references."

"I'll have to think about it," she teased, but I caught the glint of tears in her eyes as she turned her head.

I squeezed her waist. "You do that."

"I might want to use her bedroom as an extra office. You'd have to share my room."

I sighed heavily. "I suppose I could live with that."

We stopped at the end of her driveway. The porch light was on, its glow a warm welcome.

"You really want to stay here?"

I looped my arms around her waist. "I know it's fast, and I know nothing is settled, but yeah. The thought of being here with you. This place. Your family. A real home. All of it makes sense to me in a way nothing ever has before. I always felt as if I was adrift. My apartment was a pit stop, my life on hold. Nothing felt permanent. I never felt settled." I looked around. "This place makes me feel grounded. You make me feel as if I belong."

"You do."

I looked down at her, knowing what I was feeling, what I wanted, was right. I wanted a life that included her. She would hate LA, but I would love it here. And she would be my world. My career came second.

"Then we'll talk about it again once everything settles. But my future contains you, Mila."

Her eyes glowed. "Okay."

CHAPTER TWENTY-TWO

NICHOLAS

Amber stared at me. "Nick, that is horrible."

"I know. I'm still reeling from it all."

"How are you coping?" she asked.

I took a sip of coffee, looking around as grips and set decorators ran around. The ABC offices were perfect for the scenes when Duncan confronted Roxie at work. They were putting the finishing touches on the rooms, and we would start filming tomorrow.

"I'm settling. Luckily, it was discovered before too much damage was done. Thanks to Mila."

"And MJ?"

"Will be gone soon enough. She texted last night to see how I was doing. I couldn't help grinding in her failure, so I called her and gave her the whole story of how I tripped and the pills landed in a sink full of water, and I had to go get a new prescription." I grinned at Amber. "It was a stellar performance."

"How did she react?"

"Let's say acting will never be her strong point. She was furious but trying to hide it. She hung up not long after, and I haven't heard from her since." I finished the coffee, thinking it still wasn't as good as when Mila made it for me. "Nothing will happen until we wrap. I won't jeopardize this film."

She waved her hand. "I'm not worried. Frankly, I'm glad you're going to leave her and the bigger studio behind. You'll have more freedom."

"Exactly. I'm thinking of trying my hand at directing."

She nodded. "You're a natural."

"I have a lot to learn."

"We all have to start somewhere." She sat back, crossing her legs. "Another change for you."

"Yep."

She eyed me speculatively. "Will there be a change of residence in your future?"

"I think so."

"I figured. You and Mila are perfect for each other. I watched you on set. She lights up, and you relax. You're both so aware of the other one."

"I know."

"I'm happy for you."

"Thanks, Amber." I cleared my throat. "Mila wanted me to extend an invitation. They do brunch at the Hub on Sundays. I gather it's a bit of a free-for-all. You are welcome to join the party."

She grinned. "I'd love that. I can meet all these men I've been talking to."

"I think Aiden wants to discuss his character arc."

She laughed. "I can't wait to meet him."

"They're amazing. The entire family. I've never experienced anything like it."

She smiled. "You deserve that, Nicholas. Believe it."

"I'm beginning to."

"Good."

I leaned close to Mila. "I don't think I've ever been in a room with this many people who are related to one another."

She grinned. "Mostly by love, Nick. My uncles didn't have families, so they created their own. It grew beyond anything they imagined. But it's wonderful. They're my safe place."

"You're mine."

She touched my cheek. "You're my rock."

I liked being her rock. I had never been that.

"My mom would have loved you," I murmured. "I wish you'd met her. She always supported me. When I started acting, she came to auditions with me, made sure I had money when the roles didn't pay much." I paused. "She treated MJ like a daughter. I think at one point she thought we'd get together, but she figured out it would never work and we were best as just friends." I frowned. "I've been wondering how much influence MJ had on Mom's decision not to tell me how sick she was. When I think back, I have a lot of questions I'll never have the answers for."

"I'm sorry," Mila whispered. "But I don't want you to dwell."

I kissed her. "I know. I'm not. It's just nice to be able to say what I'm thinking for a change."

"You can tell me anything."

A shout of laughter interrupted us. I looked over, a smile pulling at my mouth. Aiden and his sons were wrestling. Five large men acting like kids, rolling around, laughing, and talking trash. Bentley observed them, shaking his head.

"Don't break the furniture this time!" he called.

Mad Dog slapped his shoulder. "Good luck."

Beside Mad Dog stood Richard VanRyan. He was a tall, good-looking man with an engaging smile. His very presence commanded the room. Amber had taken one look at him and decided he needed to be in the wedding scene. That made Aiden pout until she told him she was using him as well. In fact, she wanted all the BAM men and women in the wedding scene. But Richard got a speaking part. He was the minister marrying Duncan and Roxie.

He had grinned, delighted. He nudged his wife, Katy, and winked at her. "I'm still a big deal, sweetheart. You prepared to be married to Hollywood's next superstar?" He ran a hand down his torso. "The ladies will be lining up for a piece of this."

She had scoffed loudly, chuckling as she walked away. "Go fuck yourself, VanRyan."

They made me laugh.

Aiden was the security overseeing the event—with a long, damaged past, he informed Amber. She had laughed and patted his arm. "You work on that tortured look, Aiden. I'll make sure to get a close-up."

"Excellent." He beamed.

Amber met my eyes, her gaze wide as she watched them rolling on the floor, bumping into furniture. "They are hilarious."

"Wait until they say..." Mila started, stopping when her mom came from the kitchen.

"Food is ready!"

"Stand back," Mila advised.

"Guests first," Bentley said in a loud voice as the wrestling stopped and they all got to their feet.

I looked at the tables, shocked. I had never seen so much food. Surely to God even this lot couldn't polish off the banquet set out. Eggs, meats, platters of pancakes, waffles, toast, and bagels. Hash browns, salads, and a massive roast that Van was carving. Desserts, cheeses, fruit. It was a spread fit for a king. An entire kingdom, to be exact.

I picked up a plate, handing it to Amber and then one to Mila. "What happens to the leftovers?" I asked.

All the women laughed. "There won't be any."

I found it hard to believe until I watched the food disappear. More platters appeared, and those vanished as well. I met Mila's amused gaze.

"Told you."

"Where do they put it all?" I wondered out loud.

"Football after lunch!" Ronan shouted. He grinned at me. "Friendly, of course. But you're kinda scrawny, so I'll let you be on my team. I'll protect you."

Scrawny?

I scoffed. "I think I can handle you lot."

He lifted his eyebrows. "You wanna make a little wager on that?"

"Sure."

"You're on, Hollywood."

I chuckled at the catcalls and taunts, as well as the nickname. It was said with no malice, and I kinda liked it. I laughed harder as voices shouted they wanted in on the action.

"I'll take Hollywood!"

"I've got ten on my team!"

"Don't touch his face," Amber called out. "I need it on camera tomorrow."

"Thanks for the vote of confidence," I huffed.

"Maybe you should pass," Mila said.

"You too, Mila?" I gasped.

"They are freakishly strong and fast. I would hate for you to get hurt."

"I'll be fine." It was a friendly game of football. How bad could it be?

"Okay, *Hollywood*," she replied. "I'll be cheering you on."

I sat in the hot tub, stifling my groan as the heat hit my sore muscles.

Realization had hit me ten minutes into the "friendly" game.

I *was* scrawny.

And I was going to hurt like a bitch by the time the torture was over. I was almost grateful to be sent to the sidelines.

Mila slipped in, gazing at me across the water. "You okay?"

"Never better."

She laughed. "Will you be all right tomorrow?"

"If my legs can move, I'll be fine."

"I warned you."

"Who won the bet?"

"Richard. He guessed you'd last thirty minutes. You lasted twenty-nine."

"Liam took me out with an unnecessary hit."

"You had the ball. It was legal."

"I think he rearranged my kidneys."

"He barely touched you, Nick. He rolled so you landed on top of him."

"And he's like a freaking stone mountain."

She moved closer. "Poor baby. Can I help? Maybe kiss it better?"

I cracked one eye open. "Maybe."

She got in closer. "Tell me where it really hurts, and I'll make it all better...*Hollywood.*"

"Everything from my neck down."

"Then I had better get to work."

I groaned again as she wrapped her hand around me. "Yes, you had."

"Cut!"

I rolled my shoulders, looking to Amber.

"Good. Take five, everyone."

I wandered to my director's chair, smiling when I found it already taken.

"Hey, Shortcake." She was on set most days, and I loved having her around again.

With a grin, she handed me a coffee. "How's it going?"

I sat beside her, taking a sip. "Far better today."

"Has everyone recovered?"

I regarded her seriously. "Mila. No one will ever recover from yesterday."

She bit her lip. "It was pretty damn funny."

"It was the most awesome thing ever," I agreed. "I'm not sure I have ever seen a film set disintegrate into mayhem so quickly before."

I chuckled again, thinking of the day.

It started normally enough. We filmed Duncan and Roxie's wedding. It took all day with the angles and all the extras, including almost the entire BAM clan. Amber had joked she'd never had so many extras with their own wardrobe. Every man owned a black tux. All the women had lovely gowns.

The most stunning of them all was Mila, who wore a red dress. I had seen it and begged her to wear it. Pleaded with her to be in the scene. "It's your book. Your story. You need to be in it."

She had finally agreed, and I had trouble taking my eyes off her until I slipped back into the role of Duncan.

Once the wedding scene was done and Richard gave his stellar performance, there was a quick scene outside on the large dock. "Guests" were to be milling around, and Richard stood to one side, supposedly having a conversation with Aiden, who was informing him someone was demanding to speak to the groom. It was the moment leading up to the big reveal in the book.

Just a quick but needed scene.

Until Aiden got too close to Richard, who backed up. "Watch it, Tree Trunk. You're hogging my spotlight." He pushed him away. Aiden bumped into Maddox, who growled.

"Watch it. This is Armani."

Bentley groaned. "Behave, you jackasses."

"Who you calling a jackass?" Aiden responded, shoving at him.

"You." Bentley pushed back. Aiden stumbled as Amber yelled at them to cut it out. "The scene is done. Get up here!"

But it was too late. Aiden fell into Richard, who grabbed at Maddox. He grappled at Bentley, and they all toppled into the water. Cursing and shouts filled the air. Laughter began among the crew watching the debacle.

Chaos ensued, and before I could blink, Aiden had yanked both Reid and Halton into the drink with them. Van stepped back, his hands up, refusing to be part of it. Ronan bent, laughing, extending his hand to his father, who pulled him in. That led to a free-for-all. The rest of the guys followed, pushing and shoving one another, dunking and splashing. The women ran off the dock and out of their reach. Amber jumped from her chair, marching toward the melee, and I held my breath, knowing they were all about to get a major dressing down. Except, when she bent over to scold Aiden, he wrapped a hand around her ankle and dragged her in with them. She came up sputtering, and instead of yelling and cursing them, she started to laugh and dunked Brandon, Halton's son.

I couldn't believe it. I walked to the edge of the dock, shaking my head. I met Van's bemused eyes. "What idiots."

"Are you calling me an idiot?" Amber asked, looking affronted.

"If it looks like a duck and acts like a duck…" I trailed off.

She glared then looked at Van. "Hit him."

The water was bloody cold as I went under. But luckily, I took Van with me.

That began the most epic water fight that ever had been seen. Luckily, one of the crew was smart enough to film it, and I planned to use it one day.

It was hours before things were back to normal, and I still laughed when I thought about the grown men heading up to the winery, dripping wet and still cavorting. Their daughters and wives all looked resigned, talking among themselves about our behavior. No one paid them any mind. I chased Mila, but she refused to let me get her dress wet. I got other parts of her wet later in my trailer when I changed.

I noticed Amber trailing behind with Brandon. I had spotted them talking a lot at the brunch the week before. Seen them wander to the beach together on a walk. I had noticed him around the set even on days no extras were required.

I grinned as I wondered if the magic of this place was weaving yet another spell.

Mila's giggle brought me back to the present.

"Things are calmer today."

"Yes." I finished my coffee. "We're going to wrap this fast, Mila."

"I know."

"I have a few retakes to do in LA. And I have to close out my life there. End it with MJ so I can start here."

She glanced away. "I know."

"Will you come with me, Shortcake?"

She glanced up. "You want me to?"

"Yes."

"I would love to."

I picked up her hand and kissed it. "Thank you."

"That's a wrap!" Amber called. The crew and cast began to clap.

There was always a bittersweet feeling attached to those words. I was glad filming was over. Aside from a few retakes, maybe some ADR, my part was done. It was now up to Amber and the production crew to work their magic. That took longer than the actual filming of the movie, but I was glad this part was complete. I was anxious to move on to the next step in my life.

I hugged Lacey and shook Bradley's hand. Embraced Amber. Then found Mila with my eyes. "Let's hear it for the author!"

Everyone clapped and she blushed, looking pretty and bashful. I still loved the fact that she had been so comfortable with me as quickly as she had been. To the rest of the world, she was still shy and quiet. I loved knowing a side of her no one else did or ever would. That was my Mila. No one else's.

I cupped her face and kissed her. "We're done, Shortcake."

"No more coffee."

I laughed, pressing my mouth to her ear. "I'll need coffee in bed now. Served by a sexy, naked Shortcake."

Her blush deepened, and I kissed her again. "Time to party."

"Privately or with the cast?"

I had to laugh. "Both."

CHAPTER TWENTY-THREE

NICHOLAS

Mila was quiet on the flight back to LA. Jacob, Tom, and Andi traveled with us, and my future was already changing. We booked the same suite she'd had on the last trip, and I looked around with a grin. "Hotel, sweet hotel."

She smiled, although I saw the anxiety in her eyes. I traced a finger down her cheek. "Everything is going to be fine, Shortcake. Jacob is meeting with the studio shortly. All of us will meet with MJ tomorrow morning. He is sure they'll let me go. They'll want zero negativity, and the bottom line is, if they force me to stay, I'll be such a pain in the ass, they will regret it. This is all going to be over soon."

"Will it?"

"MJ won't risk her deceit coming out. She can't stand to be thought of as anything but the best. She has other clients she wants to keep. She still gets her cut of my earnings for our shared projects."

"Including this movie? My book?"

"Yes. But it's worth it to be rid of her." I sat down, pulling her next to me. "Jacob has already put me in touch with an immigration lawyer. For the first time ever, I'm thrilled my celebrity status can do something. It will help fast-track my immigrating to Canada so we can be together."

"Are you sure that's what you want?"

"You doubt that, Shortcake?"

She glanced away, and I slid a finger under her chin, making her meet my eyes. Her fingers were fidgeting with the hem of her skirt, and I stilled them. "What?"

"You're very clearheaded now. Your meds have kicked in."

I nodded. "Fully. That doctor I saw in Port Albany recommended an additional medication that has really helped with the anxiety. I'm picking up my files for him so I can transfer to his practice. And I've spoken to the therapist he put me in touch with. I liked him a lot. We've chatted a few times, and I plan to go see him regularly." I stopped talking as I realized her worry.

"Shortcake, what I feel for you has nothing to do with my disorder, or the fact that I was spiraling toward an episode. I fell for you instantly. Hard. Permanently. Disorder or not. I didn't make a rash decision based on the emotion of the moment. It was based on the need of a lifetime. I love you, Mila. Then and now. Forever." I cupped her face in my hands. "You could never be a mistake, baby. I love you. I want a life with you." I met her eyes so she saw the sincerity in my gaze. "You hear me?"

"Yes."

"I love you," I repeated.

"I love you," she whispered.

"So, we're clear?"

"Yes."

"Good. Glad we had this conversation."

We spent the day doing errands. I visited my doctor and got my files. Picked up a few boxes and headed to my apartment. Mila was surprised as she looked around.

"Not what I expected," she admitted. It was simple, the furnishings modern, and it looked more like a hotel room than a home.

"I know. I told you, I was never settled. I didn't want the huge house or the grandiose lifestyle. No point in buying a condo. This was just a place to shut the door and be alone. MJ chose the furniture and filled it while I was away on a shoot. I didn't like it, but I didn't care enough to change it. I'm leaving it behind—they can do what they want with it."

"You rent?"

I nodded. "I was never interested in homeownership. Once it was discovered where I lived, I was surrounded by paps, so I'd have to move. And frankly, I never thought I'd settle down enough to want that. I've been here for about two years. A long time for me." I laughed, looking around. "You wouldn't know that, would you?"

"No."

"I have some personal things to pack, and that's it. The fridge is already empty, and I doubt there is much in the cupboards. I just ate out a lot."

She looked incredibly sad, and I wrapped her in my arms. "It's okay, Shortcake. That's all behind me now. Right?"

She looked up. "Right."

"I'll pack up the bedroom if you want to take the few pictures down here and put them in a box."

"Okay. I'll look around and see what else should go."

"We'll drop them at FedEx and ship them home."

She beamed at the word home. "Okay."

I sat on the edge of the bed, relief flowing through me. "Really?" I said into the phone.

Jacob chuckled in my ear. "It's funny how, as soon as you mention causing mental duress, forging the truth, and tarnishing their reputation, a person can be deemed expendable by a studio. Of course, they insisted the information MJ gave them was different, but they decided to release you from the contract. Papers are being drawn up."

"What about the franchise?"

"I suggested the next installment could be rewritten at the start with the lead having had an accident and then having facial reconstruction. A new, more handsome, younger lead could easily take your place."

I laughed at his dry wit. "So, as simple as that? A little threat, a suggestion, and it's done?"

He paused before he answered. "No. But I handled it, because that is what you hired me for. I can fight as dirty as they can, but you don't need to know all the details. Unless you want them."

"Maybe later."

He laughed. "One down, one to go."

"I fear MJ is going to be the hard one."

"That's why you have a team now, Nicholas. We have your back."

"It's a great feeling."

"Get used to it. We'll meet in the morning and go through everything. Has MJ contacted you?"

"She's tried. I haven't taken her calls, like you told me. She knows something is up, and she isn't happy. She's pissed about having a meeting. I'm sure she'll have lots to say tomorrow."

"We'll handle it."

Mila came in, and I told her the news. "Thank goodness," she breathed out.

I looped my arms around her waist, pulling her close and resting my head on her stomach. She scratched at the nape of my neck, her touch gentle and warm. "One down," she whispered, repeating my words from earlier. "One step at a time."

I nodded, looking up at her. "I called Manny. He can get us in later tonight if you want."

"I'd love that."

There was a noise from the other room. "Oh no, I think a box tipped over," Mila muttered. "I left one on the arm of the sofa." She hurried out of the room.

I stood to finish packing, except I heard her low gasp. I raced to the other room, stopping when I saw what had caused her distress.

MJ stood there, a scowl on her face.

"What the hell are you doing here?" she spat, glaring at Mila. She looked at me. "What the hell is going on?" She took a step forward.

There was no thought. I placed myself in front of Mila, shielding her from MJ.

"I think the question is, what are you doing here, MJ? In my apartment without me knowing?"

She waved me off. "Checking to see why you're ignoring my

calls. Came back without letting me know. My source at the studio called. I know there was a meeting that involved you. One I wasn't invited to." She narrowed her eyes. "What sort of shit has that little bitch cowering behind you talked you into, Nicky boy?" She barked out a laugh. "Thinking with the little head now, are you?"

I glared at her. "Show some respect for me and Mila. I've told you not to call me that. You'll find out what the meeting was for tomorrow. Now, leave."

"I don't think so." She crossed her arms. "Whatever you think you're doing won't happen."

I was tired of her. Of her threats. Her dire warnings. Of her darkness.

"It's already happened, MJ. I've broken my contract with the studio." I paused, watching her eyes widen in shock. I reached behind me for Mila's hand, needing her quiet strength. "And you."

"What did you just say?"

"We're done, MJ. I won't let you control me anymore."

"You think you can hire some two-bit lawyer and get rid of me?" she laughed. "After everything I've done for you, you ungrateful little prick?" She shook her head, her gaze ice-cold and her voice furious. "I helped make you. And I can destroy you."

It was my turn to laugh. "Everything you've done for me? Hiding my disorder, letting the world think I'm an addict of some sort? Choosing roles for me you knew would push me toward an episode so you can keep controlling me?" I shouted. Then I went in for the kill. "Changing my meds, MJ? Did you think you'd get away with that forever? Or just until you killed me?"

Her ire turned to panic. "I would never."

"We have the evidence!" I roared. "It's finished, MJ. Done. All of it. We. Are. Over."

She paled. "But I love you, Nick. I've always loved you."

"You loved me?" I replied, incredulous. "You don't know what love is. All you care about is MJ. That's all you've *ever* cared about."

"No, you have it wrong. I love you. I've waited for you to stop looking everywhere and see what was in front of you."

I blinked. She was in love with me? It was never like that for us. We were friends and nothing else. And that friendship had died a painful death a long time ago.

"I don't love you," I said quietly, meeting her eyes so she knew I was sincere. "My heart and my life are Mila's."

I should have expected the slap. She'd done it before. Her fury returned in the blink of an eye, and she lost control. This one landed with the full force of her wrath. My head snapped back from the power in her swing. I gripped Mila's hand, refusing to let her out from my protective stance. I heard her gasp of horror, and I squeezed her fingers. I met MJ's anger with the one thing I knew she would hate. My indifference.

"Get out."

MJ began to shout obscenities. Cursing me. Mila. She spewed threats. I slid my hand into my pocket. "I'm calling the police," I said calmly, refusing to let her see the pain radiating through my cheek or how upset I was. I hadn't wanted it this way. I wanted a clean slate and to walk away, knowing it was for the best but had been handled well. Of course MJ wouldn't allow that.

She turned and headed to the door. Mila slipped out from behind me, staring in horror at my rapidly swelling cheek. "Oh my God," she murmured. "She is vile."

MJ spun on her heel, lunging the short distance.

Mila turned in front of me, calm and steady. As MJ pulled back her arm, I reached to yank Mila out of the way.

But there was no Mila to grab. She bent, avoiding MJ's attack. She twisted, coming up behind her and taking her down in a move so smooth and lethal I blinked. One moment, MJ was right there; the next, she was facedown on the carpet, Mila bent over her, MJ's arms held against her back.

"He told you to leave," Mila seethed. "He gave you the chance, you horrible excuse for a human. He doesn't love you. He told you that. He doesn't want you. Now, you have two choices. Wait for the police and the charges that we will both press. Assault. Attempted murder for switching his meds. Or you get up, you walk out, and you never bother him again. You attend that meeting in the morning, and you sign the papers. If you don't, we will still press charges. Do you understand?"

I blinked at the tone of Mila's voice. The fury and determination in it. I had never seen her like that. A protective lioness defending her mate. Me.

I was shocked, thrilled, anxious, and, frankly, a little turned on.

"Get off me."

"Is Nick calling the police?"

I saw MJ's shoulders drop in defeat. "No. I'll go."

Mila got up, keeping her hold on MJ's arm. She walked her to the door, opening it and pushing her out. "Think before you do something stupid, MJ. Nick is giving you the break of a lifetime. I wouldn't be so generous."

"You are such a sanctimonious little bitch," MJ hissed, rubbing her arm. "You will regret this. I'll make sure of it." Then she nodded my way. "He isn't worth the trouble."

Mila cocked her head. "Do your worst, MJ. And by the

way, he is. And it's not trouble when you really love someone. It's called support. Empathy. You should try to learn that."

She slammed the door, locking it.

We heard MJ's rants all the way down the hall.

Our gazes locked, and I shook my head in wonder at the incredible woman standing there.

Fearless. Strong. Mine.

"You should probably call Tom and Jacob," she said as her left eyebrow twitched.

I caught her before she hit the floor.

CHAPTER TWENTY-FOUR

MILA

I opened my eyes, meeting Nick's concerned, dark gaze.

"Hey, Shortcake." He pressed his lips to my forehead. "There you are."

"Oh God, I went down again."

He smiled, brushing his finger over my cheek. "Not before you pulled some cool Charlie's Angels moves on MJ. You threw her out of here like last week's trash." He shook his head. "How did you learn to do that?"

I smiled ruefully, pulling myself up. We were on the sofa, me cradled protectively in his arms. "Have you met my uncles? Aiden and Dad made sure all us girls knew how to defend ourselves. Sammy can flip a man twice her size in the blink of an eye."

"Remind me not to get you angry with me."

"She's gone, right?"

He looked upset. "Yes, thank God. I texted everyone while you were out. We're meeting at the hotel once we're done here. I told Andi what you did."

"I was out that long?"

"Only a few moments. My voice-to-text was fast. She said you sometimes were out longer than usual if the trauma was intense."

I sighed, leaning my head on his shoulder. "That's one word for it."

"I'm sorry, Shortcake. I didn't want her near you at all. She's poison."

I cupped his face, frowning at the bruise already forming. "You took the brunt of it. That bitch."

"It's the last time."

I frowned. "Was there a first before today?"

He nodded with a shrug, and my heart hurt for him. "Never again, Nick."

He smiled. "No. Never again. Now, you finished out here?"

"Yes."

"Good. I'll be done in ten, and we'll load up and head to the hotel."

"Okay."

He pressed another kiss to my head. "Okay, baby."

A couple of hours later, I looked at Andi, who met my gaze calmly. Jacob and Tom had been busy. When Nick expressed his worry over her retribution, they had assured him everything was locked down.

"All your accounts are safe. Passwords changed. Access limited. We've notified those needed that she no longer represents you as your business manager slash agent. You brought all the contracts from your safe?"

He handed them the files. "Yes." He drew in a deep breath. "She might not show tomorrow."

Jacob sat back, crossing his ankle over his knee. He shrugged. "At this point, it's moot. She knows. She's angry. We need to brace ourselves for her pushback." He pointed to Nick's cheek. "I want pictures of that. I think we should prepare a statement and be ready to file an assault charge if she refuses to go quietly."

Nick nodded, and Andi took some pictures. I handed him some ice, which he held to his cheek, wincing as it came into contact with his skin. He grinned at Andi. "You should have seen our girl. Kicking ass, telling MJ exactly how it was going to go down."

Andi grinned back. "I've heard her and Sammy talk about Aiden and Van teaching them. Never thought she'd use her ninja skills."

"Oh, she used them, all right."

I rolled my eyes. I barely remembered it. I reacted, knowing she was going to hurt Nick again, and I couldn't allow that to happen. I knew he wouldn't strike back—he would never hit a woman, even one as vile as MJ. One moment, she was advancing, and the next, she was down. The rest was sort of a blur until I woke up in Nick's arms.

"Enough," I groaned. "Not my finest moment."

Nick leaned over and kissed my cheek. "I disagree. You defended me, Shortcake." He dropped his voice. "It was fucking hot."

I looked away, trying not to blush.

Tom looked at his phone with a frown. He stood and went to the balcony, his low voice obviously angry. He came back into the room and went to the TV, turning it on. He flipped through the channels, settling on a show I never watched.

Gossip and celebrity news filled the time slot, and I had no time for any of that. "I think we have a problem."

The face of a commentator known for his malicious streak came on. His smile was smarmy, his expression filled with vindictive delight.

"Tonight," he began, clapping his hands in glee. "I have the story of the month. The year." A picture flashed behind him. It was of a couple, their faces blocked out, caught in an embrace.

I recognized my yellow dress. Nick's hand wrapped around my waist.

"The ever so popular, ever so secretive author has been spotted with a male in a lead role. Or as I discovered, a supporting role. Who is the lady behind the mystery? And who is the troubled actor addicted to her words?" He smiled again, evil and twisted. "What else is he addicted to, and what lengths will he go to in order to cover it up? Come back tonight at ten, and I'll fill you in on all the gossip."

The room was silent for a moment. Then Tom shook his head. "That bitch."

Nick was on his feet. "That was the night we went to Manny's. I knew she was behind the whole pap swarm."

"And now she is going to reveal Mila's identity and smear Nick's name. All from behind the scenes. Even if we sue, which we will, the damage is done. And that show is notorious for getting away with shit," Jacob muttered. "They cross the line just far enough to inflict injury and keep their ratings high, but not get shut down." He slammed his hand on the table. "Dammit."

Andi sat beside me. "It's okay, Mila. We'll figure this out."

I stood, my mind going a thousand miles an hour. "How quickly can you call a press conference?"

Tom frowned. "Why?"

"Let's beat her to the punch. Announce Nick and I are together. That I am a Canadian citizen, and my name is Mila." I laughed. "I am not very exciting, so if she thinks outing me will bring her some sort of retribution, she is wrong."

"Mila," Andi admonished. "Your privacy."

I smiled. "We knew this day would come. My publishers have been dying for me to do some signings. Maybe it's now. It'll boost the movie. And once a couple of days go by, who will care? There are a hundred other authors far more interesting than me."

"Not involved with Nick."

"I'm protected in Port Albany. No one knows where I'm from. We'll grant a few interviews and be done with it."

"I'll come out about my disorder at the same time. That will be far more newsworthy," Nick said. "They'll focus on me. It'll take the meat out of that asshole's scoop, and MJ will have nothing left to threaten me with."

"It would work," Andi agreed. "Mila, are you sure?"

I was anything but. Except I knew I had to do this. As Nick had pointed out, if we were together, my identity would eventually come out. At least this way, we controlled the message.

"Yes."

Tom smiled. "If I call a press conference, they'll catch wind of it and release the story early. I have an even better idea."

Nick looked curious. "Tell us."

I sat next to Nick, my nerves flying. He looked so good dressed in a button-down with the sleeves rolled up and dress pants. I wore a skirt and blouse Andi got in the hotel lobby shop, the pretty colors suiting me. I swallowed as Nick leaned over. "Relax, Shortcake. This will be easy. We're just gonna answer some questions."

"In front of a few million people. How did Tom do this so fast?"

"Magic."

Gloria Hanes, the interviewer, joined us. Well-known, well-respected, and clearly surprised, she sat across from us, offering us a smile. "So, we're going to wing this. I'm going to let you lead, Nick. I have the questions Tom has given me, and I'll let you tell your story. You can join in when you're comfortable, Mila. We're going to keep this to twenty minutes, and it will air live at eight, preempting the show that was planned. Once it hits the airwaves, his story will be worthless. It'll kill that gossipmonger's ratings." She smiled widely. "That'll be worth it."

She leaned forward. "Any chance of a sneak peek at your latest book, Mila? I am a huge fan."

I laughed. "Andi will get you one. I'll send the whole collection to say thanks for doing this."

She settled, waiting until her mic was clipped on. "The author falling for the star? The actor with a hidden secret? Uprooting his entire life to be with the woman he loves. My God, that's a book right there." She looked past us with a nod. "Okay, you two ready?"

Nick squeezed my hand. "We're ready."

I swallowed and lifted my head, remembering what my dad had said to me when I called to tell them what was happening.

"Show them who you are, Pumpkin. Strong, fierce, talented, and beautiful. We're so proud of you."

"Ready."

An hour later, I sat, bemused, as Nick and his team shook everyone's hand. The interview had been easier than I expected. Gloria was charming, intelligent, and blunt. Her questions were direct and formed in such a way they could be answered without implicating anyone.

She downplayed my identity.

"You write under another name. I know many authors do. Why?"

I shrugged. "I'm boring. My life when I'm not writing is simple. There is no news. I used that name in a contest and it brought me luck, so I kept it. I'll still keep it. A.M. Archer is the artist. Mila is just along for the ride." I laughed lightly.

Nick entertained her with the whole gofer story and my nickname. She laughed in delight, but I was glad he never mentioned the pool.

Then they discussed his bipolar disorder, not giving too much away. She cocked her head. "And the studio allowed the story of you being in rehab? They preferred you being a drug addict to the truth?"

He had smiled and shrugged. "What happened or what was done is in the past. I'm looking toward the future." He drew in a deep breath. "But I will say this. If you need help, ask for it. Go to your doctor. A friend. Reach out. You don't have to suffer with pain on your own." He found my hand. "You can find your support. I did, and I'm stronger for it."

She turned to me. "So, Mila. I understand you live with a disorder as well."

I cleared my throat and talked about vasovagal syncope.

"How extraordinary," Gloria mused. "I had never heard of that until now. So, you could pass out at any given moment?"

"It's much more under control. But I don't drive or operate heavy machinery," I quipped, making her laugh.

"And you found each other."

Nick smiled, his megawatt superstar smile that made women melt. "She bolsters me, and I hold her up when needed. We're a great team."

Gloria nodded. "So, a new page, Nicholas. A new life, new management, a new goal. A clean slate, so to speak."

Tom had insisted that line be in the interview. It sent a clear message to the world that MJ was no longer part of his career.

"All of which I'm looking forward to," he replied.

"And love."

He nodded, pressing a kiss to my temple. "And love."

She looked at the camera. "Only in Hollywood, folks. The writer falls for the star. The star changes his life and finds healing in revealing the truth. Then they ride off into the sunset together." She smiled at me. "Sounds like a great book to me."

I smiled. "That is one story I plan to never end."

Gloria ended the program with phone numbers and websites for mental health.

And it was over.

Nick sat beside me, resting his arm on the back of the sofa. "You were amazing, Shortcake."

"So were you."

Andi sat down. "Well done, you two. My phone is blowing up."

Tom chuckled. "Mine as well. We should get to it."

"What about tomorrow?" Nick asked.

"We'll handle it. You two have done your part. I doubt MJ will show. If she's smart, she'll send her lawyer to sign the papers and the NDA. Tonight killed her revenge. They are pulling the show that was to air. She has nothing left to hurt you with." Tom smiled at us. "You two relax tonight. Your part is over."

They left, and I nestled into Nick's side.

"Who knew all of this would happen when you wrote this book," he mused.

"I know. The final draft was way different from the first one."

"Oh yeah?"

I nodded. "You never would have filmed in Port Albany. The wedding would have happened in Vegas."

"Vegas?"

I sat up, pulling my hair from the clips that held it back. "They eloped."

"What changed your mind?"

"It didn't work for them. I realized Roxie wanted the big white wedding, and I had to give it to her."

"Because that's what you want too?"

I shocked him when I shook my head. "No. I'd be fine with Vegas. My husband and I. The thought of the whole thing, all the people looking—even if they are mostly my family—it just doesn't do it for me. I want small, private, and fast."

"Your parents would be so upset."

I laughed. "They wouldn't be surprised. I always told them that. I said they could have a party after. As long as they could celebrate, they'd be fine." I began to stand. "One day."

He grabbed my hand, his gaze intense. "How about today?"

"What?" I asked, confused.

"Let's be Roxie and Duncan. That's who you wrote about when you crafted the book, Mila. Us. I saw it in every word. Let's give them the original ending."

"What are you saying?"

He stood, cradling my face in his hands. "Marry me, Shortcake. Tonight. We'll fly to Vegas, get married, and spend the night. We can be back in the morning. Give our story the ending you first wrote."

I felt the rush of tears. "You want to marry me?"

"I want it all with you. We'll get married and head home together. Face your father. Have a freaking party to end all parties. Start our life. You heard Gloria. A new page. A new story for us." He paused. "Please."

I could only say one word.

"Yes."

CHAPTER TWENTY-FIVE

MILA

Andi glowered at me from across the aisle on the plane. "Your father is going to kill me. When we started this, I promised to make sure you were okay. When he finds out you got married, he is going to use some of those power tools of his to dismember my body."

I laughed. "He'll be fine. I'm not saying a word until we get home."

She sighed. "Who knew my little shy Mila could cause all this stir?" She leaned forward, mock glaring at Nick. "This is your fault."

He grinned at her, leaning over and nuzzling my cheek. "I'll take full responsibility, Andi. You're safe."

He smiled at me, pressing a kiss to my cheek. "You okay, wife?" he whispered, making me shiver. He'd been calling me that since the minister pronounced us married two days before.

We'd been on the last flight out that night, arriving in Vegas just before midnight. Nick had already been busy on his phone, and he pulled me to a limo and we went directly to a chapel. He'd thought of everything. A pretty bunch of flowers. A hotel room for the night. He'd dragged me to the jeweler's in the lobby, and he picked out a ring—a simple, heavy platinum band. He made me leave the store after getting my ring size, and he slipped a beautiful band on my finger when we said I do. The pavé diamonds caught the light and reflected the brilliance.

"I'll buy you a big diamond if you want," he promised.

"No. I love this."

He kissed me. "I love you, wife." He smiled against my mouth.

We went back to the hotel and spent the night celebrating. He was loud and vocal. Demanding and sweet. Loving and relentless.

We celebrated so much, I had trouble walking the next morning. I was still a little achy.

Jacob, Andi, and Tom met us at the hotel suite in LA in the early afternoon. Tom let us know MJ had sent her lawyer and all the papers had been signed. Jacob smiled.

"I will work out all the details and make sure you're protected."

"Thanks." Nick put out his hand to shake, and Andi yelped.

"What the hell is that on your finger?" Then she grabbed my hand. "Mila!"

He grinned, wrapping his arm around my waist. "We eloped last night."

I had never seen Andi speechless before.

She hadn't shut up since she recovered.

The plane touched down, and I felt the nerves in my stomach kick in. Despite what I told Nick, I knew my dad would be sad about my eloping. He was sentimental and old-fashioned.

I hoped he wouldn't be too upset. I knew I'd already caused enough of a stir with the film, Nick, and everything else.

Nick lifted my hand in the car, kissing my ring. "We'll get

married again if they want," he promised me, knowing what was on my mind. "I'll marry you a hundred times, Shortcake."

I smiled. "Once was enough, Hollywood."

"We'll see what your father says about that."

My parents, uncles, and aunts were all waiting for us at the Hub. We dropped our luggage at the house and wandered over. I saw all the people inside and groaned. "We'll get it over with all at once," Nick assured me. "Think of it this way— your dad can't kill me with all those witnesses."

"Or they can provide him an airtight alibi," I muttered.

Nick stopped beside me, not opening the door. "What?"

"Nothing."

"You're funny, Shortcake."

"Let's go in."

We were greeted warmly, coffee poured, cookies set out. Everyone wanted to hear the whole, real story, and Nick indulged them, giving them the scoop. When he got to the part of me taking down MJ, he stood, reenacting it. His ring flashed in the light, but no one seemed to notice. Aiden whooped and hollered, giving me a high five. The diamonds on my band caught the light, glittering and sending a rainbow over the wall.

No one even blinked.

Finally, I yawned, and my mom patted my shoulder. "You're tired, my girl. Go have a nap. We can do dinner later if you want. Aiden already ordered Chinese."

Nick grinned. "Awesome."

"Sammy's back at the ranch. Is she doing okay?"

"She's very happy. She'll call you later."

"Okay."

I felt strangely disappointed. Not a single member of my family had commented or asked about our rings. I'd purposely pushed my hair back, letting my hand linger, but there was no reaction. I looked at Nick, who seemed confused.

"So, Mila and I have some news to share."

"Oh my goodness," Mom said. "We've had all the news we can take. Save it for later."

My dad yawned and rolled his shoulders. "Yeah, I think I'll go work out. You coming with, Aiden?"

Aiden stood. "Sure."

But his tone was off, and I saw him trying to hide his smile.

I jumped out of my chair. "Oh my God, you know. You all know!"

Aiden began to laugh. "Who says we can't act?"

It turned out Andi had called and told my parents. She'd seen a picture of Nick and me in Vegas snapped by some random fan, with the headline of something along the lines of "Nick's New Life Starts Early." She'd wanted them to know before the story broke wide.

My family had decided to play a joke on us.

Once they explained how they knew, the hugs and voices became loud. I went from one set of arms to another. My mom was a teary mess, my aunts beaming. Nick was jostled around like a sack of potatoes until we both ended up in front of my dad. I met his eyes, seeing only his love.

"He makes you happy, Pumpkin?"

"Yes."

"You plan on keeping her that way, Hollywood?" he asked Nick.

Nick slid his arm around my waist. "Always, sir."

"And you're staying here—in your house—right?" Dad asked me.

"Yes," both Nick and I answered.

"Then there is only one thing I can do."

"Which is?" Nick asked, tightening his arm on me.

"Throw you a major party that your mother and I plan. Whatever we decide goes."

Nick grinned. "Deal."

My dad opened his arms, and I ran into them. He enfolded me in his embrace.

"I love you, Daddy," I whispered. "I couldn't bear to leave you."

"Good, Pumpkin. I couldn't face both you and Sammy being out of the nest so close together." He held me tighter, kissing my head. "I love you too. Be happy, my girl."

I sighed.

I already was.

EPILOGUE

NICK

I ran a hand through my damp hair. I'd been in meetings all morning in Toronto, and when I got back to Port Albany, I worked out with Aiden, then showered before coming home. I was trying to leave my wife alone so she could write.

We'd been married six months, and I still hated to be away from her for long periods of time. A few hours felt like forever.

My life had changed. I had changed.

I'd never known happiness like this existed until Mila came into my life. She was my constant. Living here was incredible. The privacy, the peace. Her—*our*—incredible family.

I worked out with Aiden. Talked at length with Bentley. Shopped with Maddox. Doted on Sandy. Geeked out with Reid. Sought Halton's counsel on more than one occasion. I joined the men on their cigar nights, listening to their stories as we sipped expensive booze and enjoyed life.

I got along well with all the cousins. We hung out. I wasn't Nicholas Scott, celebrity, here. I was Nick, Mila's husband—a role I loved having. I was part of something. A group of people who truly cared for one another.

All the women mothered me. Fussed and clucked. Staunchly supported my movies. Fed me constantly. There was always one of them around if I wandered to the Hub while Mila was busy.

I found a new therapist. One I trusted. I stayed on top of my meds. Realized how it felt to feel almost normal. I had my moments, but I didn't feel as if everyone were waiting for me to fall. Instead, they made sure to keep me lifted up. The combination of this less anxiety-driven lifestyle and the support around me made a huge difference. I didn't have to hide myself. I could just be me.

Or "Hollywood," as they all called me.

Except Liv.

She called me "her boy," and I liked that. My mom used to call me that, and it made me smile. Feel loved. I knew she was looking down at me and was happy I had found my place.

I got to the house, peeking in the office, surprised Mila wasn't at her desk or in her big chair she liked to curl up in to write. I walked to the kitchen, still in awe of this place. Mila and I had bought some new pieces together. She had discovered my sketchbooks when we were unpacking my things and had framed several pieces, hanging them on the walls. She loved it when I would show her new sketches, and I enjoyed the tranquility of sitting and drawing out the vistas and quiet beauty of this place.

My favorite sketch was the one I drew of her when I first met her. Before I knew who she was. I had still captured her sweetness. It hung in the room I used as an office now, and I often lost time gazing at it, until I had to go and see the real thing. Hold her and feel her against me, knowing this was my life now. Mila filled every crevice and dark spot with her lightness and love.

Not finding her, I headed upstairs, stopping in the doorway. Mila was on our bed, leaning back against the headboard, watching the TV. I stared at her for a moment, noting the loose T-shirt she wore. One of mine. She loved putting on my clothes. I loved taking them off her.

I did a double take when I saw what she was watching, and I strode into the room, standing between her and the screen, glaring at her.

She pulled off the headphones. "What?"

"What did we agree, Mila? No porn watching. I'll give you whatever you need."

She waved her hand. "You were at work. I need inspiration. Move."

I shook my head, crawling up on the bed toward her, tossing the headphones away. "Not without me."

"Stop. It was getting to the good stuff. The moaning and writhing were about to start."

She looked adorable, defending her need to watch the movie. I cocked my head, leaning close and dropping my voice. "You wet, baby? Has watching made you wet?"

"Maybe," she responded.

An idea hit me. I recalled what she told me once. How she could get off just watching porn. We'd never discussed it again, but suddenly, I needed to see that more than I needed anything else. I pulled her forward, sliding in behind and settling her between my legs. Using my feet, I opened her legs, wrapping an arm around her and holding her tight to my chest. I grabbed the remote and restarted the movie.

"I want to watch," I murmured in her ear.

"With me?" she breathed.

"No, I want to watch you watch them. I want to see you come."

"I don't know if I can with you here."

"You can, baby. I'll help."

She whimpered a little as I grazed my fingers across her breasts, finding her nipples tight and hard.

"You're so turned on, aren't you?"

She nodded, her eyes fixed on the screen. I slid a finger between her legs, feeling the dampness of the cotton that covered her.

"Oh baby, let's see you go."

The movie was more sensual than dirty. More artistic than porn. But she liked it. I tugged her legs open wider, letting my hand cup her. She pushed back into me, my growing erection trapped between us. Her hands moved restlessly on my legs, gripping at the material. Her breathing became choppy, sounding harsh in the room. As the woman on the screen began moaning, her lover's face between her legs, Mila's body stiffened, her back arching. Her toes curled, and she whimpered in her release. I watched her, fascinated at the flush on her cheeks and her body's response to the stimulus. I slipped my finger inside her underwear, finding her hard clit. She gasped as I stroked her, another orgasm bearing down on her. She cried out, riding my hand, turning her head so I could capture her mouth in a searing kiss.

I gentled my touch, withdrawing my hand, but my little spitfire wasn't done. She turned, pulling off my shirt and yanking down her underwear.

"Down," she begged, tugging on my legs.

I slouched, letting her pull off my shorts. Then she slung her legs over mine, presenting me with a glorious view of her back and ass. She guided me inside and rode me, reverse cowgirl style, her eyes still on the screen. She was tight from this angle, and I gripped her hips, guiding her. Listening to her noises. The catch in her throat. The raspiness of her voice. The way she tightened around me.

"Jesus, baby, yes. Again," I demanded, sitting up and burying my face into her neck. "Ride me until you come."

Then my world exploded, and I clutched her harder. Thrust deeper. Heard her cry out one more time before going limp and quiet in my arms. I turned off the TV, no longer wanting the images.

I helped her climb off, her legs shaky. I pulled her back into my embrace and lay down, taking her with me.

"No more porn watching without me," I said. "But that was the hottest thing I have ever seen, baby."

She mumbled something unintelligible. I kissed her head. "Are you inspired now?"

She nodded, already drifting.

"Sleep, Shortcake. You can write it out later. If you need more inspiration, or a reminder, I'm right here." I paused. "It's a hard job," I stated. "But someone has to do it."

She tried to slap my chest and snort. She managed neither, her hand sort of waving in the air and her snort of derision more like a snore.

I kissed her head, loving her. Every part of her.

FOURTEEN MONTHS LATER

I stepped into the elevator, Tom following me.

"Good day," he muttered. "Lots of positive reviews and comments. Great job with the interviews."

"Yeah," I agreed. "Thanks for being here."

He clapped me on the shoulder. "Of course."

My relationship with Tom was nothing like the constant battle I had endured with MJ. He was calm, decisive, positive. He offered advice, smoothed troubled waters, and supported me in all my decisions. He'd flown to LA with me for some interviews and press leading up to the release of the movie. There was lots of interest in it, and the early reviews were great. Mila was here as well, but she preferred to stay in the background. Her face and her name were out there, but she didn't do much to call attention to herself. Andi made sure she was still protected, and her public persona was rarely seen. Simply the thought of attending the screening of the movie made her anxious enough. I didn't like my wife anxious.

We exited the elevator, and I headed to our suite, after Tom reminded me of our breakfast meeting. I waved at him, already dropping the business mode and looking forward to seeing my wife and taking her out to dinner.

I found her on the lounger, glaring at her laptop. On the table beside her was a glass of iced tea and a forgotten sandwich. She looked up as I strolled out onto the balcony. I bent and kissed her, chuckling. "Problem, Shortcake?"

"Damn character," she muttered.

I laughed and pulled a chair over, sitting beside her. I picked up the sandwich, taking a bite. Then I pressed it to her pouting lips. "Eat, baby."

She let me feed it to her, although I ate more of it than she did. I would make sure she ate well tonight. I had gotten used to her odd habits when deep in writing mode.

"What am I doing that is not pleasing you?" I asked.

"It's my character, Nick. Not you."

Laughing, I chucked her chin. "We both know you think

about me whenever you write a lead male character, Mila. I'm your muse." I sat back, flashing her a smile. "That's why they're all drop-dead gorgeous, sexy, and fabulous in bed."

She sniffed and rolled her eyes. "And full of themselves."

I laughed. "And they love their woman with every part of their being."

She smiled, resting her head back against the lounger. "I can't figure out his reaction in this scene."

She looked tired, and I knew she needed to stop. I also knew she wouldn't stop until she figured this out. I stood. "Let me help. Scoot forward."

I slipped in behind her and had her scroll back a couple of pages. I read the scene slowly, frowning. "So basically, she's pregnant and not sure how he is going to react? Your leads are always thrilled. Unless I'm missing something?"

Her voice was low. "This one is nervous about his wife getting pregnant. He worries over her too much. He worries over the future."

"Still, I think he'd welcome the news. It's a baby. Babies are miracles."

"Yes."

"Write it."

She tapped away, and I read the last words. *You're going to be a father. Please be happy.*

Then she stopped.

"Finish it," I encouraged.

"I'm waiting for his reaction," she replied.

Then it hit me. I *was* the character. This scene was us. My breath caught in my throat. Mila knew I wanted kids, but I was worried. Bipolar disorder was thought to be hereditary. My mother had suffered from what had been labeled depression and was often on medication. When I spoke to my doctor and therapist, they both told me it was believed the disorder came from the maternal side, but there was no solid proof yet. So perhaps a child of mine would not suffer the way I did. Still, I was hesitant, although we both wanted children.

Yet, looking at the words on the screen, all I felt was...*joy*. The worry and fear didn't seem as important. If they had the same disorder, they would have us. Our family. A huge support system I once only dreamed of.

I leaned forward and typed two words.

I am.

At the sound of Mila's soft sob, I shut the lid of her laptop and set it aside. I wrapped my arms around her, resting my hand on her stomach and my chin on her shoulder. "Our child is right here, Mila?"

"Yes."

"We're going to be parents," I breathed out.

"Yes."

I had to see her. It took some maneuvering, but I got her turned around. I cupped her face. "Shortcake, tell me. Let me hear your words."

"I'm pregnant."

"I'm going to be a daddy," I said with wonder.

"I'm going to be fat," she sobbed.

"You're going to be the cutest damn pregnant woman I've ever seen." I kissed her. "And the best mommy. Mila, this child will be so loved, no matter what. I'll make sure they grow up strong and healthy. You'll nurture their creative side, I'll watch over them. Oh God, your parents are going to go crazy."

"So you're really happy?"

I gathered her in my arms.

"Totally."

The next few days flew by. The premiere was good, the film well received, and I'd heard the word *Oscar* more than once. Mila was with me to walk the red carpet, and she enjoyed seeing the movie, although she turned her eyes away at the sexier parts. I laughed and kissed her head, murmuring silly words to make her smile. I, myself, couldn't stop smiling, but it was because of the news she had shared even more than the premiere or the exciting projects I had signed on for while there.

I arranged for a private screening of the film back in Toronto for her family. Mila still protected their privacy as much as possible. We would watch it with them when we returned and have our own after party.

One thing about the BAM clan was they loved a good party. Any excuse was used, and they were always ready to celebrate. We'd have a double celebration this time.

We sat in the first-class lounge, waiting for our flight home. Mila sighed, resting her head on my shoulder.

"Glad to be heading home?"

"Yes."

I understood her feelings. Despite the fact that LA was where I grew up and lived for so long, the sleepy little hamlet of Port Albany felt more like home than LA ever did. I loved the privacy, the peace, and the people. I pressed a kiss to her head. "Me too."

We linked our hands together. "My parents will be so happy when we tell them."

"I know. Your dad might like me."

She laughed, nudging my shoulder. "He already does."

I had to chuckle. "I know." Van and I got along well. I

secretly thought I had the edge over Luke since I'd moved to Port Albany and didn't take Mila away, but I kept that information to myself.

"I want you to pull back a little when we get home," I said, lifting her hand to my mouth and kissing her knuckles. "I already told Tom I'd be adjusting some dates."

"And he was okay with that?"

I smiled. "He'll make it work. He's awesome that way."

She nodded. "A definite upgrade."

I chuckled. "Did I tell you what I heard about MJ?"

Mila frowned. "No."

"She lost the rest of her clients and left LA. She's managing some third-tier wrestling wannabes somewhere in the Midwest."

Mila's eyebrows rose. "Oh my. Quite the fall from grace."

"Yep. It's vastly amusing to me. Bad acting and bad management. She deserves it."

"Do you ever think to reach out?" she asked. "I know you have a lot of history."

"Nope. She is the past. The worst of it. You're the best. You, my wife, are my future." I lowered my voice, drifting my fingers along her stomach. "You and our little one."

She smiled, her eyes bright with tears. She went from happy to sad back to happy a lot. I should have clued in on the whole pregnancy thing faster than I did. I would next time.

She sniffed and wiped at her nose, then tapped something out on her phone, scrolling for a bit. I sipped my coffee, glancing up when she giggled, then looked at me. "I found the website."

Of course she did. Research was one of her many talents. "Oh?"

"Oh, it's so awful," she murmured. "The names. The Grim Rapper. The Scottie Hottie."

"Does he wrestle in a kilt?" I asked dryly.

Her eyes widened, a grin tugging on her lips.

"What?"

"One guy's name is Pack'em & Rack'em."

I grunted. "Nice name. Catchy."

She shook her head, trying to hold in her amusement. "Bad choice. His opponents call him Packed Rectum."

She began to laugh. Loudly. She covered her mouth to stifle the sound and snorted. I laughed with her, bending close to kiss her, and shutting off her phone. "Forget her."

They announced a delay to our flight, and I let my head fall back with a groan. Mila patted my arm, still giggling quietly.

"When you're done laughing over that unneeded information, Shortcake, I need a coffee," I informed her.

"Are your legs broken, Hollywood?"

My lips quirked. "I married you so I'd have my little gofer around all the time. Now, do your job."

She laughed again and stood. I felt the press of her lips, and I grasped the back of her head, kissing her far too passionately for a public place. But I didn't care who saw us.

I loved this woman. Every side of her. The sweet and funny. The serious and quiet. The deep thinker. The silly prankster.

My Mila. Unscripted, unexpected, and perfectly imperfect.

Perfectly scripted for me.

IT'S A WRAP - SERIES EPILOGUE

SANDY

Twilight was approaching, the shadows moving in and stealing the light. It was one of my favorite times of day here in Port Albany. The way the last of the sun's rays danced on the water. The easing of the day before nightfall. I glanced around the room. There were people everywhere. On both floors. The food had arrived, and as usual, families drifted together, congregating naturally toward parents and siblings. It happened every get-together.

Jordan smiled, covering my hand. "Everyone," he breathed out. "Everyone came for this. How wonderful."

I flipped my hand, squeezing his fingers. "I know. Bentley and the boys are over the moon. I have no idea how the girls did it, but everyone is here. Although, I'm not sure an invitation was issued as much as a motherly demand. Whatever it took, the girls made it happen."

He chuckled. "The girls aren't girls anymore."

I smiled. "They'll always be girls to me."

He lifted my hand and kissed it. "You're the prettiest one here."

"I'm the oldest."

"Doesn't matter. Still the prettiest."

"Charmer."

He winked and smiled toward Emmy, who brought us our dinners. At our ages, we needed all the help we could get, and once we sat down, we rarely moved. She slid the plates onto the table in front of us. Bentley followed her, and he sat beside me with his own plate.

"Go, eat with your family," I protested.

He met my eyes, shaking his head. "You are my family."

"Bentley."

"Look, I had to pull rank to get to sit with you. Aiden and Mad Dog are still pouting. Let me enjoy my victory. They get coffee and dessert with you."

I laughed, patting his hand. "Fine."

I glanced over at Bentley's family. His daughter, Addison, and her husband, Brayden, sat with a child on each lap, making sure they ate, while picking at their own meals. Bentley's other daughter, Chloe, was curled up on the sofa, her husband beside her. They were sharing a plate, him feeding her as she chatted to her mom and held the small rescue dog that went everywhere with her.

"Look at them. Isn't that lovely," I murmured.

Bentley chuckled. "Newlyweds still."

"Since you thought she'd never get married, I love seeing her so happy."

He nodded around a mouthful. "Samuel is a great guy. He gets her. Of course, the fact that they're both vets is a big help.

They work well together." His voice softened. "And he treats her the way she deserves to be treated."

"The farm going well?" Jordan asked, referring to the animal rescue shelter Chloe opened.

Bentley smiled. "Very well. Their program is thriving. Samuel moved his practice onto the farm, and they are flourishing. They took on six new kids this past spring."

Chloe and her husband brought in foster kids who were aging out of the system. Gave them jobs, a place to live and belong. Some stayed, some left, and there were always new faces, but it gave the kids a solid starting point. All the BAM men had thrown in their support when she decided to open it, Reid especially. Anything to do with kids needing help got him involved. He and Becca often went to BC with Emmy and Bentley to visit the farm and help out.

"You must be so proud," I observed.

"I'm proud of all of them," he replied, his voice warm with affection. "They have the best of Emmy and me in them."

I squeezed his hand. "Thomas looks good. It's lovely to see him here."

"He does. Emmy is thrilled to have him home. And, of course, Natalie. They're rarely around." He leaned my way. "But we should see them more. Natalie is pregnant. So instead of skipping around the world saving whales, they're going to have a permanent base in BC. I bought them a house."

I patted his arm. "That is wonderful news. The man who insisted he would never find a woman who understood him and settle down has changed."

Bentley laughed. "My stubborn son, yes. I'll never forget the day he called to tell me about the volunteer who informed him he was a stuffed shirt who liked to hear himself talk too much. I knew right then that girl was going to be important. He complained about her for weeks, and then suddenly, she was perfect." He looked at his son fondly. "I think he still thinks she is."

"Like you think about Emmy."

Everything about him softened at the mention of his beloved wife. The sweet girl who'd brought him out of his shell and taught him what was really important in life. "She is pretty perfect."

"Perfect for you."

His smile said it all.

Maddox laughed at something Brayden said, clapping him on the shoulder. He leaned down, taking their granddaughter and lifting her high. She saw Bentley and waved, calling his name. "Grampa! Come save me. PopPop is eating me!"

Bentley chuckled and excused himself. He and Maddox doted on the grandchildren they shared. Addi and Brayden had known each other their entire lives, and it surprised no one when that turned into love, forever tying the families together. Bentley went over, picking up Ella and giving her a raspberry. Her sister, Skylar, watched, smiling and staying close to her mom. She was the shyer of the two, preferring to stay within her family circle. Addi and Bray always made sure to sit between the two families so the kids got both sets of grandparents close.

I smiled as I watched Shelby, Maddox and Dee's daughter. She was always quiet, her head in the clouds or a sketchbook. She'd been busy today, sketching everything and everybody. I knew she would finish the drawings in more detail later, and everyone would be given copies as gifts. Her husband sat close to her, watching with an indulgent smile. Simon owned an art gallery and had fallen in love with Shelby quickly. It took him a long time to convince her to give him a chance, but once she did, they moved fast. They were married and settled in Toronto. She painted and sketched and helped him run his successful gallery. She built up her reputation and was a sought-after artist. They fit each other perfectly, and Maddox often stated she couldn't have a better partner.

Bentley bent down and spoke to Emmy, and Reid took full advantage, sliding onto the vacant chair.

"Finally," he groused. "The bastards didn't even include me in the challenge."

Bentley looked up, frowning, then laughed and sat beside Emmy. He waved his hand in a magnanimous gesture. "Good one, boy wonder."

Reid chuckled. "Haven't been called that in a long time."

"You'll always be that to them."

He smiled. "I know." He glanced at my plate. "Do you want something else, Sandy? Jordan?"

Jordan shook his head. I smiled. "No, my boy. I'm good. It was delicious."

"It was good. Not as good as when our wives cook, but I'm glad they took the day off. Becca is enjoying having everyone here."

I followed his gaze. Becca was on the sofa, surrounded by her kids and grandkids. Reid still looked at her as if she'd hung the moon. Theo and Anne were laughing at something Jenny said, no doubt teasing her little brother, Carter. Lily and her partner, Daphne, were smiling, their two rescue dogs on their laps being fed tidbits.

"Lily looks so happy," I murmured. "So settled."

Reid nodded. "She is so busy at ABC, running their systems. Theo says she blows me out of the water," he boasted, not at all put out. "And Daphne is amazing. She was just offered head trauma nurse. Lily is so proud. We all are. She's a great partner for Lily. I'm glad they found each other." He sat back, lowering his voice. "Melissa and Timothy found out their adoption of Michael has been approved. We're going to need another party to celebrate." He grinned. "Maybe a touch smaller."

I laid a hand on his arm. "Reid, how wonderful."

He smiled fondly as Michael came over, his little face wreathed in smiles. "Gramps," he said. "Gramma said I get two pieces of cake since I ate all my supper."

Reid lifted him onto his knee. "Even your vegetables?"

Michael nodded. "All of them."

"Then you do get two pieces. I'll make sure they're big ones."

Michael beamed, throwing his arms around Reid's neck and hugging him. My heart warmed, seeing the affection.

When Melissa and Timothy found out they couldn't have kids, it had been a sad time for them. Then they decided to adopt and met Michael. He was three and was a sickly toddler, going from foster home to foster home. That changed once they decided he was going to be theirs. Given Reid's history, he threw himself into helping Michael, and he was now a healthy child, always smiling and happy. Knowing he would legally be a part of this family was the best HEA I could think of for any child.

Never one to stay in place long, Michael jumped down, stopping to offer me his sticky lips. I bent, and he pressed a gentle kiss to my cheek. "Lub you, Nana."

"I love you," I replied.

He high-fived Jordan and returned to his parents, who watched him with love.

I sighed. "So many good things."

Reid leaned back, chuckling. "Did you hear what Liam's boys did this week at school?"

I shook my head. All of Aiden's children were now married with families of their own. Ava and Hunter had two boys who kept them busy. Austin and Knox loved following their dad around and "helping" him build things. He insisted they were the future builders of ABC. Aiden couldn't be prouder.

Ronan and Beth were constantly on the go with Evan's teenage schedule, and their kids, Luke and Zoey, were the apple of Ronan's eye. Jeremy and Kim had a daughter, Lana. Paul and Diane had a son, Joseph, and a daughter, Joanna. But Liam beat them all and had five children. He'd adopted Paige's daughter, Lucy, had two other daughters, Shannon and Erin, plus a set of twins, AJ and Brock.

Prank-loving, keep-you-on-your-toes twins.

"What have they done now?" Jordan asked, amusement lacing his voice.

"They snuck into the science lab and took out all the fish from the tanks, then filled them with green and yellow Jell-O and plastic fish that they put in upside down. It looked as if the water had turned and the fish were dead." He chuckled. "They missed one camera. Otherwise, they would have gotten away with it. Liam spent a day overseeing them cleaning the tanks and restocking them." He grinned widely. "They are grounded for a week."

Jordan shared a glance with Reid. "They'll break out in two days."

Reid shook his head. "I give them a night."

I had to laugh. The pranks were usually harmless, but they kept Liam and Paige on their toes. Aiden found it vastly amusing since he'd had to deal with his triplets causing trouble growing up and had little sympathy for Liam, although he tried to keep a straight face most of the time.

Laughter came from the corner, and Brandon, Halton's eldest son, stood and executed a bow. He was the comic of the family, the most gregarious of them all. He had shocked everyone when he had followed Amber Grey back to Hollywood and married her. They had met while she was here directing the movie adaptation of Mila's book, and it had been a whirlwind romance. They divided their time between here and LA, him always traveling with her when she went on location. His consulting business enabled him to go anywhere as long as his laptop was with him.

"I'm sure Halton and Fee are thrilled to have all their kids together. Bethy was over yesterday, visiting Jordan and me." We called Halton's youngest Bethy, so as not to confuse her with Ronan's wife, Beth.

Reid grinned, relaxing back in his chair. "Entertaining you with her archaeology dig stories? She has the best ones."

"They're certain the team is onto a huge discovery," I replied. "Who knew home-loving little Bethy would be such an adventure seeker?"

"She always loved digging in the dirt."

I laughed. "Darius seems nice and he can hold his own with this crew, so that is saying a lot. Another surprise wedding," I added, looking over at the couple. Darius was a fellow archaeologist, and they had met on her last trip to Egypt. Now, they were inseparable. He was charming and funny, and it was easy to see how much he adored Bethy. Halton saw it as well and was pleased his daughter had found someone so loving.

"We seem to have a lot of those. But when you know, you

know. Did she show you the pictures of them getting married by the ruins? Those were spectacular."

"They were. Halton and Fee are planning a visit. Now that Elise has taken over the practice full time, they have lots of free time."

"Did you see the article on her and the firm in the paper? Top ten family lawyers in the city. Her husband, Jeff, too. The firm is doing well."

"Halton and Fee are very proud. And Craig and Joseph's furniture company is booming. They've had to hire more people."

"Joseph says his partner Duncan has an exciting new line he is designing. I can hardly wait to see it. Becca loves his stuff." Reid crossed his ankles. "Halton has some talented kids."

I hummed in agreement.

"Craig's wife, Alannah, told me they're getting a couple more foster kids," Reid continued, sounding pleased. "They already have three, and they figure one or two more will fit in just fine." He shook his head. "Those kids are damn lucky to have them."

I knew he was thinking of his own painful childhood. I reached over and squeezed his hand, but he shook his head. "I wouldn't change it, Sandy. I have this." He swept his arm out. "I wouldn't trade this family for the world." He leaned forward and pressed a kiss to my cheek. "Especially you." He smiled. "But I'm grateful for families like theirs who take in kids and show them what a family is really like."

We shared a smile, my heart full of love for this man. The boy I first met was still there—the one desperate to belong somewhere and afraid to hope for it. Except now, he'd found his place and tried to make sure others did too. He volunteered both his time and money to make sure to help the most vulnerable of kids. I was incredibly proud of him.

Aiden and Maddox came over. "All right. You stole enough time."

Reid laughed good-naturedly. I smiled at them, shaking my head. "You all see me every day. Every. Day."

Reid leaned down and brushed another kiss to my cheek. "Today's a special day. And it's never enough, Sandy. Never enough."

He strolled back to his wife, Becca, who was watching him with a soft smile. She knew how close we were.

Aiden and Maddox sat beside Jordan and me, sliding a tray with coffee and several pieces of cake on it between us.

"All that cake?"

"Well, you know, I couldn't decide." Aiden winked. "Jordan loves them all."

Jordan scoffed, but I saw the delight in his eyes.

"I'm glad we catered this, but it wouldn't be the same without our Beth's cakes," I murmured.

"I know," Aiden hummed in agreement. "They are the best."

Sammy stood, heading for the table, her husband, Luke, following.

"I can never get used to Luke without his cowboy hat," Maddox mused.

Aiden chuckled. "I know."

I smiled, watching Van with their kids. They adored him and Liv and enjoyed coming to visit. Sammy and Luke had adopted siblings, Allison and Jacob, but they were loved as much as all the grandkids were. They were simply family. It made no difference to this diverse group. We all loved it when they came for a visit, especially Van and Liv.

Heather and Reed sat on the floor, Heather between Reed's long legs. Their son, Tyler, was eating cake and entertaining his younger cousin, Rosie, Mila and Nicholas's daughter. Mila was nestled against Nick, curled up in the corner of the sofa, happy and content.

"I hear Nick is up for another Oscar for the last film he produced and directed," Jordan said, then took a sip of his coffee. "Of course, he was too modest to tell us himself. It was brilliant. The story and how he handled bringing it to the screen."

"Yes. Another one of Mila's books." Maddox grinned at me. "Our little Mila. Quiet, shy, and bursting with talent."

"Still waters and all," I quipped. "They are good together. He says she's the best thing that ever happened to him. That everything good in his life began when they got together."

Aiden smiled. "Well, he won best actor for his work in the first film. The film won best adapted screenplay. Now this one is garnering a lot of attention. His little Rosie, whom he adores. Another babe on the way. Plus, he got all of us. That right there is like gold."

We all chuckled. Nick had fit in with us so well, and everyone loved him. He was good to Mila, and she adored him. And Aiden was right; his career took off in a positive direction once he met Mila. It was wonderful to see.

"Are Richard and Katy staying for good?" I asked Maddox. "Not going back and forth as much?"

He nodded. "Yes. They sold the house in BC. They bought a small condo close to Matthew's place so they can go visit. They're going to make Port Albany home now. Gavin and Matthew promised to visit more."

"You must be pleased."

He grinned. "Having my partner in crime here all the

time? Absolutely. The four of us are planning some major golf rounds."

Aiden nodded, equally delighted. Richard VanRyan wasn't a part of BAM, but he was as close to being family as everyone.

"Heather and Gracie are so happy about it. Richard and Katy can fly easily to England, so Penny is pleased too. Gavin and Amanda are planning on spending more time here as well, so everyone is happy."

Maddox chuckled. "Poor Phillip always looks a bit shell-shocked when he's here."

"I don't blame him. Penny says his family is much smaller and proper."

"It's good for him," Aiden insisted. "Lady Peepee gives him the normalcy he needs."

"He's pretty laid-back for a lord. Great dad," Maddox mused. "And Penny looks very happy."

"She does. So does Matthew. I have to say, I've never seen him look so relaxed."

"The last to fall," Jordan murmured. "Always the sweetest. He said he would never get married. No kids. Now he has a wife and one child here and, from what I heard, one on the way. Richard is hoping for twins. Not sure how Matthew feels about that. But Madison is good for him. She made him realize he needed a life outside of being a doctor."

"And Ashley and Luc fit in so well, you'd never know they weren't part of us all this time," Maddox murmured. "Their son looks so much like his namesake, it's scary."

"Acts like him too. No doubt who his hero is. He worships Gramps."

We all glanced toward the VanRyan clan. Richard was being smothered by his youngest grandkids, loving every second of it. The businessman was put aside now, the loving husband, father, and grandfather in his place. Katy observed them, a smile on her face. She was happiest when her children were around, and today, she beamed with delight.

It was good to see.

It was incredible to have them all here. To live long enough to see all my boys and their families, happy, healthy. There had been scares and traumas for everyone, but we all persisted.

I glanced at Bentley, who was leaning on the doorframe by the kitchen. He had a cup of coffee in his hand and was gazing around, the look on his face saying everything. The once-lost man was home. These were his people. His family.

He glanced toward the microphone then back to the room. I met his eyes with a slight nod and a smile, encouraging him. Nothing was planned, but somehow I knew the day wouldn't be right if Bentley didn't speak.

I smiled as he set down his coffee cup and picked up the microphone.

BENTLEY

I grabbed the mic we usually used for karaoke. I took a minute to look around the room at all the faces. The smiles. Listen to the laughter. Feel the love that permeated this place. I tapped the mic to get everyone's attention.

I smiled at their confusion. We hadn't planned speeches. I had just wanted to celebrate this occasion with the people I loved the most. But I found myself wanting to say something. I cleared my throat.

"I won't take up much of your time, but indulge me for a

minute. It's not often we have everyone—so many generations gathered together at once." I met Emmy's eyes, still beautiful and captivating after all these years. She nodded and blew me a kiss.

"Never would I have imagined when I opened the doors of BAM fifty years ago that I would be standing here today. Celebrating our achievements." I took in a breath as emotion suddenly swamped me. "BAM was, and is, more successful than I ever dared to dream. ABC is the extension of that dream, run by some of our children and upholding the values we stood for all those years. It is a legacy I am proud of. One of many."

I cleared my throat. "I never dreamed the day I went to find a place to live and ran into Aiden that this is where we would end up."

"I was your good luck charm!" Aiden yelled.

Everyone laughed, and I joined them. "My best friend," I said. "Then and now. We added Maddox to the group, and he became our third musketeer."

"All for one!" Maddox called, sitting next to Jordan.

"When it was time for me to start my business, I knew there were no others I could trust or depend on more than my two best friends. No one I wanted to share that journey with more. To this day, I have never once questioned that decision. Together, we created an empire that we could all be proud of."

There were choruses of awws and some whistling. I grinned. "And of course, we'd be nowhere without our Sandy. Our queen."

That got a wild round of applause. Sandy laughed and waved her hand to stop, but I could see how pleased she was.

"Our company was strong, our days busy, but we weren't complete until three wonderful women entered our lives. I know Emmy made me a better man, the same way Cami and Dee did for Aiden and Maddox." I paused. "They were, and are, the best parts of us."

Aiden and Maddox stood and clapped. I tucked the mic under my arm and joined them. There was more applause, and all the women looked teary-eyed.

"We grew again with Richard, Reid, Van, and Halton. Their wonderful wives and children. Our friendships became our focal point. Our compass."

I paused to take a sip of water.

"We found this land, built this complex, and our families expanded. Developed in number and strength. Grew up together. Always more than friends. Family. We added more houses and this incredible gathering place we all love so much. Where we come together and celebrate as a family. Sometimes all together, sometimes in smaller groups, but it is the center of our little hamlet. The place we call home. The people we call family." I paused. "I will always be proud of our company, but it doesn't compare to the successes that happened outside the professional world. The greatest of which is found in this room. This family."

I shook my head. "I don't know where the years went. How my babies went from being safe in my arms to successful men and women with families of their own. How you all grew and became the people, we, your parents and grandparents, are so incredibly proud of. Watching you develop and become the people you are, the parents you are, is incredibly humbling."

I had to pause before I could speak again.

"And as I said before, you are the greatest accomplishment of us all. BAM and ABC will carry on—legacies that will outlast me. Outlast many of us. But no legacy, nothing else I have been part of, will ever come close to making me as fulfilled as the people in this building. The beating, wonderful hearts of our families. That is the legacy I am most proud of. The one I will treasure and hold the highest in this life."

I swallowed. "You. All of you."

I was pretty certain there wasn't a dry eye in the place.

Maddox and Aiden joined me, Aiden taking the microphone. His voice was thick as he spoke. "Since Bentley started this, I want to add my two cents in. This building—" he paused and looked around "—was a dream project for me. A place that we could all gather and celebrate. The heart of our group. We all feed it. With the love that saturates every corner and crevice. The laughter that has echoed in every room. The tears we shared. The celebrations."

"The revelations!" Ronan shouted out, making everyone laugh.

Aiden nodded. "Those too. And wow, we've had some whoppers. But we made it through every single challenge, event, and occasion as a family. Like Bentley, I am in awe of what we built, but he is right. Our legacy is those we brought together, here in this building we created to celebrate the one thing the three of us never thought we would have. Family." He paused to clear his throat. "These two men beside me are my brothers. My closest friends. They believed in me when I couldn't believe in myself. I will always be grateful..." He paused, and I wondered if his emotions were going to overtake him. But then he grinned, finding the humor the way he always did. "I will forever be grateful that Bentley was too snobbish to really live in a dorm."

Everyone began to laugh, including me. I looked at Maddox, raising my eyebrow. With a shrug, he took the mic. "Might as well finish this up the way we started. The three of us talking together. I agree with everything Bent said. No accomplishment or success is as great as our family. Nothing will ever come close. And Tree Trunk is right, this building is the beating pulse of all of us. I want to thank Aiden for being Aiden. Always looking after us. Teaching us. Showing us how to overcome adversities. Being the pillar of strength for every person here."

He paused as the applause broke out, the two of us joining in and Aiden looking shell-shocked.

"And as for Bent, there is no one on earth I admire more. Focused, determined, loyal, and always leading this family with his greatest asset—his heart." He chuckled. "I guess we're like the Wizard of Oz. We were looking for something we already had. Brains, courage, and a heart." He smiled. "And the way home. We found that with one another and built this into our own Kansas, Sandy leading us on like our own Dorothy."

"Who's Toto?" someone asked, trying to be funny.

The entire room roared as Aiden looked straight into the room, focusing on one person. "Reid."

More guffawing broke out. Reid came to join us, grinning. Aiden ruffled his hair the way he used to do in order to drive him nuts. Now that hair was streaked with gray—just like ours.

I waved Van and Halton up to join us. "I have no idea where you two are in the Oz thing," I mused as they joined us.

Halton grinned. "Oh, I'm the mother bad witch."

Van laughed. "I guess I'm the good one. I do have a thing for glitter."

Richard strolled over, handing us all glasses. "I guess that makes me the Wizard. Let's face it, boys. I've always been the one behind the curtain, pulling the strings." He winked drolly, and everyone laughed again, because it was Richard being Richard.

It took a few moments for the room to settle down. I saw Mila scribbling something in a notebook, and I had a feeling some of the funny lines were going to end up in a book somewhere.

I was fine with that.

Richard raised his glass.

"To Bentley, his vision, and his amazing brothers. The people I'm proud to call my family and friends. And to his toast. Fucking epic."

Maddox laughed, lifting his glass. "To our families."

Everyone stood. Someone yelled out, "Live long and prosper!"

I lifted my glass.

I could drink to that.

Thank you so much for reading UNSCRIPTED WITH MILA. If you are so inclined, reviews are always welcome by me at your retailer.

As I stated early in the start of the book, this was not an easy book to write. I have so many people to acknowledge for their guidance and love.

If you'd like to get a look at what happened at the Oscars, download a copy at https://BookHip.com/ZDJFAJV

If you haven't read Richard and Katy VanRyan's story, you can meet them in The Contract. You meet an arrogant hero in Richard, which makes his story much sweeter when he falls.

Another story that I touched on mental health is Harvest of Love. Dani suffers from anxiety and learns that change is good–especially in the arms of organic farmer, Noah.

Enjoy meeting other readers? Lots of fun, with upcoming book talk and giveaways! Check out Melanie Moreland's Minions on Facebook.

Join my newsletter for up-to-date news, sales, book announcements and excerpts (no spam)–visit https://bit.ly/MMorelandNewsletter

Visit my website www.melaniemoreland.com/shop for signed paperbacks and merchandise.

Enjoy reading! Melanie

ACKNOWLEDGMENTS

As usual, a few thanks.

Lisa, thank you for your input, your comments that make me laugh and your encouragement.

Your dislike of snarling will live on to infinity.

Beth, thank you for your insightful feedback and assistance. Your contributions always make the story better.

To my sensitivity reader, thank you for sharing your personal experiences on having the difficult conversations. Your advice on molding Nicholas was invaluable.

Thank you to Heidi and CARS team of Milwaukee County BHS for their medical input in making sure I got the facts straight.

Melissa, Trina—thank you for your encouragement, laughter, and support.

Deb—thank you for your eagle eye and help. You keep me on track!

Sisters Get Literary – thank you for your keen eyes and enthusiasm.

Karen's team—words cannot express my gratitude. I am so glad Karen talked you into joining us! Atlee, you are a joy and to our Girl George – you are rocking it!

Karen— I never know how to say thanks enough, so I love you and you mean so much to me will have to do. Keep doing

it since my world would crumble with you in it. And PS —
GOOD JOB. PPS I gave you your reward so hush now.

To all the bloggers, readers, and my promo team. Thank
you for everything you do. Shouting your love of books—of
my work, posting, sharing—your recommendations keep my
TBR list full, and the support you have shown me is deeply
appreciated.

My reader group, Melanie's Minions—love you all.

MLM—for all you do I cannot say thank you enough. I
wish I could hug you all. Maybe one day.

Matthew—my forever love. My one sure thing, my ride or
die. I love you. I love our life. Thank you for being mine.
Always.

ABOUT THE AUTHOR

NYT/WSJ/USAT international bestselling author Melanie Moreland, lives a happy and content life in a quiet area of Ontario with her beloved husband of thirty-plus years and their rescue cat, Amber. Nothing means more to her than her friends and family, and she cherishes every moment spent with them.

While seriously addicted to coffee, and highly challenged with all things computer-related and technical, she relishes baking, cooking, and trying new recipes for people to sample. She loves to throw dinner parties, and enjoys traveling, here and abroad, but finds coming home is always the best part of any trip.

Melanie loves stories, especially paired with a good wine, and enjoys skydiving (free falling over a fleck of dust) extreme snowboarding (falling down stairs) and piloting her own helicopter (tripping over her own feet.) She's learned happily ever afters, even bumpy ones, are all in how you tell the story.

Melanie is represented by Flavia Viotti at Bookcase Literary Agency. For any questions regarding subsidiary or translation rights please contact her at flavia@ bookcaseagency.com

facebook.com/authormoreland

twitter.com/morelandmelanie

instagram.com/morelandmelanie

bookbub.com/authors//melanie-moreland

ALSO AVAILABLE FROM MORELAND BOOKS

Titles published under M. Moreland

Insta-Spark Collection

It Started with a Kiss

Christmas Sugar

An Instant Connection

An Unexpected Gift

Harvest of Love

An Unexpected Chance

Following Maggie

Titles published under Melanie Moreland

The Contract Series

The Contract (Contract #1)

The Baby Clause (Contract #2)

The Amendment (Contract #3)

The Addendum (Contract #4)

Vested Interest Series

BAM - The Beginning (Prequel)

Bentley (Vested Interest #1)

Aiden (Vested Interest #2)

Maddox (Vested Interest #3)

Reid (Vested Interest #4)

Van (Vested Interest #5)

Halton (Vested Interest #6)

Sandy (Vested Interest #7)

Vested Interest/ABC Crossover

A Merry Vested Wedding

ABC Corp Series

My Saving Grace (Vested Interest: ABC Corp #1)

Finding Ronan's Heart (Vested Interest: ABC Corp #2)

Loved By Liam (Vested Interest: ABC Corp #3)

Age of Ava (Vested Interest: ABC Corp #4)

Sunshine & Sammy (Vested Interest: ABC Corp #5)

Unscripted With Mila (Vested Interest: ABC Corp #6)

Men of Hidden Justice

The Boss

Second-In-Command

The Commander

The Watcher

The Specialist

Reynolds Restorations

Revved to the Maxx

Breaking The Speed Limit

Shifting Gears

Under The Radar

Full Throttle

Full 360

Mission Cove

The Summer of Us

Standalones

Into the Storm

Beneath the Scars

Over the Fence

The Image of You

Changing Roles

Happily Ever After Collection

Heart Strings